P9-BBP-936

if i should die

A MALI ANDERSON MYSTERY

grace f. edwards

BANTAM BOOKS
NEW YORK TORONTO
LONDON SYDNEY
AUCKLAND

This edition contains the complete text of the original hardcover edition.
NOT ONE WORD HAS BEEN OMITTED.

IF I SHOULD DIE

A Bantam Book / Published by arrangement with Doubleday

PUBLISHING HISTORY
Doubleday hardcover edition published May 1997
Bantam paperback edition / March 1998

ISBN-0-553-57631-3

Published simultaneously in the United States and Canada

Bantam Books are published by Bantam Books, a division of Bantam
Doubleday Dell Publishing Group, Inc. Its trademark, consisting of the
words "Bantam Books" and the portrayal of a rooster, is Registered in
U.S. Patent and Trademark Office and in other countries. Marca
Registrada. Bantam Books, 1540 Broadway, New York, New York 10036.

PRINTED IN THE UNITED STATES OF AMERICA

OPM   10   9   8   7   6   5   4

Also by Grace Edwards

In the Shadow of the Peacock

If I Should Die

A Toast Before Dying

No Time to Die

To Perri Edwards
and the members of the
Harlem Writers Guild

acknowledgments

Special thanks to William H. Banks, Jr., the director of the Harlem Writers Guild, as well as the workshop participants. I thank Donis Ford for her long-distance patience and expertise. And Earl Hunt, Allen Judge, John Harris, M.D., Theodora DuBuisson Lopez, Walter Dean Myers, William Ponder, and Clarinda Wilkins and Martin Brown for their much-needed assistance.

if i should die

chapter one

Wait a minute, Ruffin. Owners have some rights too, you know, so be patient . . ."

The dog was in danger of breaking my wrist so I untangled the leash and moved away from the stoop and toward the curb. The sky was slate gray for April—not my favorite color—and the temperature could have used a little juicing up also. Just a few minutes outdoors and already my feet felt as if I had stepped in a bucket of ice.

. . . Maybe I just oughtta walk the dog and go back in the house. Let that boy come home in the rain without his jacket. That would teach him a lesson, but then, I'd probably be up all night nursing his cough.

. . . Just like an eleven-year-old, never wants to hear anything that resembles advice. Told him the weather wasn't going to warm up anytime soon but did he listen? Now I had to call him at rehearsal to wait there until I bring his coat.

. . . Well, I get a chance to walk the dog again, or

trot beside him if he decides to slow down. Sometimes I can't figure out who's walking whom . . .

. . . I shouldn't complain. Alvin's adjusted to the group. He likes the singing, and the nightmares are not nearly as bad as they used to be . . .

I lingered for a minute and gazed down the block, a row of three- and four-story brownstones with iron filigree balconies and narrow, French-curtained windows. They called it Strivers Row because of the black professionals who owned property on the block.

I was born here thirty-one years ago, and as far as I could remember, the houses had remained unchanged through the years. Now the gray and brown facades took on a silken sheen from the mist that hung in the air.

The branches of the trees were still bare, but several gardens showed signs of life. From Adam Clayton Powell Boulevard to Frederick Douglass Boulevard, behind old iron railings layers of forsythia, shaped into rounded hedges, had bloomed into brilliant yellow almost overnight.

They looked warm and inviting and hinted at spring but I was still cold. I pulled my hat down and jacket collar up and steered Ruffin toward Powell Boulevard, listening to the light *tip-tip* of his paws on the wet pavement. The delicate sound was deceptive for a Great Dane.

The rain had driven all but a few hardy souls from the street, which was fine. It was Saturday afternoon and the wet weather meant fewer children to watch out for and Ruffin wouldn't have to be reined in quite so tightly.

On the avenue, we passed the old Renaissance Casino dance hall near 138th Street, which had been boarded up for years. Under its weather-worn marquee, the long-haulers who regularly drove up from Georgia and South Carolina were already set up and selling their produce despite the rain. We usually bought smoked hams, pig tails, collards, yams, and jars of honey here, and in another month or so, we'd buy string beans, corn, and watermelon fresher and cheaper than the local stores but, still, it was depressing to look at the faded marquee overhead.

Lately, I had begun to feel differently. When David Dinkins and Charles Rangel arranged to have Abyssinian Baptist Church buy the hall, my depression lifted. "That grand old ballroom will be renovated, it's going to reopen," I said. "Harlem's coming back."

My father had raised one eyebrow and smiled. "My dear girl, Harlem never left. It can go through a million changes and never change. Harlem," he said, "is a state of mind, an essence. It's not defined by one building. Of course it helps to see that place open and functioning again, and I tip my hat to those guys who tapped the mortgage, but they gotta get the deed in the hands; gotta get title to the place."

"What if they don't?"

"Well if a general loses a fort doesn't mean he's lost the war. It means he has to revise his battle plans."

Listening to him was like opening a history book, only better sometimes. "You're just kids," he used to say to my sister and me, "but I'm gonna show you anyway so you'll know where all the old neighborhood dance halls, nightclubs, and after-hours spots used to be. And why everybody, not just from downtown, but from around the world, wanted to visit at least once. This is history, and since you're Harlem babies, I want you to know it."

And he had walked us, two little girls, into the past, pointing out the Club Baby Grand on 125th Street where Willie and Ray, the deejays, had broadcast their rhythm and blues; the old Cotton Club, where the black chorus girls couldn't be any darker than the cream in the white gangster-owner's coffee. The Savoy, "Home of Happy Feet"; Minton's Playhouse, the serious jazz hangout. And

Jock's Place, Smalls' Paradise, and the Red Rooster. That was just for starters.

My father, Jeffrey Anderson, teaches music. When he was younger, he had spent weekends rolling his bass fiddle from one club to another and then into one of the after-hours spots to greet the dawn.

He had jammed with the best jazz men in town, out of town, and those just passing through town, and spoke of the politicians and movie stars he had met in the clubs: George Raft had once lit his cigarette with a solid gold lighter. Adam Clayton Powell, Sugar Ray Robinson, and Willie Mays had shaken his hand. He had small-talked with big-time gangsters and had been tipped a whole week's salary by a numbers baron just for a solo. And more times than he cared to think about, he had gotten out of a joint just minutes before it was raided by the cops.

"Folks scramblin' for the door like they was rushin' off the *Titanic*," he said. "Those were hot places and some hot times, man."

Those times and all of those places gone, but somebody said that was progress. My sister is also gone—dead two years—and I wonder who else could point out the exact spot on Lenox Avenue where the Golden Gate Ballroom and the Savoy and the Club Sudan once stood. Dad misses those old times, but he still has his students, more than he can make time for. And I have Alvin, my sister's son, and am showing him these places, the same way Dad showed me.

Ruffin continued to pull on the leash, as if he knew exactly where we were going.

. . . I'm glad I called that boy to let him know we're coming. Especially today. Sometimes he takes a different route even though I tell him not to . . .

I cut through 138th Street, a block much like my own with old brownstones, small front gardens, and bare-limbed trees lining the curb. The street was deserted now because of the rain.

Midway into the block, I saw Ruffin's ears perk up. Then I heard the commotion. A car had halted several yards away and a struggle was taking place near the car's rear door. The cries, high-pitched and frightened, moved through the driving rain.

"Lemme go! Naw! Lemme . . . go!"

Instinct, a dangerous and sometimes necessary thing, took hold, and before I knew it, I was running forward, forgetting I was no longer on the force, no longer carrying a weapon, and had only Ruffin trotting beside me.

Through the downpour, the cries came at me. Desperate. This was not the crying of a stubborn child, but a terrified one.

Habit got the better hand and I opened my mouth.

"Police! Don't move!" My voice seemed to float somewhere outside of me. I hadn't shouted those words in two years, but to hell with that now. I yelled again and unclipped Ruffin's leash from his collar, tapped him on his side, and yelled once more.

"Get 'im, Ruffin!" hoping that whoever was trying to harm that kid would appreciate the size of a Great Dane and have sense enough to get away from the scene while he still had legs.

Ruffin's bark should have been enough. He looked like a young colt as he leaped away, covering the distance to the car in less than a second.

I heard a muffled shout and a light pinging sound. A hand shoved the child away from the car and the door slammed shut. The automobile, a black, late-model Cadillac, accelerated and turned screeching onto Seventh Avenue.

I caught sight of "HO" on the plate before it disappeared in the rain.

The child, ten or eleven years old, sat sprawled on the curb in a daze, his hand bleeding and his jeans and jacket rain-soaked. Ruffin paced the ground beside him, quiet now, then trotted over to the middle of the street where a man lay, motionless.

I knelt beside the man, took a closer look, and pressed my hands to my mouth. My friend Erskin Harding, the tour director of the Uptown Children's Chorus, lay in the rain-soaked street, his eyes wide, seeing nothing.

chapter two

Yellow tape cordoned off the scene, and the uniformed officers kept the crowd back. The detectives sent someone to get the child's mother while the EMS workers examined the boy and bandaged his hand.

I remained near the yellow tape, watching the forensic unit snap several rolls of film. I held tightly to Ruffin's collar, concentrating on the photographer because that was easier than trying to absorb the reality of the body lying there in the street.

Erskin was in his early thirties, perhaps even younger. And handsome. He had long curling lashes and a trace of mustache and I remembered his smile, especially after a concert when the applause was still ringing in his ears. His shirt and tie, pale gray, were spoiled now by the bloodstains. I looked at his loafers—one still on and the other about ten feet away near the curb—and idly wondered why a shoe always came off when the spirit leaves.

When the car had sped away, it looked as if it had been a hit-and-run. But then, when I had knelt down and pressed lightly under Erskin's throat, the pulse was no longer there and I saw the small round hole over his left eyebrow, neat and effective.

When I had finally found my voice, it brought out neighbors from both ends of the block.

I remained near the tape, feeling the crowd move around in a ritual of activity. The detectives looked busy and the uniformed cops looked anxious, though the crowd was still small. The rain was coming down hard one minute, then slacked off, as if a giant hand had discovered a faucet and couldn't decide what to do with it. My jacket was soaked through and droplets were easing under my collar. It was time to leave. Just then I felt, rather than saw, someone approach, and turned to face my old nemesis from the precinct.

"Mali, I understand you were—"

"Miss Anderson, sir."

I stared hard into the blue eyes of Sergeant Cotter as I corrected him, letting him know that I was no longer under his command and I was still not taking any foolishness from him or anyone else. A pinkish color flared above his collar as if the air had suddenly been cut off and I knew, word for word, what he was calling me under his breath.

Words that would remain unspoken because the weight of one lawsuit against the NYPD was heavy enough.

I was exactly his height, five feet nine, and did not have to look up or down, but directly at him, staring straight into his eyes, knowing that most people found it easier, after a minute or so, to look away from me. Folks sometimes had trouble matching pale gray eyes with dark brown skin.

When I was growing up, older folks frowned and came right to the point: "Where you get them eyes, girl?"

I was well mannered then and held my tongue. Now I say, "Got 'em from the same place you got yours." And my eyes are more prominent since having my hair cut close, finally giving up what Dad had tactfully called my "Angela Davis do."

At fifteen, caught up in the remembered rapture of Huey, Rap Brown, and Eldridge, I had taken Angela as my heroine and my father had stared in amazement at my sky-high afro.

"Where are you going with all that hair?"

"To join the movement . . ."

Mom had moved to lock the door and Dad called our neighbor, a practicing psychiatrist. Luckily, he was available and agreed to see me in exchange for music lessons for his twin sons.

"Two lessons for one session?" my father had protested.

"Mali is a difficult case," Dr. Thomas had said.

Some say I'm still difficult and I still wear my hair in its natural state—allowing no wigs, weaves, or waves—but now it's cut so close that Dad says he can read my thoughts.

With less hair to frame the face, the eyes were . . . well, to be frank, sometimes I scared myself. Especially on a morning when I'd woken up hung over and staggered to the bathroom unprepared for the sight in the mirror.

I continued to stare at Sergeant Cotter, waiting for him to speak.

"Look," he said, averting his eyes and sidestepping the issue of Miss, Mrs., or Ms. by not calling my name at all, "I understand you were on the scene when this occurred."

"No."

Silence. If he wanted more information, he would have to pull it out of me, syllable by syllable.

"But you witnessed the incident?"

"Which incident, sir?"

"Was there more than one? We have a body here with a bullet in it. I have no time for games."

"Neither have I. I wasn't sure which incident you were referring to—the murder of that man or the attempted kidnap of the child."

I hadn't meant to refer to Erskin as "that man" but the anger I felt toward Cotter—an old and corrosive anger—outweighed my grief. He had protected the cop who had gotten me fired. What little information I now had would go to the detectives eventually assigned to the case, not to this man.

Cotter stared and his expression told me that he could have wrung my neck and would have smiled as I gasped my last breath.

I turned away from him and saw that more people were gathering despite the rain. Umbrellas grazed against each other and I tried to listen, hoping to hear a reason for another senseless death. Instead, the predictable comments drifted back and forth:

"Why did it have to happen here? This is a quiet block."

"Still is. The dead don't talk."

"Anybody seen him before?"

"Some big shot in the Children's Chorus . . ."

"You kiddin' . . . why anybody wanna shoot him?"

"What about the child? Lookin' like he scared to death . . ."

I listened but learned nothing more than what I already knew. The boy's name was Morris, he was eleven years old, and had been returning from rehearsal, the same Uptown Children's Chorus rehearsal where I was going to meet Alvin.

An involuntary chill went through me and I held

Ruffin's leash tighter. This boy was the same age as Alvin, same small wiry build. Suppose, if this was a random unplanned kidnapping, and I had not called to have Alvin wait for me, the man in the car could have somehow snatched him instead.

Then again, suppose it wasn't random. The Uptown Children's Chorus was a Harlem institution and a world-wide attraction. The several small groups which made up the Chorus had appeared at the White House, traveled across the country, and performed in Europe and Asia at least three times in any given year.

. . . Why would someone want one of the choristers? Why would they want a chorister badly enough to murder the tour director?

I tried not to take the thought any further. My friend was lying in the street, dead. Worse yet, my nephew could have been sitting on this curb, crying.

Before the police had arrived, I tried to get some answers.

"Morris, why did the man grab you? Did you know him? Was there more than one person in the car?"

I had asked the questions softly while the boy stared at Erskin's body without blinking. As if he wanted to remember something to call up in another time.

Finally, a murmur. "I don't know . . . I don't . . . I don't know . . ." He had rubbed his hand and the blood was smeared over his knuckles. "The man in the backseat . . . he was choking me so I couldn't breathe. I hit him in the mouth, punched him three times . . . hard as I could . . . then Mr. Harding tried to help me, yellin' at the man to leave me alone. Now look, Mr. Harding is dead. Maybe if I hadna punched the man . . ."

He could not stop crying. There was nothing any-one could do for Erskin, but I held Morris to me, knowing that I was going to hold Alvin the same way when he found out.

"It's not your fault, Morris, it's not."

I had whispered this over and over but he had not heard me.

I moved away from the crowd now, easing up on Ruffin's leash as we stepped back onto the sidewalk. My free hand moved into my pocket and fingered the tissue that held a bridge of three gold-edged tooth caps with a small diamond chip which I'd picked up from the ground near Erskin Harding.

Kneeling beside his body, I'd seen the bullet hole in his forehead, the shoe in the gutter, and the gold caps glistening on the dark, wet ground.

. . . I'll call Tad, give these to him to trace. If they assign him to this case, all the better. He'll know what to do. Maybe these caps have no connection. Maybe they were in the street before all this happened. But Tad is good at his job. He'll find out.

Sergeant Cotter called again. "Mali—Miss Anderson. We'll need you to come to the station later . . . Witness."

I acknowledged him with the barest shake of my head and continued to study the photographer documenting the position of the body and the angle at which the bullet entered. Another detective searched the area for a deformed bullet—one that had been fired. Then I heard Tad speak.

"So. You can't stay off the job, it seems."

His voice was quiet, deep, and familiar as he moved through the crowd toward me. Even in the rain, Detective Tad Honeywell looked good. How could someone look so good in the rain?

I managed to smile in spite of the confusion, in spite of myself, and in spite of all the heated debates—arguments—we'd had at the precinct and sometimes over dinner.

"Hardheaded" had been his favorite term for me.

"Nothing wrong with that," I had answered. "I won't let anyone step on me, that's all."

More times than I cared to count, he had suggested: "Why don't you let that chip roll off your shoulder?"

"Who put it there?" I asked. "It didn't grow out naturally, now did it?" And he never answered because we both knew what the deal was—we were acutely aware of that ever-present undercurrent of racism that infected everything in our daily lives.

Our last date had been at Sylvia's, seated at a small table in the back. My chip by then had grown to the size of a California redwood.

Outside, on Lenox Avenue, tour buses were lined up for three blocks and the restaurant was packed with Japanese and Germans and cameras. The silverware clinked above the murmur, and waitresses moved with dishes trailing aromas that could make the dead wake up hungry. There was a mood in the place, lively and wonderful, but that evening, after what happened that day at the precinct, I had lost my appetite.

"You see how no one reprimands the white boys when they get out of hand. What was I supposed to do? Grin and bear it? Grinning days are over and I ain't barin' nothin' but my fist in their face. I joined the force to make a difference in the community, not to take crap from the people who're supposed to be protecting it."

Tad had looked around, then held up his hands, as if to push me and my anger away from him.

"Okay, Ali, take it easy."

"Mali . . ."

"Whatever. Sometimes I can hardly tell the difference."

The official letter, the notice of my termination, was unfolded and pressed flat on the table, each corner anchored

by an empty cocktail glass. The waitress arrived with dinner
but by then I had been too busy counting vodka calories.

   I had been on the force less than two years when I was
fired for punching another officer. What they couldn't understand was that the creep deserved it. He had been harassing
me from the time I stepped in the door, so I figured enough
was enough. How could he tape that picture to my locker and
expect to get away with it? Probably would have if I hadn't
come up the stairs so quietly.

   I had sneaked up on him, spun him around, and landed
a sharp punch before he knew what hit him. Then I snatched
the picture—a perfectly normal picture of two apes copulat-
ing, except that my name had been scrawled in red across one
of them.

   The cop, Terry Keenan, was fined three days' pay for
being in the female locker room, a restricted area. After two
hearings, I was terminated and went to my attorney to get my
job back.

   The rain was coming down steadily now as I stood
near the edge of the crowd, forgetting how wet I was, and
waiting for Tad to speak.

   "How's the lawsuit going?"

   "It's still going, but you know how the city takes its
time, hoping you'll be six feet under before the case comes
to trial."

   I talked but tried not to stare at him so brazenly.
Detective Honeywell was six feet three, 220 pounds, with
skin I could only describe as "well honeyed" or "honeyed
well," depending on how high my temperature peaked
when I saw him. His eyes were like burned brown butter,
soft and liquid, which belied a toughness that had surprised me.

   I recalled two summers ago when the precinct had
been on alert because a rapist had sodomized a six-year-
old girl and then thrown her from the roof of the twenty-
seven-story project building where she lived. Honeywell

had spent his vacation tracking a slim lead until he caught up with the man in a one-light town in Tennessee. When he finally pulled him into the precinct, somehow both of the fugitive's kneecaps had been rearranged.

"Son of a bitch tripped. Running too fast," was all Honeywell had ever said about it. The DNA test did the rest.

I gazed at him now, wanting to tell him that he was the only thing I missed at the precinct.

"The lawsuit is still alive. But even after I win, I won't be coming back. I've nearly completed my thesis and I've decided to look into a Ph.D. program."

The faintest smile crossed his face, and I knew that when he got back to the precinct, he would drop that bomb on them in his usually casual way. (Yeah, you know Anderson, who used to work here? The one with those eyes? She's about to get her master's degree and will enter a Ph.D. program. Isn't that great?)

And I knew he would smile again at the stony silence that greeted his news.

"Still interested in sociology?"

"Of course."

"Still think you can make a difference?"

I looked at him closely, trying to decide what I heard behind the question. Of course I could make a difference. Social work had been my first choice before I had detoured into NYPD.

Finally, I said, "Why not?"

"I was just wondering. With all that academic activity, will you have time for any socializing?"

Try me, I wanted to say. Except I wanted the words to come out the way James Brown breathed them when he was down on his knees with his white cape and curled hair and face washed in sweat.

Try me . . .

Instead, I bit my tongue and whispered, "I manage to come up for air every now and then."

"I'm glad to hear that."

Our eyes met briefly and I was the first to turn away. "Got to get going, pick up my nephew . . ."

Tad reached out to touch me lightly on the shoulder but Ruffin rose abruptly and I had to pull him away. With four feet on the ground, Ruffin's head came as high as my waist.

"Sit!"

He sat and his head was still as high as my waist. But Tad did not step back as most people usually did. Instead he smiled.

"Can I call you tomorrow, Mali?"

I felt my temperature rising and knew that the stammering would start if I remained near him much longer.

"Sure. Sure . . . tomorrow's okay . . . why not?"

"Good. Be seeing you . . ."

He smiled again and walked away to speak with another detective.

. . . Thank God. Come on, Ruffin. Time to go . . .

"Miss . . . wait a minute . . ."

I turned to see a woman pushing her way through the crowd. She looked to be about forty with smooth brown skin, sturdy build, and medium height. Her hair was in rollers partly covered by a plastic rain cap and she wore slippers with the backs turned in under her heels and probably had a housedress on beneath her raincoat.

A light film covered her face and I wasn't certain if it was rain or perspiration but she seemed to be out of breath. Looking at the slippers, I knew that she had left home in a hurry.

"Are you the lady? Yes, you're the one. The one

with the dog. You saved my son. I don't know how to
thank you . . . what to say."

Her nervousness overwhelmed her and she put her
hands to her chest and began to cry. "I don't know how to
thank you . . . So much is goin' on. Poor Mr. Harding.
So young. Young. Why'd they have to shoot him? Leave
'im layin' in the street like a old dog. Life just don't mean
nuthin' no more."

"I know . . . I know how you must be feeling,
Mrs.—"

"Johnson. Mrs. Johnson. I'm Morris's mother. He's
my only child and I would've died if somethin' happened
to him. I would've just laid down and not got up no
more . . ." She looked at me again and shook her head.
"You saved my boy from bein' stolen, maybe even killed.
God is gonna bless you . . ."

"That's all right, Mrs. Johnson."

The woman fumbled in her coat pocket and
brought out a tissue to blow her nose. I decided to let her
talk. Now was not the time to ask questions.

"I don't know why they did this. Who would want
my boy? Why?"

Mrs. Johnson shook her head as she looked into the
crowd and at the few policemen remaining at the scene.
The rain had slacked off into a fine drizzle. I followed her
gaze. It would be some time before the medical examiner
arrived and before Erskin Harding's body could be
moved. Until then, the crowd would remain and might
get even larger.

Finally, Mrs. Johnson sighed. "You know, the
Chorus was the best thing that ever happened to Morris.
He used to run in these streets somethin' awful. He was
gettin' way outta hand, but then one a his teachers heard
that voice of his and said it was almost like Michael Jackson, you know.

"Anyway, she recommended him to try out for the

Chorus and he did and he been all right ever since. Kept his grades up and everything. I mean, they did a lot for him, but I'm a let them know he ain't goin' back. I need my boy alive. I can't take too much. My pressure. I got to take my medicine every day just to get out of bed . . .

"Now they want me to bring him to the station for more questions. The boy is too scared for that." She pointed to her chest. "Me. I'm scared too. My nerves is not strong anymore." The tears came again and her shoulders began to shake.

I reached out and touched her arm. "Mrs. Johnson, listen to me. Tell them you can't go to the precinct, that you're too sick and you're taking your son home. Tell them to send a detective to your house if they want to question him any further."

She dried her eyes slowly and looked at me with new interest, her confidence buoyed somewhat. "Yes. You're right. Let 'em come to my house. I can't thank you . . ."

"And call me." I reached into my pocket and gave her my personal card. "Call me if you or Morris hear anything at all. As a matter of fact, call me anyway. My nephew belongs to the Chorus and I need to look out for him too."

She read my name and phone number and nodded her head. "I sure will, Miss Anderson. Thank you." Then she dabbed at her face and looked at me again. Closely. "You sure got some pretty eyes. They ain't them fake-color contacts, is they?"

"No, ma'am, they're my real eyes. Call me when you get a chance."

The crowd shifted as she eased her way through and I was able to gaze at Erskin's body again. A quick glimpse.

The rain-soaked shroud covering him made him seem less personal, less likely to have a mother, father, lover, or sister—someone who would scream and fall down when they heard the news. But I remembered his deep-set eyes, and his smile after the last concert, and I turned toward Seventh Avenue, crying in the early evening rain.

chapter three

The confusion greeted me before I opened the door at the rehearsal hall. As I secured Ruffin's leash to the parking meter, I had recognized the unmarked car at the curb but I was not prepared for the scene inside the hall.

Several of the younger members were huddled together crying, and the secretary, an elegantly dressed older woman with graying hair, was leaning against the desk in the reception area in tears.

The news had traveled swiftly, even for Harlem, and several parents had already crowded inside the lobby. Many more were in the auditorium, where the two detectives and the administrator tried to speak above the noise.

I listened for a minute as the director of the organization spoke. Lloyd Benton was tall and slim with smooth beige coloring and regular features. His eyebrows were thick, and when he frowned, they seemed to come together in a straight line. He was visibly shaken and his voice could barely be heard above the crowd.

"Please. Rest assured that we're doing everything we can to get to the bottom of this. We are working very closely with the police and they—"

"And they ain't gonna do shit," a voice behind me whispered matter-of-factly. "Ain't gonna do shit!"

I turned to look at the man standing just inside the doorway. He glanced at me, then looked away. He had a hard handsomeness about him, tall and lean, his mouth drawn in a straight line across his smooth face. Everything about him seemed expensive—his dark suit, highly polished shoes, navy silk tie against mauve shirt. Even his fragrance spoke for him. He was probably in his mid-thirties, but when he moved, he walked with the practiced stroll of an old, old gangster.

He drew his breath and swore again, softer this time, as he turned away, heading for the door. I watched him go. He looked vaguely familiar, though I couldn't remember seeing him at any of the concerts. I wondered which child in the Chorus was his.

I turned again to the auditorium and scanned the crowd. These were ordinary working people—truck drivers, postal workers, teachers, nurses, clerks, single parents, couples—all showing the strain of grief, worry, and confusion. Suppose it had been their child?

They pressed in shoulder-to-shoulder, their apprehension rising to spread across the room like a wave.

"How did this happen?"

Lloyd Benton was unable to answer, and one of the detectives stepped to the microphone and held up his hands for quiet.

"Please," he said. "Please. Give me a minute." I watched the room quiet down expectantly as Detective Danny Williams lowered his arms.

"I'm sorry, truly sorry about this incident. This is a fine organization and you are all caring and concerned parents. Something like this should never have happened and I want to assure you right now that we're assigning all available manpower to this case. This will have our top priority and we won't stop until we get results. We already have a witness to the incident so we should have a solid lead very soon."

The crowd stirred as some of the tension lifted.

"A witness? Who? Wonder what they saw?"

I felt a sudden anger toward Danny Williams. Why would he advertise the fact that he had a witness? Even though he hadn't called my name, I felt that any minute, every face in the room would turn toward me. I ignored the hard knot forming in the bottom of my stomach and continued to scan. Alvin was not there.

I eased out of the room and returned to the lobby. Several people shook their heads. No one had seen him. Someone else said, "Maybe he's upstairs. I don't know . . . This is terrible. Terrible."

No one seemed to know anything. Other parents were calling for their children. I glanced around and walked quickly up the marble stairs leading away from the confusion.

The second floor had four offices facing a long narrow corridor which made up the administrative area. This area should have been cordoned off but Lloyd, the director, had probably resisted. Appearance and propriety meant everything and he had probably argued against any yellow tape. Erskin, after all, had not been murdered in *this* establishment.

I knocked at the first door. No answer, but a dim light inside was suddenly switched off and the door was locked when I quietly turned the knob.

I moved down to the end of the corridor and heard my heart pumping despite the noise that drifted from the auditorium below.

Please, God, please. Let me find that child. Let him be all right. I can't take any . . .

He was crouched on the floor, his knees drawn up to his chin and his head resting on the door of Dr. Harding's office.

"Alvin!"

He did not answer as I lifted him to his feet, at the same time turning the knob to the empty office. The door opened and we went inside.

I switched on the lights and watched him carefully as he looked around the office. Perhaps being here would help in some way, though I wasn't sure how. I glanced around and prayed that Lloyd would not come up and catch us.

The room seemed undisturbed. Books were stacked on the glass-enclosed shelves of the floor-to-ceiling bookcases and a small calendar was on the large oak desk, turned to today's date. There were piles of sheet music on the filing cabinets in the corner.

"Why did they kill him?" Alvin asked.

He walked around the desk and touched the arm of the worn leather chair, then turned as if he expected Dr. Harding to come through the door at that moment and explain everything.

"Why did they have to kill him?" he asked again.

I, too, felt that Erskin would walk through the door and explain even as I fumbled for an answer to a question that had no answer.

"Alvin, these things . . . happen and . . . sometimes there's no explanation, none we can understand . . ."

He continued to move around as if he were alone in the room, then paused near the window.

"Here's the cassette," he whispered. He reached over behind the chair, pushed the plant of hanging ivy aside, and snapped the tape deck open. "This is the tape Grandpa wanted him to hear. An old recording called

'Profoundly Blue.' Grandpa taped it and I brought it to Mr. Harding last Saturday."

He held out the tape and I recognized my father's precise handwriting: "For Erskin Harding, Ph.D. A Man Who Recognizes the Only Original Art Forms Made in America. Jazz & Blues. Best Wishes. Jeffrey Anderson."

I slipped the tape into my shoulder bag.

. . . Quite a long title, Dad. Why didn't you simply write "Profoundly Blue" on the label and be done with it? The title alone tells the whole story . . .

But then it wouldn't be Dad if he missed a chance to teach, preach, or otherwise inform.

I reached across the desk and for no reason I could think of, slipped the small calendar in also. And closed my purse just as the door opened.

"Who . . . are you? What . . . what are you doing in this office?" the man asked.

I flashed a glance at Alvin, signaling him to keep quiet. Then I spoke. "We all heard the news. My nephew was feeling sick, so we came in here until he calmed down."

I gave the man my most direct stare until he looked away. He was short, with round shoulders and a hairline that had begun a serious recession, although he couldn't have been more than forty years old. The cut of his black silk suit and white silk collarless shirt let me know that every time he walked down Madison Avenue, he left the Calvin Klein Men's Boutique a few thousand dollars richer. His nails were manicured and carried a hint of a dull, discreet sheen.

His face was pale and colorless. It reminded me of a wax mask, capable of reshaping itself according to the temperature of the particular room he entered. His forehead was highlighted by a large port wine stain on the left side, like the former Russian president, and his nose reminded me of a fighter who had gone ten rounds and lost.

He seemed on guard, as if he expected someone else to come down the corridor and surprise the three of us.

"Is this your office?" I knew it was not but I asked anyway, prepared to apologize for trespassing.

Alvin had moved from the back of the desk to stand beside me. "This is not his office," Alvin said quickly, breaking the silence.

I looked down at him and tried to squeeze his hand but he ignored me and rushed on in his hurt and childish way to get the information out.

"He's Mr. Mark. He's only the director of development, the fund-raiser. His office is down the hall, not in here."

Only the fund-raiser. Alvin made this last pronouncement proudly, as if he had appointed himself to protect the space and memory of Dr. Harding.

The three of us faced each other in the room. Muffled sounds rose from below and I guessed that most of the parents were still in the auditorium, seeking answers which Danny Williams and Lloyd Benton had not been able to give.

"I'm Gary Mark, the director of development," the man finally said in a voice just above a whisper. He did not extend his hand and I wondered how friendly a fund-raiser was supposed to be. Weren't they professional handshakers, extracting thousands of dollars with each shake? Either Mr. Mark was derelict in his duty or he had sized me up, come up with an estimate of my (zero) bank balance, and decided I wasn't worth a handshake.

Actually, it was neither. Gary Mark dabbed lightly at his forehead with a linen handkerchief as he glanced around the room, every movement telegraphing a vain attempt to control his emotions. It seemed that Erskin's death had had a tremendous effect on the children, the parents, and the staff.

I wanted to stay and talk to Gary Mark but I

needed to get Alvin home where Dad and I could sit with him and try to make sense, try to come to terms with everything that had happened.

And I certainly did not need Lloyd to walk in here and accuse me of trespassing.

I glanced down at Alvin. "Do you feel well enough to leave? We could stay longer if you like—"

"No. No." He looked around, deciding that this was probably the last time he'd see the room in this state. His gaze swept over the desk, the old leather chair, the bookcase, and the dark red carpet.

I followed his gaze and noticed the small square outline on the desk where the calendar had rested. A faint coating of dust had settled around everything else and the square was visible. I dropped my bag on the space and waited. I thought about fingerprints but I'd visited Erskin often enough in this office, along with a hundred other folks who had probably left prints. His office had been open to everyone who cared to drop by and chat.

Alvin, who had closed his eyes, now opened them. "I'm ready," he said. "Let's go."

I paused at the door, wondering what else to say.

"Mr. Mark, sometimes when these things happen, there's no . . ."

He held up his hand and closed his eyes. "No. No. Don't . . . I'll . . . Everything will be all right . . ."

I looked at him for a minute. He trembled slightly and I wanted to touch his shoulder. Instead I said, "Yes. Yes. Of course. Everything will be all right."

He stepped aside and I pressed my shoulder bag to my side and walked out of the room.

chapter four

Even on his answering machine, Tad Honeywell's voice was extraordinary and I had a hard time remembering why I had called. I left a message, vague and neutral, and the name "Hard Head," then hung up.

. . . Damn, Tad. Please call. Please. There's something about this calendar that's just not right. Call me, dammit . . .

I paced the floor of the living room, annoyed by the sound of my own footsteps. Alvin had finally gone to bed and Dad had canceled his gig so he could be within crying distance if the boy needed him. Nevertheless, he had decided to drop in on his buddies across the street for a round of poker. He was only a phone call away and would probably play until dawn.

I had taken out my notebook and, in this quiet time, attempted to go through Erskin's calendar entries, day by day, trying to reconstruct his life by reading his notes.

There were the usual luncheon and dinner appointments, reminders for birthday greetings, sympathy cards, flowers for someone hospitalized, a callback to the head of the Ford Foundation, and confirmation for visas and new passports for two of the choristers. From the looks of it, Erskin kept his own calendar, so apparently he didn't have his own secretary, although he might have shared a clerk with the other administrators.

There was a dental exam scheduled for a few weeks from now, an appointment he would never keep—the only hint that he had had a personal life.

I settled on the sofa to concentrate. Everything on the pages related only to his professional life. The many occasions I had met him, usually after a concert, he had kissed me on the cheek and had seemed in great spirits, almost buoyant. Thinking back on those times, I realized that he was like most artists, especially performing artists —and the buoyancy was there because he was still coming down from the high excitement of the event itself. I thought of Dad and the nights—more like early dawns— when he had come in from a gig, not exhausted as one would expect, but still full of the energy that had earlier driven his performance.

My sister, Benin, and I used to go to bed before the streetlights came on in order to wake up and run downstairs as his key hit the door. Then we'd sit in the kitchen as he brewed the usual pot of Blue Mountain coffee. And as he relived the entire evening for us, he was alive, effusive, entertaining.

"This was a society gig at the Audubon," he told us one night. "All the doctors, lawyers, and chiefs were there. Not a fried chicken leg in sight. Just skinny little hors d'oeuvres and skinny flutes of Moët. And everything was going great till Mrs. what's-her-name spotted Miss so-and-so waltzing through the doors with this tall, young, fine-lookin' cat draped on her arm. Problem was Mrs. what's-her-name had been seeing and most likely supporting this cat on the side while playing house with her lawful lawyer husband. Next thing everybody knew, she had left her old man standing in the middle of the dance floor and ambled on over to fine-young-cat. Didn't say one word to him but snatched his girlfriend's wig right off her head and said out loud, 'I know I paid for this crap 'cause Jesse ain't never had two dimes to rub together in his whole life.'

"It was one of those red, curly wigs too. Mop had so many curls and waves we thought it was Shirley Temple when she first walked in.

"And before the girl could say 'boo,' Mrs. what's-her-name had wound back with a left that could've put Satchel Paige out of business. I mean she threw that wig so far it landed in the punch bowl on the buffet table, way on the other side of the room.

"What we usually do when a fight starts is ditch the slow music and scramble into a kind of fast tempo, a calypso, something to get everybody out on the floor and draw attention away from the catfight. Well, everybody got up from their tables, all right, but not for no hip-shaking calypso, no sirree. By that time, the two women were down on the floor tangled like a pretzel, the fur was flying, and there was this big circle crowded 'round, with people in the back jumping up and down trying to get a look-see over the shoulders of the ringsiders. I even heard bets being called, and the cat they were fighting about was nowhere to be seen. Heard later that he had snuck out with somebody else's wife."

The life of the artist, Dad said, is filled with incidents that happen in other people's lives, incidents that the artist knows are worth recording. Even so, there is a life apart from the art which sustains him. How many of Dad's musician friends knew what brand of coffee he drank at 5 A.M.? Or that he took his daughters on late afternoon walks, pointing out architectural treasures that anyone could have seen if they had bothered to look?

Erskin, like Dad, must have had something beyond his music but he'd had no children to tell it to. There's a diary lying about somewhere, somewhere just out of reach. I know there is . . .

The last page of the calendar, behind the space marked "Coming Events," had a smaller page taped to it. The notation read "Check the end of the year."

The end of the year. I spent the next hour looking at the calendar, but the entire space for December 1995 was blank.

My message to Tad had been deliberately vague. Who knows who might have access to his machine at the precinct? I couldn't take that chance.

I continued pacing the floor.

. . . I've got to remember to ask him for his private number. At home. Wait a minute. Is his divorce final? He might be involved with someone else, might have someone living with him . . . Fine as he is, he wouldn't last a hot second before some other sister . . .

Hell with that. I still need the number . . .

I stopped in the middle of the room and squeezed my eyes shut. "Call, Tad . . ."

I raised my arms toward the ceiling and drew my breath in and held it. "Call. This is important."

Sometimes this worked. Sometimes it didn't. When it did, I always managed to say a prayer of thanks. I did so now as I breathed out.

The phone was ringing.

I lifted the receiver and was about to say, "What took you so long?" when a woman's voice, small and breathless, came on.

"Miss Anderson? This is Mrs. Johnson, Morris's mother? I'm callin' 'cause I gotta talk to you. This boy is tellin' me some stuff I think you ought to know about."

"Okay. Okay. Don't say any more. Give me your number and I'll call you back in half an hour." I jotted down the number and hung up, intending to go out and use a public phone.

Who knows? Ever since I started that stupid lawsuit, the crank calls have been coming in, so who knows? My line may very well be wired.

Anyway, there's nothing like a healthy dose of paranoia to get me through the day . . .

The phone rang again and I picked it up on the second ring. Tad's voice: "Don't you believe in call waiting? How do you expect Ma Bell to make any money if you stick to just basic service?"

I heard the lilt of laughter in his throat and had to sit down. My knees had suddenly gotten weak.

"What's going on, Hard Head?"

"Everything. Could you come over?"

"Now?"

"Yes. Now. I—"

"What is it, Mali? What's—? Are you all right? Talk to me."

I held my breath and let it out slowly. I hadn't meant to alarm him.

"Tad, I'm all right. I just need you to—I'll tell you when you get here. It's important."

There was a second of silence in which I heard the light sound of his breathing. Then he said, "Whatever it is, just hold on. I'll be there."

Twenty minutes later, as Tad settled himself on the sofa, I went over near the piano, pressed a strip of wood on the wall nearby, and a large panel slid open, revealing a mirrored, glass-shelved bar.

"Sorry I sounded so upset on the phone, but I have

Dr. Harding's calendar and there's something peculiar about it. I can't quite figure out what it is."

I pointed to Erskin's calendar lying on the table in front of him. He picked it up and began to turn the pages slowly, as I had done earlier.

I placed two glasses on a tray. "What are you having?"

"Walker and water, please . . . I won't ask how you came by this . . . piece of evidence . . ."

. . . Evidence. This was a piece of evidence. Damn . . .

I paused and he returned my gaze steadily. He had me so mesmerized that for a second I had forgotten that he was a detective, a very good one, and the traits that made him good were always present, like a second skin.

Finally, I said, "Go ahead, ask me. No, I'll tell you. Save some time. I found it at the rehearsal hall earlier this evening when I picked up my nephew."

He was quiet now but I thought I detected a slight frown.

"You're telling me that this calendar just fell off a shelf and into your pocketbook . . ."

"I'm not telling you anything of the sort," I replied, beginning to feel like a suspect. "I'm only saying that I have it, I tried to figure out something of the man's life from the notes, and there's a message on the last page which I bet no one can figure out."

"Well, why are you so interested in his life? Shouldn't that be our job?"

He was right, but Erskin had been my friend. I did not want his death to become one of those open-ended "still under investigation" cases that languished in a file gathering more than its share of dust. I intended to find out everything I could about his life so I could understand his death.

I placed the tray with the Scotch and glasses on the

table and curled up on the sofa opposite him. He picked up the calendar again.

" 'Check the end of the year,' " he said. "Maybe what Harding meant was a check check. As in bank check, bad check, blank check, check for a certain amount of money he expected to receive."

"Like a bonus or something? Lots of folks receive bonuses—if they have a job. Why would he be so cryptic about it?"

"I don't know." Tad leaned back against the pillows. "Check the end of the year. What? Where? And with whom?"

The question, when he repeated it, took on a soft, singsong cadence that I might have listened to all night.

He shrugged and lifted the glass to his mouth. I watched, gazing at him over the rim of my own glass. He was forty years old and already his hair was edged with gray. Was that the result of the tension on the job, or was it because of his personal problems? I couldn't do anything about the job, but I had some ideas about how to help him privately.

"Perhaps," he continued, "Harding knew he was jammed up. Maybe he knew it a while ago. And now that he's gone, there's something somewhere that someone is supposed to look into . . . But why wait till the end of the year?"

Why indeed? I continued to gaze at him. He had taken his jacket off and leaned back. I wondered how it would feel to give him a massage . . . Start around those great shoulders and work my way . . .

He had stopped talking and was gazing at me, smiling. "You're making me nervous, girl . . ."

I lowered my eyes, looked around the room for something else to interest me, then laughed. "I'm sorry. Bad habits die hard."

"Hey, I'm only teasing you."

He looked around also, attempting to focus on something. His gaze took in the piano, the bar, the paintings, the fruitwood mantel over the fireplace, and the oak staircase in the foyer.

"This is a beautiful place, Mali. In fact, the whole block is beautiful. Strivers Row. I walk through it every chance I get."

Every chance he got. I suppressed a sigh, a deep one. Had I known that he strolled the neighborhood, I'd have propped myself up in the window wearing less than a New Orleans working girl. I'd have even gotten one of those velvet swings.

Instead I said as casually as I could, "Lived here all my life. Born a short walk away."

"Harlem Hospital?"

"That's right. My mother liked to tell the story of how she walked there at two A.M. The night I was born, my father was at an all-night gig. He never lived it down. She wouldn't let him, I suppose. They laughed about it a lot."

I felt relaxed, but somehow I curled up tighter on the sofa, drawing my legs under me. Now that he was here and we had run out of ideas about the calendar, at least for now, I needed to gather some other, more personal information. I needed to catch up, to fill in the gaps that needed filling in this relationship, this friendship really, that previously had not gotten anywhere beyond precinct talk, a few dinners, and late night phone conversations.

I knew now that I had hesitated at the time because he was stepping out of a bad marriage and had been busy with attorneys and alimony and ulcers.

He had been busy, and when he finally called, something had happened in my own life and I could not speak to him.

Now I settled back into the pillow, determined.

"One month after I was fired from the department, my older sister died. I never got the chance to tell you because everything happened so fast. She and her husband had been vacationing in Europe. Hiking in the Alps between France and Italy. They stepped on an ice shelf and it caved in under them. That was nearly two years ago. Dad and I are raising their son."

Tad looked at me. His eyes seemed deeper than ever. "Mali, I'm sorry. Jesus. I didn't know. How old is the boy?"

"Alvin's eleven. Nice, bright . . ." I looked down at the floor, trying to concentrate. "I'm raising him, or trying to, but I don't know . . . At times I wonder if I'm doing the right thing . . . like not allowing him to join the Scouts because I can't stand the idea of him going hiking. When he goes to camp in the summer, I take him there personally to tell the administrator that my nephew is not to go hiking.

"The only thing I feel comfortable with is the Chorus. But now with this kidnapping attempt and Erskin Harding's death—his outright murder . . ." My voice trailed off and Tad waited patiently before I was able to continue.

"Alvin was very close to Dr. Harding and this is the boy's second loss in two years. I don't know what to . . ."

Tad leaned over and his fingers covered my hand.

"Listen, Mali, I can understand how you feel but maybe . . . maybe . . . at times we don't realize how easily we can spoon-feed our own fears into someone else, into children especially."

"I know it, but I can't help it. He and my father are all the family I have left. I have no children of my own so my family ends with my nephew. I can't help it.

"My sister taught school and her husband had just finished his internship. He planned to specialize in pediatrics. It was a terrible blow. None of us has gotten over it and I'm especially worried about Alvin. For a long time, he had screaming nightmares. They had begun to fade, but now they'll be back. Since Dr. Harding was killed, I know they'll come back again. Sometimes, I think—" My voice was about to leave me and I put my hands over my eyes. "I don't know what to think. It's been one thing after another without a minute to catch my breath."

"Mali—" Tad leaned across the sofa and pulled me to him. My head rested on his shoulder and his voice was soft near my ear. "I remember now. You never spoke much about your family except to say that your father's a musician . . ."

"I know . . ."

I let it go. "Keep your own counsel," Mama had always said. "Especially among strangers." And I had found soon enough that nothing was stranger than the NYPD. If I hadn't been fired, I certainly would've quit.

"I know," I said again. I could feel the steady reassuring weight of his hand on my shoulder as he spoke.

"I read about that accident in the *City Sun*. But I didn't make the connection because the last name was different than yours. I didn't realize it was your sister.

"Mali, you had a hell of a lot happen. Your family. The problems with the department. Now this . . . I'm sorry. I'm really sorry." He turned my face up to meet his eyes. "Listen. I don't know if this is the right time or not. If it isn't, or if it isn't what you want to hear, just shut me up. But since we're finally talking, I may as well tell you.

"When you didn't return my calls, I was really confused. And angry. I didn't know what was going on. I thought of writing to find out what was going through your mind. I thought we'd meant more to each other than just that good-bye card you left on my desk.

"The day you left, I put your card in my pocket and went home and earned a king-size hangover the next day.

Then I called and called . . . and you were never there or you were too busy to come to the phone."

He pressed the palms of his hands to my face and I felt the strong pressure of his fingers.

"Mali. Baby. I missed you. I'm—"

I put my fingers to his lips to quiet him but he opened his mouth and drew them in lightly.

"Listen, Mali . . ."

His hands slipped down the small of my back and I had no idea what the next few minutes might bring. A light massage. Or a heavy one. Starting from the shoulders down. And ending somewhere around my legs. Or no massage at all, just moving directly to the heart of the matter. I had imagined this and dreamed of this for so long, day and night, that I knew exactly how I intended to help him get started.

I had wanted to reach now for the lamp and turn it off but I heard the loud scrape of the key in the lock and Dad's familiar noisy movements as he opened the front door and made his way through the foyer.

He was whistling. Probably left the game early because he had won all there was to win.

Damn! His good night had certainly ruined mine.

"Dad."

When I called, I was so out of breath, I did not recognize my own voice.

"Dad, I'm in the living room. I want you to meet a friend . . ."

I watched the two men shake hands. My father seemed cautious; Tad looked uncomfortable—like an overgrown kid who'd just been caught with his hand in the honey jar.

I wanted to laugh but I still had trouble breathing.

"We're going out for a walk, Dad. Can I bring you anything?"

"Nope. Did all right by that game. Henry and the

fellas'll be better prepared next time." He patted his pocket and turned. "Nice to meet you, young man."

He climbed the stairs and I waited until I heard the heavy sound of his bedroom door closing. The door needed planing and was in danger of etching a serious semicircle in the wood floor. God knows when it would be repaired. Dad always promised but his music came first.

Outside on the steps, the street was quiet, and when Tad spoke, his voice was low. "Where would you like to go?"

"Anywhere, as long as we pass by a phone on the way. I have to return a call."

"Want to drive or walk?"

"Walking's fine. I need the exercise."

"Okay by me," he said.

I watched as he walked over to check the lock on his car. It was a black late-model Cadillac parked at the curb and the "HO" on the license plate stood out under the lamplight.

chapter five

ord, when I come to the end of my journey . . ."

At the Cathedral of St. John the Divine, the voices of the Uptown Children's Chorus rose toward the vaulted ceiling, then flowed down against the stone piers to touch the crowd gathered to pay their respects.

All of the choristers were present, each group—tenors, altos, bass, and sopranos—distinguished by the individual colors of their robes.

A tall, stately woman from the borough president's office, with hair worn in tight locks, spoke of the tragic loss to the family, community, and friends. She stepped away from the pulpit and the voices rose again. I looked around me.

I'm not comfortable sitting in the first row of anything—classrooms, buses, theaters, airplanes, and certainly not funeral services—but now I sat as close to the front as I could manage in order to watch Alvin.

He had insisted on attending, and singing with the

group. Even Dad had agreed: "Let the boy deal with this
the way he knows how. You didn't want him to attend his
mother's funeral because you thought he was too young.
Wouldn't understand what was going on. He was nine
years old, for God's sake, and you insisted he was too
young.

"Well, that may be why he keeps having all those
nightmares. He never got the grief out of his bones. Let
him make it through this one for Harding. Do 'im good."

There were huge banks of flowers and the fragrance
mingled with the smoldering incense to drift heavily in
the air.

Alvin was one of the taller boys and stood in the
third tier surrounded by candlelight. I could not distinguish his voice from the others but his mouth moved, he
held himself erect, and he appeared calm. I guess Dad was
right again. I'll have to tell him so later.

Several people spoke of Harding's life. I listened,
trying to read between the lines and trying to listen to
those around me, hoping to find some connection to the
memo on the calendar. In between, my thoughts wandered back to Tad's license plate, then I simply dismissed
it. There were probably hundreds of plates in the city
with those same letters. I tried to refocus on the eulogy
but learned nothing and two hours later moved outside to
the steps and watched the procession file out.

As Erskin's mother passed, a man reached out and
touched her arm. She looked at him, surprised, and drew
back.

"Don't you dare touch me. My son is gone. All of
those flowers. They don't mean a thing to me. Get out of
my sight!"

She moved away and walked quickly to the waiting
car.

The man, exquisitely dressed, was the person who
had sworn under his breath in the rehearsal hall the night

Erskin was killed. He nodded his head slightly, turned, and disappeared into the crowd.

I watched him move away and wondered about his connection to Mrs. Harding. I did not see Alvin and Dad approaching until they were nearly in front of me. Alvin's robe was white with a purple yoke and he appeared older than eleven years. The set of his jaw seemed hard.

"How're you feeling?"

He looked away, scanning the crowd, which had thinned now to those small lingering knots of mourners who always remain after such events and long after the procession of cars, their headlights ablaze, had moved from the curb and out of sight.

I wondered what he was thinking but before I could ask, he said, "I'm tired."

"Come on, kid," Dad said immediately. "You're tired. I'm hungry. Let's head on down to Majestic's and pick up an order of fish 'n' chips on the way home."

"Sounds good."

The slant of Alvin's jaw softened somewhat but tightened again when I said, "You two go on. I'm waiting for someone. I'll catch up later."

"Shall we get something for you?"

"Probably not. I don't know how long I'll be out."

Five minutes later my eyes met Mrs. Johnson's and she made her way over to me.

"Didn't mean to keep you waitin'. You know how these services are. Everybody got to get in a word or two about how well they knew the deceased. Happens every time. Betcha most of 'em never even said hi to 'im. And I'm sorry about the night when you called back. Clarence was there and I couldn't talk."

"Clarence?"

"The person I wanted to tell you about."

"What about him?"

She looked around and didn't answer. We walked

to the corner of 110th Street and Amsterdam Avenue as three yellow cabs sped by, ignoring our outstretched hands.

"Do you want to walk?"

"Not in these damn heels," she said. "I'm gettin' a cab if I have to lay down in front of one."

Luckily, a gypsy cab finally stopped and we headed for Singleton's Bar-B-Que, a small restaurant on Malcolm X Boulevard and 136th Street. It was jammed with Harlem Hospital staff but there was an empty table in the back which we rushed to claim. Once settled, I apologized.

"I didn't want to talk to you on my phone, Mrs. Johnson, because I'm an ex–police officer and I'm suing to get my job back."

Mrs. Johnson looked across the table at me, her eyes wide.

"I knew there was somethin' about you . . . a don't-take-no-stuff attitude that I like. Well, we face-to-face now. This is always the best way."

We stopped talking when the waitress, a young girl clad in jeans and a "Free the Juice" T-shirt, approached with the menus.

"Be back in a minute, ladies."

We waited until she moved away. I opened the menu and laid it flat on the table but did not look at it.

"Mrs. Johnson, what's going on? Is Morris all right?"

Mrs. Johnson scanned her own menu carefully, then glanced around before she spoke. When she did, her voice was low, nearly lost in the floating din of general conversation.

"Morris is okay. Still scared some but he's okay. You know, when that first big wave of fright hits you, you forget things, sometimes it could be so bad, you forget your own name. Well, Morris, he started rememberin' and tellin' me certain things once he quieted down."

She looked around again and her voice went even lower, forcing me to lean over the table.

"Morris said he overheard somebody threatenin' Dr. Harding the Saturday before he got killed."

She drew a breath, and a frown covered her face, as if the whole situation was too much for her to handle alone. She needed support, someone who would tell her what to do.

With the pink rollers gone from her hair, she did not look like the housewife who had come out of the crowd the night of Erskin's death. Her dark brown hair was now swept up and over to the side and held in a deep stiff wave which added at least three inches to her height and cut ten years from her age. She wore very sheer white stockings—a vivid counterpoint to the dark suit and patent-leather high heels. The three-strand pearl necklace completed the picture of a very well dressed, stylish woman.

Funerals will do that, I thought, looking at her.

"Did Morris say who it was that threatened Dr. Harding?"

The frown deepened and her fingers played along the menu, curling the edges. "Said it was Clarence. Boy used to be a problem but somehow he started actin' right even before he joined up with the Chorus. Used to hang out on the basketball court all hours of the night, even past midnight, sometimes playin' ball out there all by himself. Felt sorry for him. 'Specially when it was cold. Talk travels in those projects so I know for a fact that many a times that boy would open his fridge hopin' that for once, the food stamps had been used to buy food. I mean how you expect a child to study fractions and French while his belly button is pressin' on his backbone?

"Most of the times, I just call out the window for

'im to come on up and eat dinner with Morris. Even though there's a difference in their ages. Clarence probably seventeen now—" She closed her eyes to calculate, then said, "Yeah, he's seventeen and Morris ain't but eleven, but when a boy's starvin', you don't look at age, you just try to step in and help out . . . but I want to tell you God has blessed me for what I did 'cause you stepped in and saved my son."

She sucked her teeth and avoided my eyes as if anticipating my next question.

"Clarence's mama got a little problem. Ain't too straight right now."

She said no more and I let it go. There were so many euphemisms for crack addiction.

"What did Morris hear Clarence say?" I kept my voice low and tried not to sound too eager.

"Seems like Dr. Harding had called Clarence into the office to tell him he wasn't gonna go on that trip to France. He had failed some grades in somethin' or other, Morris wasn't sure."

"How did Morris hear all of this?"

"He was standin' right outside the office, waitin' to bring some sheet music Harding had sent him for. The voices was so loud, Morris said he was embarrassed just bein' there, but he didn't know what to do. Said Clarence even used some street language with Dr. Harding and I know for a fact that kinda stuff just don't go in there . . . they don't stand still for nuthin' like that."

I shook my head, remembering the long, grueling orientation session I had attended when Alvin joined earlier. If a child survived that lecture, he could survive anything.

That day the goals of the organization had been stressed, along with the responsibility of each chorister to "act as an ambassador representing every Harlemite who ever lived, past and present."

Three thousand singers had applied and one hundred had been chosen to join. The incoming hundred, fifty boys and fifty girls, had to dress, act, think, and speak with the utmost decorum. Just as the other, more seasoned choristers had been taught. That meant no profanity—"off-language" the director had called it. No oversize T-shirts, no gold-capped teeth that did nothing but cause bad breath, no baggy trousers falling off the hips, and no short skirts.

As I saw it, the director didn't care if it was the style for the nineties, if the pants couldn't stay up and the skirts down, he wasn't cuttin' no slack. The kid was out the door. Plain and simple.

I often wondered how anyone could have delivered a four-and-a-half-hour speech that didn't include lunch.

At the end of that day, everyone, parents and new choristers alike, had straggled from the auditorium in a daze, the choristers only too happy in their newfound roles as cultural ambassadors.

I had gone home, taken two aspirin, and put on a Wynton Marsalis tape to calm my last nerve before falling into bed.

"What does Clarence look like?"

Mrs. Johnson shrugged. "Tall, thin, gangly, like he ain't never had enough to eat since the day he opened his eyes. Kinda brown-skin with one a them flattop fadeaway haircuts. Don't look too nice on him, though, 'cause his face is real thin."

"And you think . . . Morris thinks . . . Clarence might have had something to do with Dr. Harding's death?"

"Might have. But who knows? Who knows? I, for one, don't buy that but he did threaten him. Last thing he said when he rushed out the office was 'You ain't seen no attitude, Mr. Harding. You ain't seen nuthin'.'"

"Morris said Clarence stomped so hard the steps

shook when he ran down . . . Now, I suppose ain't no-body gonna parlez-vous anytime soon 'cause all the trips have been canceled."

I said nothing, wondering if the trips had been canceled out of fear and general confusion or merely post-poned out of respect for the dead.

"Where does Clarence live?"

"In the same projects as me, only he's in a different building."

She opened a patent-leather purse and slipped a piece of paper across the table. "Here's his address. And his phone number. Lord, I hope he ain't mixed up in none of this. He got a voice that was heaven-sent. I mean that boy can sing."

"Did he sing today?"

"Matter a fact, he did. He was with the senior chorus, standin' toward the left, on the very end. I didn't even think to point him out to you."

"That's all right. Here comes the waitress again. At last."

We ate in silence. I did not mention the well-dressed man who had touched Erskin's mother. Instead I wondered about Clarence.

Seventeen-year-old kids committed murder often enough that it was no longer front-page, but did a seventeen-year-old find enough nerve to attend the fu-neral and sing over the casket?

Did he know how to drive? If so, whose car had he commandeered or stolen? I thought of the HO plates and decided that I needed answers to a lot of things—answers that didn't seem possible.

chapter six

The "Welcome" banner hung limply over the precinct's entrance, and the main lobby was crowded as usual. An old woman with an empty carrying case was screaming at the desk sergeant because someone had stolen her two Persian cats while she was out shopping for pet food. A short stocky man wanted the police to put out an all-points bulletin for his girlfriend who had disappeared from the Half-Moon Bar while he was taking care of business in the men's room. Two adolescents sat hunched over on the bench cocooned in their sweat hoods, coating their fear with loud meaningless talk.

People moved around them, in and out of the area. The air had a slightly medicinal odor which I had never noticed the whole time I'd worked here. I saw that the beige rubber tile floor still had the same indelible coffee stains and gum marks, and the spool of flypaper still hung ineffectually from the ceiling.

I walked in just after the evening shift had come on.

The cordiality surprised me and several officers approached to shake my hand, though several of the others hung back, pretending not to see me.

I signed in and was accompanied up the stairs to the investigation unit. On the landing, I encountered the man who had caused me to lose my job. Patrolman Terry Keenan smiled and stepped out of the way with an elaborate flourish.

He was five feet ten, with a thin, pockmarked face, stooped shoulders, and concave chest that seemed to fill out and look healthy only when he donned his bulletproof vest. He said nothing but I remembered that thin nasal voice, whining about never making enough money for this dangerous job and how his taxes alone seemed to be financing the entire welfare system.

The high point of his career happened when he, in a mob of a thousand other officers of the law, egged on by a prosecuter who bore a striking resemblance to Frankenstein's monster, stormed City Hall, threatening and cursing Mayor Dinkins. Keenan and several others had been caught on camera but Keenan still had his job. His father was a captain somewhere in Brooklyn so I supposed that counted for something.

Still, I paused long enough to size him up and regret that I had not punched him twice as hard when I had had the chance. I took comfort in the fact that I'd named him in my lawsuit against the department.

At the top of the stairs to the left, the door to the investigation unit was open. Detective Danny Williams rose from the desk and approached with his hands outstretched. "Come on in, Miss Anderson—Mali. Good to see you again despite the circumstances."

Danny Williams was Tad's partner and everyone said they made a good pair. Both were as tenacious as pit bulls once they got hold of a clue, no matter how slight or where it led them. But the similarity ended there. Tad lived in a two-bedroom co-op apartment in the Riverbend complex on 140th Street facing the Harlem River, but Danny had recently moved from a brownstone on 128th Street to a split-level on the tip of Long Island.

"Nobody's gonna get back at me through my kids," he liked to say. Yet he remained in the neighborhood spending as many off-work hours as Tad. He tracked down leads and most of the time he was successful, but rumor had it that his wife and daughters rarely saw him.

At one time, Tad had hinted that Danny might have some other reason for hanging around Harlem so much. A lot of calls came in on Danny's line, and when Tad offered to take a message, a woman's soft voice usually said, "No message," and hung up. Of course, he could have traced the calls if he wanted to, but what Dan did was his business. Tad was trying to get a handle on his own problems at the time and had no interest in another man's personal stuff, even if he was his partner.

I looked at Danny now and wanted to shake my head. Here was this slightly chubby, middle-aged man with a wife, three daughters, a new car, and a house mortgaged up to his eyeballs. Was he still trying to burn his candle at both ends?

He pulled out a chair for me, then walked around his desk to sit facing me. His movements were languid, and although he did not weigh as much as Tad, the roundness of his stomach made him appear heavier.

Up close, I saw that he had less hair than when I had last worked in the precinct. His suit bore the hallmarks of very good tailoring and his dark brown face was clean-shaven, but under the fluorescent lights, he appeared tired.

"So how's it going, Mali? Private life must be all right. You look like you just stepped off the cover of *Essence*. Our mutual friend mentions you all the time.

Talks my ear off. Hey, a Ph.D. I'm damn proud of you and I'm glad to see my man smiling again."

I had dressed carefully for this visit. Fresh haircut, small gold Nefertiti earrings, and shoes and shoulder bag to complement a beige wool suit. At five nine and 120 pounds, people often mistook me for a model or a disciplined athlete. Now I felt uncomfortable, wondering if Tad had been smiling because of my schoolwork (my graduate study) or my "homework" (my activities with him). But I hadn't made love to him yet, so what was he so happy about?

The safest answer was no answer at all so I smiled and remained quiet. Danny fingered his notebook and spoke of his family. "Teenagers are the hardest thing to raise," he complained. "They think they know everything."

I thought of Alvin, who was not yet a teenager but who also pretended, once upon a time, to know everything. Now the silences have grown longer, and when he does speak, it is the echo of grief I pretend not to hear.

Danny unfolded a wallet-size collection of pictures. "This is Harriet, the oldest. That's Claudia, and the one next to her is Louise."

His fingers moved across the surface pointing out the split-level in the background complete with the brick barbecue grill. The final picture was that of a small, light brown woman seated in a wheelchair near a curved sofa inside the house.

"This is my wife."

I smiled, waiting to hear her name, but he folded the collection up and slipped the wallet in his jacket again.

"It's wonderful that your children have such old-fashioned names."

He leaned back in the chair. "Yep. I left that decision to my wife."

I nodded again, waiting for him to continue, to at

least talk about why she was in the wheelchair, but he said nothing more.

I looked around the small room with its two desks, the battered chairs, and the three filing cabinets in the corner supporting a huge spathiphyllum plant, its leaves grown wide as palms and pointing up toward the lights.

A row of "Wanted" posters hung from the wall at eye level in stacks as thick as telephone directories. They were suspended from large hooks with photos and sketches of America's Most Wanted. The wall nearest Danny's desk was covered with a glossy "Just Say No" poster and next to that was the sector map with its black, yellow, white, and green pins representing the incidents of homicide, rape, burglary, and robbery.

I glanced at the map and wanted to ask "How's business?" but knew that I'd be there all night if I had to listen to his answer.

I was beginning to wonder if this was a social call when he finally got around to the first question. I gave my statement, describing the event as well as I remembered but omitted finding the gold caps. Let Tad discuss that with him. I'd had enough of a lecture when I'd given them to him four nights ago. I didn't need a further reminder about "tampering with evidence." If indeed it was evidence. But I did mention speaking that night to Mrs. Johnson, the boy's mother.

Danny looked up from his report sheet.

"Oh? What did she say?"

"Nothing revelant. Just thanked me for saving Morris."

I also didn't mention the later conversation in the restaurant.

Danny put his pen down and leaned across the desk. "We all thank you, Mali. I mean it. You know, when I look at my daughters, it hurts to see something like this . . ."

I nodded, wondering if, in his busy schedule, he got the chance to look at his daughters. It was common knowledge in the precinct that he wanted to take on every homicide case that came in. And when he got a case, he submerged himself in it. I wondered if it was his way of crowding out the situation at home.

"I dropped by to see Mrs. Johnson yesterday," he continued. "She was just coming in from the funeral so I guess my timing was off. Nice woman but nervous. I guess anybody'd be nervous trying to raise a kid nowadays with all that's going on . . . By the way, what can you tell me about the boy?"

"Nothing, except that he's a member of the Chorus and a friend of my nephew. They play ball together sometimes."

"Basketball?"

"Well, yes . . ."

"Where?"

"Around. You know, the usual places . . ."

"Kid been in any trouble before?"

I looked at him. "Which kid?"

"Sorry. I meant Morris and of course you wouldn't know that. I'm sorry."

He flipped his notebook closed and rose from behind the desk. The interview had ended.

I rose also, feeling vaguely disappointed. Weren't there more questions to be asked? It's true that I didn't get a good look at the person in the car and he seemed satisfied with that, but why ask me so many questions about Morris and what he might have seen? Where was the "solid lead" he had talked about at the rehearsal hall?

Perhaps he'd gotten all the information he needed from Mrs. Johnson. Or he's going to question Morris again. That's his method. Circle around and around like a shark and then close in.

Then again, perhaps he really has more cases than he can handle.

He seemed to be in a hurry to dismiss me so I obliged.

"If you think of anything else I might be able to help you with, give me a call," I said.

On the first floor, I glanced toward the rear where the holding cells, twenty-five in one long unlighted row, were situated. The area was quiet and the crowd in the lobby had also thinned out. There was no sign of the two boys in the sweat hoods and no one screaming, cursing, or making hysterical demands. I checked my watch and knew it would not remain that way because the evening was just beginning and there was always a peculiar ebb and flow from crisis to crisis.

A slight breeze drifted in and the "Welcome" banner fluttered as I passed beneath it. Outside, I decided to take the long way home and stroll with ordinary people who were going about ordinary business. I walked toward Malcolm X Boulevard and turned to stroll past the Schomburg Research Center. Inside the glass walls, a small crowd lifted champagne glasses, celebrating a new art exhibit, while across the avenue, an ambulance splashed a whir of red and yellow lights against the walls as it screeched into the emergency area of Harlem Hospital.

I continued to walk, not too fast, because I wanted to think about the questions Danny Williams should have asked me. Questions about the license plate. About Erskin and if he was alive when I had gotten to him. The possibility of other witnesses. Instead, he asked about Morris as if the boy was the villain instead of the victim, but that was Danny's way, his roundabout method.

chapter seven

The temperature had reached fifty-five degrees when I stepped out of Shepherd Hall on Convent Avenue and rushed to a phone. Deborah's line at the library was busy so I hung up and waited and watched the other students as they lounged about the CUNY campus, convinced that spring had finally arrived.

I tried the number again and her calm voice came on the line: "Research and Acquisitions, may I help you?"

"Deborah? My last class has been canceled. How about lunch?"

"You caught me just in time, girl. I'll meet you across the street from the Old School."

The Old School was our junior high school on 135th Street and Edgecombe Avenue where Deborah and I first met in the seventh grade. From there, we went through high school and City University together.

The walk from the campus down the steep hill near Hamilton Terrace triggered old memories of my sister and me sledding down this dangerous incline and curving

into a snowbank at the last minute, barely avoiding sliding out into the rushing traffic of St. Nicholas Avenue.
We did this in bone-freezing weather, as long as the snow
lasted, and were always sorry when winter gave way to
spring.

Walking down the hill now had a different feeling.
My sister was gone and I was glad for Deborah's long,
steady friendship.

The traffic on the avenue seemed to move faster
now and it made me dizzy to watch. As I approached the
corner, I actually waited for the light to change before
stepping off the curb.

Despite the warm weather, most of the benches
along the park were empty. I strolled past St. Mark's
Church where St. Nicholas and Edgecombe Avenues
merged. A block away I selected a bench directly across
from the school and opened my notebook. A jogger ran
by, circled back, and though he was out of breath, managed to call out: "Hey, pretty. Need some help with your
homework?"

"Not today, thank you." I smiled at the man. Despite his nice strong legs, he looked old enough to be my
father. He smiled and waved and ran on.

Minutes after I lost sight of him, Deborah strolled
across the avenue. She sat beside me and extended a large
brown paper bag.

"Here we are. Our favorite food . . ."

Before she opened it, I knew the package contained
fried chicken sandwiches from Pan Pan's restaurant, complete with french fries, catsup, hot sauce, banana pudding,
and large containers of iced tea.

Deborah seems to have been blessed with a rare
metabolism which allowed her to eat five meals a day yet
she never enlarged beyond a size 5 dress. She was five feet
six inches tall, with close-cut hair and beautiful skin. Her

earrings were the biggest things on her. I was a size 7, and whenever I looked at her, I felt fat.

"How're you doing, Mal? I heard something in your voice that said 'Urgent. Come quick. Bring favorite food.' What's going on?"

I laughed as she handed me a sandwich. The chicken leg was crisp despite the catsup. I added some hot sauce and took a large bite. Finally I said, "I'm sorry. I didn't mean to sound as if I were at death's door. I need some background on a man by the name of Gary Mark. Thirtyish, white, works as director of development for the Uptown Children's Chorus. Though from the looks of him, seems he belongs down on Wall Street. Corporate type, big time. Success written all over him."

She made a note of his name. Aside from her position as a researcher, she was also a writer who knew how to get a handle on anything in the city that needed knowing. Her mind was like an encyclopedia and her memory rivaled a computer chip. She had been that way ever since our junior high school days.

"Shouldn't be too hard," she said between bites. "I'll pull up some of the corporations, brokerage houses, and foundations. Stuff like that. If nothing pops, I'll scan the scandal sheets." She glanced at me. "Someone you're interested in?"

"Not the way you think. I sort of bumped into him the day Dr. Harding was murdered. Everyone was upset at the rehearsal hall but he was more than upset. Frightened is a better word. And I don't know why. I need some background because he's around the kids. And Alvin is in that chorus."

"Oh shit. Doesn't anyone check on these things nowadays?"

"He's not a pedophile but I suspect something else is going on. I think he might have a fondness for nose candy. Lots of it. I mean the clothes look like a million dollars, but there was something about his expression, something had terrified him . . ."

We ate in silence. Deborah sipped her tea and started on the fries. "Well, I should have something for you in a day or so."

"Good."

She glanced at me and reached out to tap my hand. "Listen, if this guy has such a shaky aura, why don't you just pull Alvin out and let it go? I don't want to pick up the newspapers one morning and read where your body was found floating off Riverside Drive. Let it go."

"I can't, Deborah. Too many things have happened already."

"Too many things like what?"

"I don't know for sure, that's why I can't say . . ."

I glanced at her face and saw the same inquisitive look she'd worn since we were teenagers. I wished I could tell her more but there was no point in involving anyone else.

"You know," she smiled, dipping back into the bag of fries, "when you left the force, I listened to your howling for weeks, but let me tell you now. I was damn glad. You were meant for better things, Mali. We went all through school together. Sweated the exams, trudged up this hill in all kinds of weather, gave up the discos to sit through summer school. And who liked to shake their booty more than you and you gave it all up to hit the books. What was the point of it? What was the point of earning a degree in sociology just to become a damn cop? A GED would've gotten you the same job."

"You know as well as I do why I joined the force," I said, trying to keep my voice even. "You remember that night we were walking down that very hill from school, and less than a block from here, we saw the cops, three of them, beating that brother, pressing his face into that chain-link fence with the heels of their shoes, using their

flashlights on his head. You remember how he looked?
His hands cuffed and his face a crisscross of swollen
welts?

"And you remember how we screamed? Two
women with nothing but our books in our arms and our
loud mouths . . . and screaming all the louder when the
cops moved toward us, calling us bitches, asking what the
fuck we were looking at? Remember?"

Memory churned up an anger in me that I thought
had grown cold, but as I spoke now, it spread to my
throat, so hot and thick I couldn't swallow. I put the
sandwich down and turned to stare directly at Deborah,
but she was looking across the avenue at the classroom on
the third floor facing the park. Our old seventh-grade
room where we had not yet learned the meaning of the
limitations of blackness.

"That wasn't fair, Mali. I had nightmares for years
after. I tried hard to forget that night."

"Well, I tried hard *not* to forget. I'll never forget it.
They were coming for us because we saw what they did
and we backed away and they surrounded us, remember?
And the only reason we're alive today, I believe, is because
other students heard our screams and had run down the
hill. And the people came out of that building across the
avenue. Came out in bathrobes and house slippers and
curlers. Dog walkers showed up. And the cops knew they
couldn't do away with fifty witnesses. So they called for
backup and yelled riot.

"I joined the force because I thought I could work
to make sure nothing like that happened again—at least
not on my watch."

"But look," she said, turning to me. "What you
really joined was a force dedicated to one thing: keeping
the natives in check. The tighter, the better. How long
would you have lasted if you hadn't hit that cop? Now
you're off the force. You were fired and you still want to

play Dick Tracy. Like I told you earlier, sometimes you have to change the world before you can change the neighborhood."

"Well, maybe I should join the Peace Corps?"

She saw my changing expression and held up her hand. "I didn't say that. But you're back in school and I'm glad. I really am. Social work is your life. Ever since I can remember, you've wanted to change things. An advanced degree will make it easier."

I wasn't so sure how much easier it'd be, but I bit my tongue and remained silent as she continued. "And this cops-and-robbers thing, I think it goes a little beyond your concern for Alvin."

I looked away. It was too simple to say that Erskin had been very special to me or that he didn't deserve to die the way he did. I wondered if I should try to explain what I had felt, kneeling that day in the rain, my feelings floating somewhere between sister love and something deeper, and brushing my fingers over his face to close his eyes. How could I tell her that when I hold my hands together, I still feel the feathery lightness of his lashes against my palm?

"Whatever I'm doing," I said, "I'll clue you when the game's over, okay?"

Friends, close friends especially, seem to have a knack for stepping on my last damn nerve.

Deborah saw this and made a big show of looking at her watch.

"For heaven's sakes, where does the hour go? Have to get back, girl. I'll call as soon as I've dug up something. Remember what I said . . . be careful."

I watched her walk away and I sat a few minutes longer trying to collect my thoughts.

. . . Shake my booty. What did she expect? I came by it naturally enough. Not too many people can brag that their mother had been a dancer with Katherine Dunham's company. And Mom only quit when she married Dad.

I opened my book again but the print on the page kept sliding away. I glanced at the cracked sidewalk and at the pigeons picking among the small patches of new grass poking through. No one strolled by and I wondered where all the people were, even though most honest folks were downtown, working at jobs they probably hated.

I felt a slight twinge of depression. "Depression," Mama once said, "is a condition that makes rich white women spend their days going from one store to another, accumulating things they'll never use."

Well, I wasn't rich or white but my AmEx card couldn't tell the difference.

Why not go shopping? a part of me said. You've got the rest of the afternoon free. Lord & Taylor is just an A train away. And while you're strolling the neighborhood, there's Saks.

Another part of me, the practical and sensible part which I rarely acknowledged, brought me back to earth and my current status. I was a graduate student with no job, living at home with a musician father. His income was good but it wasn't my income. Without my own funds to back up this plastic, having it in my pocket meant nothing. The practical side won out and I closed my book, which I wasn't reading anyway, and headed for home.

On the way, my thoughts drifted back to Gary Mark. Development directors are only as effective as their connection to money sources. Did he himself have money? How did he come to connect with the Chorus? Had he been very friendly with Erskin? Friendly with the director of the Chorus? And if he was as well off as he appeared to be, why hadn't he had his damaged septum repaired? Most of the movie stars, models, and other rich cokeheads did.

· · ·

That evening, Tad was waiting in the Pepper Pot, a small, pleasantly lit Caribbean restaurant on Adam Clayton Powell Boulevard where the patrons could talk above a whisper without competing with those seated nearby.

Our table near the window commanded a wide view of the avenue, and thanks to the break in the weather, street traffic was brisk. Teenagers, plugged into Walkmans, bobbed by to a private hip-hop beat. Vendors and hawkers were out, flashing by with mobile inventories of watches, socks, neckties, and scarves fluttering from their outstretched arms. "All items guaranteed," they called. "Check it out. Money back if not satisfied."

I made my way to the table and Tad rose to pull my chair out. He was drinking Jamaican beer and ordered one for me.

"Anything new?" he asked.

If soft lighting did wonders for a woman, it did twice as much for this man who didn't even need it. His eyes seemed deeper than ever and I wanted to touch the corners of his mouth to make certain the smile was real. My knees started feeling a little funny so I sat down quickly.

"Nothing's new," I said. "Spoke to a librarian friend earlier today. She might have something for me in a few days. I'm trying to get a handle on the fund-raiser. He seemed like real money, but there was something else about him. Something hidden. And frightened."

"You saw him for two minutes and you figured all that out already?"

I looked at him sharply. It was not his question so much as the tone that surprised and suddenly annoyed me. I was the one who had looked in Gary Mark's eyes. And what I had seen was unmistakable.

I also wanted to let Tad know that when he had walked into the precinct that first time with that prisoner,

I had figured something out immediately. In fact, what I had felt was as close to an epiphany as I was likely to get. In the time it took to blink, I had concluded that of all the men I had known and loved and hated and fought and lost and loved again, this one was going to be the very next and the very last. It had happened that quickly.

"Sometimes two minutes is enough," I said, "if you know what you're looking for."

The waitress recommended the broiled snapper and baked plantains and we ordered more beer. The soft reggae echoes of Bob Marley drifted from the CD near the kitchen and should have been enough to calm my nerves, but I was thinking of Deborah's warning: Don't let me read about you in the papers. Pull Alvin out and forget it . . .

But I couldn't forget. If she came up blank, I made a mental note to call another friend. But I couldn't sit in St. Nicholas Park and share down-home fried chicken and banana pudding with Melissa Stewart. She was one of the few black female partners in a top firm on the Street. I'd have to push my plastic and take her to Windows on the World and then probably dip her in mimosas to get her to talk. But at least she'd know of Gary Mark if he worked anywhere near Wall Street.

"What did you find out about the gold caps?" I asked.

Tad shook his head in disgust. "Nothing. Dead end. One dentist told me those caps were the cheap ones, the kind that someone can put in and snap out when they needed to. And that so-called diamond in it wasn't worth a dime. And there're no reports of any recent visits for tooth repair, at least not around here, so I guess Morris didn't do much damage to the guy who grabbed him."

"And Erskin Harding was killed simply because he tried to keep Morris from being snatched?"

"Maybe. Maybe not. He may have been in the wrong place at the wrong time but we don't know yet."

I remembered Alvin's question: "Why'd they have to kill him? They didn't have to kill him."

It was true. They didn't have to. Erskin had not been in the wrong place. It was a deliberate hit . . .

"What's Danny doing?"

"Danny seems to be up against a stone wall as well. Matter of fact, I was wondering about what you told me about that boy Clarence."

I looked up quickly, wishing I had kept my mouth shut until I found out more about Clarence.

"Tad, let me handle Clarence."

"Let you handle—uh-oh. Do I hear social consciousness kicking in? The boy comes from a deprived home, et cetera, et cetera, and will respond to love and attention and confess all."

"That's not it and you know it. I don't think there's anything for him to confess."

I was becoming more annoyed, imagining how Tad would handle the situation.

"Let me speak to him, Tad."

"Why?"

"Because somehow, I don't feel right about the idea of a seventeen-year-old murdering—"

Tad held up his hand. "Please. You haven't been out of the department that long. Have you forgotten what Riker's looks like? Place is a zoo, packed to the rafters with seventeen-year-olds. And they're not there for playing hooky."

I folded my arms and gritted my teeth.

"I don't know about the ones at Riker's. I don't feel right about *this* seventeen-year-old."

"That's what most of their mothers say: 'This is happening to my boy and it's not right,' even though the angel was caught with the gun still smoking in his hand.

They look you right in the eye and say 'My child didn't do it.' "

The waitress brought our dinner but I had lost my appetite. A minute later Tad noticed that the red snapper on my plate was untouched, so he whispered, "Okay, okay. You work on the kid. I'll see if anything else turns up about Harding."

I gazed at him across the small table. He was so damned handsome it was hard to stay angry, but I worked at it.

He's placating me. As long as he's been on the job, he should know by now that there's always more to a case, more to a clue, than meets the eye. Feelings, however vague and unscientific, do count for something, but I was not in the mood to work on changing his mind. I looked away from him.

Handsome or not, I crumpled my napkin on the table, picked up my purse, and left before my temper and tongue got the better of me.

Outside, I drew in enough breath to calm down, then headed home, which wasn't very far. The good thing about living in the neighborhood was that if you're on a date and it turned sour, you didn't need two trains and a plane to get back home. You could walk if you were angry enough. One look at your face and potential muggers on the street, most of the time, gave you a wide berth and left you and your mad attitude alone.

Once home, I intended to submerge myself in an herbal bath and listen to Dad's record, the old 78 rpm, the original sound of "Profoundly Blue." God only knows what Alvin had done with that tape. Probably stashed it as a keepsake in the bottom of his closet somewhere inside one of his smelly sneakers.

"Profoundly Blue." I don't remember ever hearing the tune or hearing of the musicians who made it so special. Meade "Lux" Lewis, Charlie Christian, Edmond Hall. Who were they?

I intended to lie back in the water in absolute silence, close my eyes, and let the answers come to me in the dark. Close my eyes and imagine the smoky club where the recording took place in front of a large old microphone hooked up in center stage after the place had closed for the night; the men—with their porkpies and stingy brims pulled low and their rolled-up shirtsleeves, open collars, and loose suspenders—playing the tune over and over until a particular chord cut through the haze sounding just the way they wanted.

Or maybe they got it right the first time. Dad said it occasionally happened that way, like the classic Miles Davis recording "Kind of Blue."

I hurried past the bricked-up windows of the old Smalls' Paradise and crossed the intersection of 135th Street and Seventh Avenue. The avenue traffic was still heavy with strollers, bikes, and Rollerbladers but faded into quiet once I turned onto my block.

The bathwater was fragrant and the cluster of scented candles near the tub threw soft shadows against the pink marble walls. The water enveloped my shoulders and I decided to ignore the noise of the phone. When the machine kicked in on the third ring, Tad's voice filled the room and "Profoundly Blue" became a small background riff against the faulty rhythm in my chest.

"Mali. If you're there, pick up! Why the hell did you walk out like that? I got some news and it's not good. I'll see you in a few minutes."

In the minute it took to stumble out of the tub, grab a towel, and reach for the phone, the line had gone dead.

I barely had time to towel off and slip into a T-shirt and sweats before the bell rang. I paused at the top of the stairs and listened to the voices, trying to decide if I had the strength to absorb any more bad news, whatever it was.

"Is Mali home?"

"Why, yes. Just a minute, she's—"

The dead tone of Tad's voice propelled me downstairs.

My father nodded and disappeared again into his basement study and Tad, moving like an old man, entered the living room.

"Would you . . . like something—Walker and water?"

"Yeah. That would be good. Whatever you have."

I gazed at his reflection in the mirrored bar, watched him sit on the edge of the sofa and rub his chin. He reached for the double Scotch and I was about to raise my own glass when he said, "You were right on the money about Gary Mark."

"What do you mean? What's happened?"

"Somebody took him out. Two bullets to the back of the head as he was getting into his car. Probably happened while we were in the Pepper Pot trying to decide what to do about Clarence."

"Could've been a robbery, a random thing," I whispered, knowing it was not.

I took a long sip from my glass, avoiding Tad's look as he continued. "Wallet, keys, credit cards, all there. It was a quick hit and the guy jumped into a waiting car."

"Where did it happen?"

"Right in front of the rehearsal hall."

"Anyone see the plates?"

"If they did, no one's talking."

A dizzy feeling came over me and I sat down. Perhaps I had swallowed my drink too quickly, perhaps it was too much alcohol on an empty stomach . . .

"Mali. You all right?"

"Yes. I think so . . ."

Two murders and an attempted kidnapping. The toll was rising. I did not want to think about who might be next.

This murder made all of the papers, the *Daily Challenge* and the *City Sun* carrying it and the major media—print and television—flooding the area with reporters pushing mikes under unsuspecting noses.

"What do you think is the major cause of crime in the area?" one young reporter asked brightly on the six o'clock news, her question interspersed with stock footage of graffiti-scarred walls and burned-out tenements.

"Let's see . . ." came the bewildered answer of one of the locals, smiling wide because he was finally being recognized on national television as the probable authority on urban decay. He blinked and smiled into the bright lights and straightened his Mets baseball cap and smiled some more.

"I'd say it was them drugs, that's what I think."

The reporter shook her head sadly and waved the mike back and forth like a wand. "So you think drugs are the problem, the major cause of crime in the area?"

"Well, yeah. Definitely. I think so."

I didn't know whether to throw up or throw my shoe at the television screen. Never mind that eighty percent of the population who are drug dependent live outside these "urban areas" and never mind that the chemicals needed to convert the plant to cocaine are manufactured in the United States and then shipped to South America—basic facts the reporter must have known as she asked:

"So what do you think can be done to solve this problem?" Flashing a smile brighter than the lights that surrounded them.

"Well, you know, the drugs—crack—is all over the

place. Police need to git on the case. Do somethin' to clean
it up. If a kid in the street know where the dealer is, how
come the top cops don't know and they gittin' paid big
bucks to know what's goin' on. How come they can't stop
these out-a-town kids from comin' into this neighborhood
to cop the stuff, and while we at it, how come every time
somethin' bad happens—I ain't talkin' about this crime,
you understan', 'cause it did happen right here—but how
come when it happen up on, say, Riverside Drive, or
Washington Heights, y'all still say Harlem? But when
somethin' okay happens, y'all say Upper West Side?
What's happenin' wid yo' geography, ma'am?"

"Well, yes, those are interesting observations but
drugs are a problem, a major problem, in many urban
areas, thank you."

Fade away to graffiti-scarred wall and burned tenement, this time with baggy-pants teenager wandering into
the camera's path and staring, bewildered, into the blinding lights, then back to reporter.

"And there you have this breaking story, folks. The
police have no suspects but the investigation is ongoing.
More at eleven o'clock. Back to you at the studio."

There had been two days of saturation coverage before the cameras disappeared. All this time, Alvin and I
had remained glued to the television and I was glad when
the news shifted to the criminal pursuits of the other bor-
oughs.

The papers treaded lightly on Gary Mark, briefly
mentioning his career as a whiz kid on Wall Street in the
high-flying eighties before his conviction on insider trading. He had misappropriated millions and was sentenced
to ten months in jail, which had been suspended in lieu of
two years of community service.

How had he wound up at the Uptown Children's
Chorus?

I called Deborah to find out how far she had been able to dig beneath the surface.

She came on the line and there was a pause. "Mali? Is that you?"

"Yes. What's going on? What's wrong?"

When she answered, the hesitation was more pronounced. "Mali, listen to me. Give it up, okay?"

And she hung up before I could ask her why.

chapter eight

Alvin sat at the table moving his breakfast around on his plate. I glanced at him for the third time in as many minutes and wondered how anyone could look at food so cold the egg yolks had congealed and the bacon had wilted. Again this morning, it seemed he was not going to eat. In fact, for the last few days, he had hardly touched any food.

I was running out of menus and wondered if I should try the corner hot dog stand next. Well, maybe not quite that, but it might be a good idea to eat out.

"I'm taking Ruffin for a stroll," I announced, pushing my chair back from the table. "Want to come with me?"

Dad glanced up from his newspaper. "I already took him out, just an hour ago."

"Well, okay. But I feel like walking anyway. Come on, Alvin. Today's Saturday. The weather's nice. Why stick in the house? We can stroll down to the African

Market on 116th Street, or maybe pick up some pies from Wimpy's and fish 'n' chips from Majestic's."

He didn't respond, even to a menu like that.

"And if you want, we can pass by the ball court on the way."

He looked up then. "Which court?"

"The one near the projects where Clarence lives."

I watched his face for a reaction. There was only mild interest, and I wondered if he had heard anything of Clarence's threats against Dr. Harding. The rehearsal hall had closed temporarily following Gary Mark's death, so any new rumors were hard to come by. Maybe I could pick up some word on the ball court.

He considered it for a minute, then smiled faintly. "Okay, let's go." He put his plate in the sink and grabbed his jacket from the back of the chair. "See you later, Grandpa."

Outside, the sky was a penetrating blue washed with the fading streaks of a skywriter. The unpredictable weather, so characteristic of late April, seemed to have come to terms with the calendar and decided to settle into a pleasant and steady springlike mode.

The Saturday crowd, taking advantage of the great weather, was out in force. The barbecue stand was already smoking on the corner of 127th Street and a ten-gallon vat nearby was filled with corn on the cob, bobbing in a boiling foam. The vendors, under the market umbrella, had stacked fresh boiled crabs in scarlet rows and had their shucking knives and hot sauce ready for the littleneck clams.

We reached the basketball court a little past noon, too early for the large crowd that usually shared the benches to watch the ballplayers or to lay something on the single action when the numbers runner passed. A few boys were under the hoop, all much older than Alvin, practicing the art of bobbing, weaving, and hustling for the ball.

One of them flew past, bouncing the ball down the court and out of bounds.

"Yo! Down for one?" He beckoned to Alvin as he retrieved the ball.

"Naw. Not yet. You seen Clarence?"

"Clarence? He don't show till the afternoon. He a night owl. Or vampire, one. He up in the dark and doze in the day . . ."

The boy dribbled the ball, turned suddenly, and executed a half-court shot that spun on the rim for a second before dropping through. Then he was gone down the court again, clapping, jumping high in the air.

We watched for several more minutes and decided to go to the market and stop by again on the way home.

Two hours later Clarence was on the court. I watched him move with the ball, turn, jump, and shoot, then he was gliding away from the hoop. His body was long and thin and he had hands that palmed the ball so that at one point he was able to lob it like a baseball.

When he approached, his sleeveless tank top clung to him and his dark skin glistened in the sun.

"How you doin', Miss Mali? I see you sometimes when you come to pick up Striver from the rehearsals."

Clarence had given the nickname Striver to Alvin when he learned that he lived on Strivers Row. Alvin must have accepted it in good humor, knowing that everyone had a nickname that symbolized something or other, but this was the first time I had heard it. It was also the first time I had heard Clarence's voice.

Although his speech was not up to the level of the cultural ambassador that Lloyd had recommended, the voice itself, as Mrs. Johnson had described, was indeed heaven-sent. He had a bass tone that rightly belonged to someone twice his weight. I listened and wondered how his lungs and diaphragm accommodated such volume. If Dad heard him, I know he'd say, "This boy could be the next Paul Robeson."

I smiled at him now. "I'm all right, Clarence. How are you doing?"

"Okay, I guess. No use complainin'."

About what? I wanted to ask, but knew he would go tight as a new zipper if I probed too far, too fast.

Then, like most young men who felt compelled to show off before a woman, Clarence tapped Alvin on the shoulder.

"Come on, Striver, let's hit it. Show your sister what I been tryin' to teach you . . ."

"She's my aunt."

Clarence looked at me, then back at Alvin, and whistled softly, "Man, you got a pretty aunt."

Then he literally ran away, knees pumping, yelling until he reached the basket, laid up a shot and hung from the rim a second before dropping to the ground again.

Alvin shed his coat and followed him down the court. Clarence had a broad smile, no sign of broken teeth, or the discoloration that would suggest he'd worn gold caps lately. Besides, if he had the money and had a choice, he'd probably take a pass on the caps and get himself some decent sneakers. The boy's shoes were in such disrepair his feet were practically on the ground.

A minute later he came to sit beside me to watch Alvin continue his jump shots.

"I'm sorry to hear about Dr. Harding and about Gary Marks," I said, trying for an opening. "I heard you singing at Dr. Harding's service" (which wasn't quite accurate: everyone sang but there had been so many choristers I couldn't distinguish one voice from another). "First, Dr. Harding, now this thing happening to Mr. Marks . . ."

I tried to read his expression as I lumped the two deaths together in a single expression of sympathy.

"One, two, just like that," I whispered. "I can't believe it."

Clarence turned to look at the far end of the court, then glanced down to study the holes and mismatched laces in his sneakers.

"Yeah. Nobody can believe it, but that's the way it went down."

"The way what went down?"

"You know. One. Two. They out."

He had regular features and rather deep-set eyes, eyes that should have been easy to read, but his face was completely without expression.

"I suppose all the tours have been canceled. What's the Chorus . . . what are you . . . going to do now?"

He shrugged and continued to concentrate on his laces. "The rehearsal hall is closed for a while. I don't know about the group. I don't . . . I don't know about me."

He suddenly turned to look at me appraisingly. "I heard what you did about Morris."

"What?"

"You know. Steppin' out for him and you wasn't even strapped. Wasn't packin' no heat." He shook his head, but his face still seemed guarded. "Man, that was somethin'. I was tellin' Striver, that was somethin'."

"Well," I said, not sure if that "something" was good or bad, "sometimes we do what we have to, when we have to. And we don't think of the possible consequences. We just . . . do it."

He looked up now and gazed toward the far end of the court. Still no perceptible change. No joy or sadness, guilt, grief, or even curiosity. No remorse or sense of loss. Was this boy alive?

The more I talked, the more he seemed to veer off

on various tangents. It was tough trying to lead him back
to his feelings about Erskin Harding and how he had
died. And he did not want to talk about Gary Mark at all.

When he shifted the conversation a third time to the
art of karate, and the various moves and stances I needed
to know in order to defend myself, I knew it was time to
let it go, maybe pick it up again further on down the line.

He rose to demonstrate a particular movement and
I tried not to glance down at his sneakers. Up close, they
looked as if they would not last another week.

He went through several stances, each one more
pronounced than the one before. His eyes finally changed
and the anger and frustration that I saw was frightening.

Alvin came over, sweating from his workout. He
pulled his jacket on and I tried not to notice the difference
in their clothing. I looked beyond them but couldn't ignore the overflowing trash cans at the end of the court,
the broken benches surrounding them, and the patches of
grass pushing through the worn asphalt. And everywhere,
the small, Day-Glo caps of crack vials strewn about, like
confetti after a parade.

I saw this and knew that Clarence saw it also. Day
after day. So much so that it had become part of a landscape that no longer registered in his consciousness. I remembered how often I had walked along 34th Street in
the shadow of the Empire State Building and had never
risked eyestrain or "tourist neck" because the building, for
all its massive presence, had always been there. And like
most born and bred and blasé New Yorkers, I tuned out
that landscape, the same way Clarence tuned out the vials
and other debris that crushed under his foot as he moved
to the end of the court. It was simply something he no
longer saw.

I watched him move and imagined his long arms
and legs—indeed his entire body—metamorphosing into

the jointed, bony plates of an armadillo enabling him to deflect all sensation.

But he sang in the Chorus, sang songs so full of feeling that he was able to pull up the pain and tears from that spring hidden within all who heard him.

I left the park, convinced that he did not own the gold caps, nor would he have stolen a car, but that flash of anger when he had gone into his karate stance was unmistakable.

chapter nine

Erskin Harding's mother lived in a five-story tan brick building near the corner of Frederick Douglass Boulevard and 137th Street. Across the avenue, construction was in the final stages of a four-block-long row of two-family homes. Young trees had been planted and new sidewalks were in place.

I paused on the corner, trying to remember what the old houses had looked like and what had happened to the cleaners and Billy's candy store and Bob's "Friday Night Fish Fry" restaurant that once occupied the space.

The lobby walls of Julia Harding's building were old pink-veined marble and the small lighting over the mailboxes still worked. I pressed the bell and walked up the four flights.

Her large living room overlooked the construction site and I took a seat by the window as she placed my gift of roses in a vase.

"Maybe I should have telephoned before dropping in like this. You're sure I'm not interrupting anything?"

Mrs. Harding shook her head and smiled. "Of course not. Folks my age don't have that many schedules. If we do, we don't have to stick to them. That's one of the privileges of age. You kinda do what you want, when you want . . . if you want. And besides, it's nice to see you again. Pink and red roses. What a pleasant surprise."

She was a small woman, with a tiny waist and soft hazelnut skin. Her white-streaked hair was pulled into an old-fashioned French twist and she moved with the airy grace of a dancer who had not forgotten certain steps. She walked the way my mother once walked.

"I wanted to see how you were doing and to let you know how much Alvin misses your son."

"Thank you, Mali. Your nephew's a fine boy. Lost his mother and father together, didn't he? God only knows why these things happen but He only gives us what we can bear."

I thought of my own mother, small, strong, non-smoker, yet dead of a heart attack before Alvin was even born.

I thought of my sister and brother-in-law and wondered about my own struggle with the ragged, on-and-off feelings of depression.

There were days when I wanted to sit in my room and do nothing, think nothing, and feel nothing. And nights when I tried to shut out the sound of Alvin's crying as long as possible before getting out of bed to go sit with him and talk, or kneel beside his bed to repeat the prayer that never failed to calm him. "Now I lay me down to sleep, I pray the Lord my soul to keep. If I should die . . ."

I held his hand and he usually fell asleep before I finished. And in the mornings, I tried not to see the lines deepening in Dad's face.

On other days, I felt okay.

I looked around the living room, gazing at the baby

grand piano, the pictures and awards that Erskin had, and the profusion of plants that blocked the window glare, though it was not really a sunny day. A fish tank took up a large space near the alcove, and there were shelves and shelves of books.

There was no television, so I imagined that Erskin had preferred to spend his time reading or practicing rather than vegetating in front of a screen.

I felt his presence more keenly now than when I had been in his office. How could I begin to question his mother? Would he have wanted me to?

"My father is a musician," I volunteered, searching for a way to begin. I moved toward the piano, not to touch it—because I knew it was Erskin's and to touch it was to touch him again. I moved close enough to stand and admire it, a Baldwin baby grand, highly polished, facing the window at an angle.

"Erskin practiced every day," Mrs. Harding said. "He'd play and I'd listen and watch the sun set. Even after he moved to his own apartment, he still dropped by to practice at least twice a week. I miss not hearing him . . ."

She walked over to the window and gazed out. "You know, I raised him alone from the time he was five years old. His father and I separated, then he divorced me. I never remarried, although I suppose I could have, many times. But I raised a son I was proud of."

She moved from the window toward the wall with the pictures. "Senior class president. College on a four-year music scholarship. Dean's list. Then he worked at doing what he loved, which was playing music." She turned to face me. "Very few people get to do what they love in this life, you know. If you can earn a living doing the thing you enjoy, it won't seem like work, it's like an endless vacation. That's the way he described his job—an endless vacation."

I nodded, understanding now why Dad had remained a musician, even when times had gotten so hard, and he and Mom had nearly lost the house. Mom had wanted to go to work—any kind of work—but Dad wouldn't hear of it. So they had held on for years by their fingernails, and eventually things turned around. The studio work picked up, there had been the commercials, then the steady gigs came again, and he was able to count himself lucky. But he never forgot those lean times, and even today he takes in more students than he can handle.

"I remember your father, knew him probably before you were even born. Heard him play at Minton's on 118th Street, Smalls' Paradise, and later at Basie's Lounge, all those places. Best bass player around."

I smiled at that. "My father had given Erskin a tape, a recording of 'Profoundly Blue.' "

"My goodness, that's really going back a long way."

"And he also came to Erskin's service. He wanted to speak with you afterward, but the place was so crowded . . ."

Mrs. Harding looked at me and her eyes filled. "I know . . . I know. It was a beautiful service. Everything was just the way Erskin would have wanted it, except—" Her eyes cleared and her voice was strong. "Except he didn't want that . . . other person there."

"Who?"

"Oh . . ." Mrs. Harding seemed undecided about going on. She seemed exhausted and her voice was soft again. "Can I offer you a glass of something? Sherry, perhaps?"

"Anything you have would be fine," I said, knowing she probably couldn't get through whatever it was she wanted to say without fortifying herself.

She left the room and returned with a small tray, glasses, and a decanter.

"I'm glad you came to see me. I don't get many callers."

She filled each glass and handed one to me. Then she offered a brief toast, and before I could blink an eye, Mrs. Harding was placing the empty glass back on the tray.

"Yes, where were we . . . The services would have been perfect if Johnnie had had the decency to stay away."

"Johnnie?"

"Johnnie Harding. He likes to call himself Erskin's brother, but Erskin never acknowledged him. I never acknowledged him either, not because his father had left me for another woman, whom he eventually married, but because, as their son grew up, he had no sense of values. From the day Johnnie was born, his father gave him every advantage he never offered Erskin: private schools from the time he entered kindergarten and at least three private colleges which he flunked or was kicked out of.

"Johnnie's mother wasn't much help. She haunted the hair salons and department stores. She was one of those young fashion plates who existed mainly to impress the bar crowd. And his father went along with it, smiling all the way. Johnnie had everything, yet he had nothing. Got into petty theft, drugs, numbers . . . whatever he thought he could get away with, that's what he did.

"Then his father said something on his deathbed . . ."

Mrs. Harding poured another glass but this time she held it in her hands, turning it round and round as she stared out of the window. The weak afternoon light cast her face in perfect profile and I could make out the faint smile playing at the corner of her mouth.

"You know what he said to Johnnie? He said,

'You're nothing. A bum. A worthless bum. I'm sorry I didn't raise my other son, Erskin.' "

"He actually said that?"

Mrs. Harding shrugged and placed the glass on the tray. "That's what Johnnie said the night he came banging on this door. Midnight. Made such a racket I didn't want Erskin to open it. But he was afraid the neighbors might call the police so he let him in, and Johnnie raved and cursed for over an hour, calling his father every name in the book. He also had a few choice words for Erskin, daring him to show up at his father's funeral."

"Did he go?"

"He wanted to, but I talked him out of it."

"What happened after that?"

"Well, that's when the phone calls started. All hours of the night, threatening calls. Then they stopped as suddenly as they had started.

"By that time, Erskin had had enough. He practically became a private detective, started keeping track of the things he heard Johnnie was involved in. Listening every time his name came up. Harlem is a small place whether we like it or not and talk does get around. Whether you're sitting in a bar, a barbershop, or a beauty parlor."

"What was Johnnie involved in?"

"I don't know exactly. Erskin compiled a list but I never saw it. I heard rumors though—of hairdressers, clubs, laundermats, restaurants, a building somewhere . . ."

She held up her hands. "Who knows for sure? Maybe Johnnie's so small-time he circulates all this talk to boost his reputation. A large part of his life is spent pretending to be something he isn't. He must have spent more than a thousand dollars packing that church with all those flowers. And I'm sure he expected me to thank him for it."

"Did he approach you as you left the church, heading for your car?"

"As a matter of fact, yes he did. What nerve."

"Assuming Erskin had made such a list, what did he intend to do with it?"

"I really don't know . . . Now I'll never know."

I was silent for a moment, wondering why a man would go to such lengths to gather information if he didn't intend to use it. Perhaps he intended it as a shield, blackmail . . . a bargaining chip to keep his brother at arm's length. And somehow, someone slipped through . . .

"Maybe Erskin kept this list in his head." Even as I said this, I thought of the calendar and did not believe it.

I wanted to talk about Gary Mark but it would have been too much for her to deal with. She was still trying to find her way through the nightmare maze of her own son's death.

I looked out of the window again but her comment brought me back.

"I suppose the police will work a little harder to solve Erskin's death now that Gary has also been killed."

I didn't know what to say. I wanted to tell her that Tad and Danny were tracking down every lead as carefully as they knew how, that they were on the case and something should break soon. But I saw the anger and resentment and couldn't say a word. I left, promising to bring Alvin the next time I visited.

Out in the street, I wondered how a dying father could set the stage for a lasting hatred between two sons and how one had to be cut down so suddenly while the other continued to flourish like a wild and useless weed.

Back in my bedroom, I kicked off my shoes, sprawled in the chair, and pressed the button on my answering machine. Dad had a separate phone line and machine downstairs in his studio and it's a good thing because the crank calls were becoming more frequent. A male voice came on now, quoted the time of the call, then said: "Bitch, watch your back because we're watching you."

There were no other messages.

chapter ten

I thought I was dreaming when I turned over and opened one eye. I had fallen asleep with the blinds up and now the morning sun washed over the bedroom. I grabbed the receiver and propped myself up on one elbow.

"Mali, you sure you want to hear this?"

It was Deborah, calling at six o'clock on a Sunday morning, the time most sensible people were in bed. She had had a change of heart but I was too sleepy to recognize it.

"All I want to hear right now, Deborah, is the sound of this phone hanging up."

There was a minute of silence and I thought that she had indeed hung up, but she continued, "I don't think so, girl. Matter of fact, there's so much stuff, not only about Mark's insider trading but stuff the media didn't deal with or doesn't know about. There's a whole lot of other folks he hung with . . . unhealthy, unlikely folks.

And seems he has an interesting connection uptown. Maybe I'd better bring this folder over."

"Now? It's practically dark outside. The sun's not even up yet."

"The sun *is* up, but not to panic. I'll drop by on my way from church."

"Church?"

"Yes, you know, that strange institution you only think of visiting once a year? It's a wonder the ceiling doesn't cave in when you show your face at the door."

It was too early to think of an appropriate response, so I simply said, "Deborah, I'll see you soon."

The phone went dead and I rolled over but I was wide awake now and suddenly remorseful. Ten minutes later I sat on the edge of the bed, rubbed the sleep from my eyes, and dialed her number.

"Deborah, you're right. I'll come over and pick up the stuff and we'll go to church together. And have breakfast afterward. See you in about an hour, more or less."

"This is a surprise! Church? You? Remember what I said about the ceiling caving in. I—"

The line went dead. I waited, then tapped the receiver.

"Deborah?"

I hung up, dialed her number, and there was that fast dial tone that signaled trouble on the line, then nothing. I quickly scrambled into my sweat suit, collared Ruffin, and started out of the house, pausing only long enough to slip Dad's straight razor into my shoulder bag. Better to be caught with something than without.

Damn, how could I have been so stupid . . .

Deborah lived in a high-rise complex two blocks away. I ran fast, not waiting for the lights and easily dodging the few cars passing at this hour. Ruffin had no trouble keeping up with me. By the time I reached the lobby, my chest hurt from fear.

The elevator to the fifteenth floor moved like a winter glacier.

I stepped out and moved down the narrow corridor just as her door opened and a man came out. He saw me and darted back into the apartment.

"Deborah!" I threw myself against the door as he tried to lock it but he was not fast enough. I wedged my shoulder bag in the opening and Ruffin's barking grew loud as he jumped up and pawed the door. The man suddenly let go and I fell in, landing hard on my knees. Ruffin leaped over me and bounded through the living room after him.

"Git that fuckin' dog away! Git 'im away!"

He ran into the dining room toward the door leading to the terrace.

"Git that dog away, you bitch! Git 'im away!"

"Fuck you! What're you doing here? Where's Deborah?"

I was screaming as I searched the bedroom. Then I heard the hard rush of water. I entered the bathroom and stopped.

"Deborah! No!"

He had left her lying in the shower. Her throat had been cut, but she was still alive. I grabbed a towel, pressed it over the wound, and ran back through the ransacked apartment. Furniture was overturned, drawers were opened, and dishes had been swept from all the cupboards. Beyond the small kitchen, I heard a thin, spiraling echo.

I ran to the terrace intending to push that man off, to kill him, but there was no one there except Ruffin with his paws up on the railing. And down below, a small crowd was gathering around the form lying spread-eagle in the courtyard fifteen floors below.

My screaming and Ruffin's barking had brought out all the neighbors on the floor. One of them, an intern at

Harlem Hospital, knew which artery to press and held the towel to Deborah's throat.

Minutes later I was pacing the corridor outside the hospital's operating room. Tad was there too, routed out of bed by my hysterical call. He walked the floor, trying to make me understand.

"Listen, Mali. I want you to lay off this case. For your own good. You gotta promise you'll let me handle it. This is my job."

"But Deborah was my friend. This happened because of me."

"Stop talking past tense. She's still alive, you understand? Your friend is still alive."

"Yes, but—"

A door swung open at the far end of the corridor and I rushed over.

"Doctor, how is—"

He removed his glasses, and the lines of fatigue were visible in his face. "We've done all we can, for the moment. She's going to the recovery room."

He described the procedure to repair the carotid artery, which carries blood to the head. I didn't understand any of it until he said, "The next twenty-four hours will be critical. That's all I can say right now."

He turned and I tried to concentrate on his green cotton surgical jacket, his nondescript trousers and soft shoes moving away from me and carrying Deborah's life with him. I concentrated on that to keep from looking at the walls, tiles, ceiling, and lights, which did not want to stay in one place.

What seemed like a second later, I was sprawled on a small bench, coughing, and waving a small vial of something away from my nose.

"Are you all right?" a nurse asked.

"I . . . guess so." Even if I wasn't too sure of where I was.

Then Tad's voice: "I'm taking her home."

Outside, Ruffin had been tied to the bus shelter pole. He paced the length of the enclosure and everyone waiting had been forced back several feet. The cool spring air revived me somewhat as it hit my face. We crossed Lenox Avenue and walked slowly past several Sunday morning churchgoers who stared in disgust at my blood-stained sweat suit, uncombed hair, and swollen eyes. Tad, leading me by the hand, did not look much better, and the churchgoers drew their own conclusions, which were easy enough to read: we were nothing but a pair of Saturday night lowlifes who couldn't take two steps to the corner without pulling a blade on each other. It's folks like us who gave Harlem a bad name. I could see it in their faces as they edged out of our way. One couple pulled their child close—a small boy with large inquisitive eyes.

. . . It's not what you think. My friend's life is hanging in the balance. In the balance . . .

But there was nothing to make them understand that.

I unlocked the door and managed to make it past the kitchen, where Dad and Alvin were fixing breakfast. Tad remained in the living room as I headed to my bedroom and changed into another sweat suit. Dad peeked out of the kitchen as I came back downstairs.

He looked from me to Tad and back again.

"You folks all right?"

"We're okay," I whispered. "We'll be better after some coffee."

He looked at me again. "Yeah, you better sit down . . . I'll bring some cups."

Once again, I started to shake and Tad held me until it subsided. I wanted to fall asleep right there in his arms.

"Take it easy . . . easy, you hear?"

I heard but could not answer. Deborah was nearly

killed because of me. I could not answer and could not stop the tears. Dad came in with two large mugs of coffee, looked at me, and placed the tray on the table. Then he frowned at Tad. "Okay. You two look like hell. Want to tell me what's going on?"

Two days later I sat by Deborah's bed and held her hand. I had promised to lay off the case, but Deborah had been my friend before she became "a case." And even though Dad had acknowledged that I'd probably saved her life, he had been shaken to the core. "When are you going to learn to mind your own business? If that man had had a gun, you'd be dead. And I'd have lost another . . ." Tears had welled in his eyes and he had stomped out of the room, leaving me wondering if I should have told him anything.

I looked at Deborah now. Her face was swollen to twice its size and her neck was immobilized, but she lifted my hand to her bandaged throat. No sound came but she recognized me.

The surgeon said there had been no brain damage despite the blood loss. She recognized me . . . Thank God. Thank God, I breathed silently, and started to cry again.

As I left her room, her mother and sister stepped out of the elevator. Mrs. Matthews was a short plump woman of fifty-five, and Deborah's sister, Martha, was small and slim, a younger version of Deborah. Both women looked as if they had not slept in a week.

"The police said it was a robbery," Mrs. Matthews said, "but we can't figure out what's missing."

"Yes, all her jewelry was still there," Martha said. "Her fur coat, even her purse had money in it."

They had flown in from Washington. Deborah's father, bedridden for years, was left at home, so Mrs. Matthews had to return as quickly as possible. Martha, however, planned to remain but she seemed on the verge of a nervous collapse.

"When my sister's able to travel, I'm taking her back to Washington to recuperate," she said. "Why she ever moved into that damn building in the first place is beyond me. She knew its history."

I said nothing. Everyone knew its history. Everyone knew that the development had been built by a major life insurance company several years ago as a compromise— after a long court battle—to keep black folks from darkening the door of their segregated residences downtown.

Martha continued to shake her head. "New York is . . . New York . . . is . . ."

Even though she had been born and raised here, she could not find the words to describe her dislike for this place.

"Deborah had called me to come over and pick up a package," I said, "something she was researching for me. When I got there, a man was coming out of her apartment. Rather than face my dog, he ran back inside, then he must have jumped or fallen from the terrace. If I had been five minutes later, Deb would have bled to death."

Martha's eyes widened. "But why would anyone do this? It had to be a madman . . ."

Even if I had known what to say, I couldn't. The tears wouldn't let me.

Night had fallen and the canopy in front of Harlem Hospital was brightly lit. I paused near the lobby door and stared at the vendors and their flower-filled carts, concentrating on the clusters of roses and gladiolas in an effort to compose myself.

It was a short walk home and I didn't want Dad on my case the minute I stepped in the house. Wanting to know where I'd gone and with whom. He was still upset about Deborah and now he worried about me. Right now I needed peace and quiet and space and a warm bath to slow the spinning inside my head.

It had been a week since Deborah's surgery and I had visited every day. Her neck was still swollen but her face appeared less puffy. The contours of her mouth, nose, and eyelids now seemed more defined but she could not utter a sound.

I had gone to the precinct, again, to answer questions. This time Danny seemed to know the questions to ask. The problem was that I had no answers. The man who attacked her, he said, had been a crackhead and petty thief from uptown named Jackson Lee who was known for his push-in robberies. And no, there was no package with my name on it in the apartment.

It had to be there, I thought. Jackson Lee didn't have it on him when he landed in that courtyard, unless, perhaps, someone in the crowd picked it up.

I wanted to mention this to Tad, but he had said to lay off, and right now all I cared about was for Deborah to get well, to be whole again.

I stood for a while under the canopy, concentrating on my breathing and feeling the deep, measured response in my diaphragm. Visitors bought flowers from the vendors and moved through the doors in a steady stream. Across the avenue, a line of cars had pulled up in front of the Schomburg Center and a large crowd had gathered, waiting to go in. I had read in the *City Sun* about the opening of a sculpture exhibit from Ghana and knew Deborah would surely have been in this crowd.

At the corner, someone touched my shoulder and I jumped away.

"Easy, Mali. Take it easy," Danny said. "I can see you're not taking this too well and I can't blame you.

Your friend's in terrible shape. That guy that did this—"
He shook his head.

The light changed and we stepped off the curb. "I'll walk you home. You don't mind, do you?"

"No. Of course not."

"Tad said you found her in the bathtub. Did she say anything?"

"No," I answered, wondering why he was asking. We had gone through these same questions in some detail already. "I told you at the precinct she was in no shape to talk. Or scream. Or cry. Or anything. Too much blood was coming from her mouth and throat."

"Yes. Yes. You told me. Too bad you had to see all that. I can see you took it very badly."

For a second I fought to keep all the anger, fear, and frustration from spilling over and engulfing the nearest object, which was Danny and his roundabout way of questioning. Dammit! What in hell did he expect? Deborah's my friend!

He droned on, sounding more like a funeral director than a detective.

"Deborah is my friend. She. Is. My. Friend," I finally said, slowly and distinctly, cutting him off. He was plucking my last nerve and I felt some heavy language creeping to the tip of my tongue, ready to roll off.

Deborah had survived, but it might be months before she spoke again. I thought of telling him that I didn't need his company, that I could make it home by myself because I needed air around me and space in which to think and let go of this anger. But he was Tad's friend and partner. In a tight spot, Tad would have to depend on him.

I gritted my teeth and quickened my pace, but he kept up with me.

"Look, Mali. I know how upset you are. I just want

you to know that we're giving this case priority. We'll find out who is behind this, believe me."

Who is behind this . . . I stole another glance at him. At the precinct, he had said it was a robbery. Open-and-shut case. The man was looking for money to get drugs and had simply picked the apartment at random.

"Yes, I'm sure Deborah and her family would like to know if this was more than a simple robbery. They'd be very grateful," I said, hoping he'd shut up.

At the door, I turned and said good night. I had no intention of inviting him in. I needed to be alone.

chapter eleven

Some folks think beauticians should earn more than a therapist or a guidance counselor. I tend to agree, at least in regard to my hairdresser.

My hair is less than two inches long, and one medium raw egg in a little shampoo under a hot shower would be sufficient to condition it. And a lot cheaper. But there's something to be said for the timeless ritual that hairdressers have perfected: the laying on of hands.

I had walked uptown from the hospital to Bertha's Beauty Shop thinking of Deborah. Though she was sitting up, eating Jell-O and sipping liquids through a straw, she was still unable to speak, and her eyes, when they drifted away from me, held a look of blank terror.

Her sister intended to transfer her to a rehabilitation center, and when her therapy was completed, Deborah would go to Washington to live. My friend, classmate, confidante, and sometimes double date was leaving, and unless I made the trip to Washington, I probably would not see her for a long while.

I opened the door to Bertha's shop and she looked at me: "Sit down, girl. Quick. Before you fall down."

Bertha was short, round though not quite plump, with dark auburn hair framing a brown face. Her shop was clean and cozy and she believed in letting her customers relax, eat the lunch they had brought, and sometimes play the single action if the numbers runner happened by.

One customer had just left, and a minute later my head was bent back over the shampoo bowl and the tightness in my forehead and scalp was being washed and massaged away.

"Mali, you got knots in your neck as big as boulders. What's eatin' you?"

"It's a long story, Miss Bert."

"Yeah, well. It usually is."

A half hour later I sat with a towel wrapped around my head waiting for the conditioner to condition and listening to Bertha's philosophy of life when the door opened and a large woman with dyed-blond hair walked in. She had a very pretty face, young, bronze-tone skin, and dark eyes as clear as a teenager's, but from the shoulders down, she spread outward, exactly like a pyramid.

She waved and headed toward the workstation near the rear of the shop.

"Hi, Bertha. Just wanted to drop my packages off. Be right back. I'm expecting two customers. If they show, just tell 'em to wait."

She waved again and was gone.

As the door closed, Bert sighed. "You see. That's what I'm talkin' about."

"What?"

"Her name's Viv. Her man cut her loose a month ago. Traded her in for a size ten and now she gotta work for a livin' just like the rest of us. He had set her up as a hairdresser, except he owned the business. Real nice shop up on Amsterdam Avenue called the Pink Fingernail. Got air-conditioning, fancy pink lights that take ten years off your face every time you look in the mirrors, CD music, everything. Even got herbal tea.

"Now the new girlfriend is in there and this one's over here, tryin' to eat herself into an early grave. Some of her customers left and came here with her, though, so she's lucky. At least she won't starve.

"I tell you, these men are somethin' else. I'm glad my name is on this deed and the combs, the hairpins, even the dirt on this floor is owned by me. My mama always said, 'God bless the child that's got her own.' And if you got half a somebody else's, that's even better, but first make sure you got your own. I'm tellin' you, a man like Johnnie Harding'll never get a chance to do me like he did her. I'm too independent for that shit, thank God."

The conditioner, whatever it was, must have seeped into my brain and caused me to nod off but I blinked awake when I heard the name.

"Johnnie Harding?" I whispered, trying to keep my voice steady. "Who's he?"

Bertha looked at me and stepped back with her hands on her hips. "Girl, where you been? In a coma somewhere?"

"Well, I heard the name, but I can't connect . . ."

"And neither can the cops. But everybody knows he's into hard stuff. Man ain't even got a Social Security card and there's more money comin' out his willie than the government got comin' outta Fort Knox."

There were no other customers in the shop so Bertha was able to talk freely. I was wide awake now.

"And the truth is, Viv really loved him. He probably went for her too when she was still small, but she kinda outgrew him. I guess that's what they mean by livin' large. She had put on a pound a month. Since he walked, she been puttin' on a pound a week. Everybody knows Johnnie likes 'em thin as a pin; small enough to get his hands around . . . Viv knew it, but I guess she figured she was somethin' special."

"I think I know who you mean. Does he drive a red Benz?"

"Naw. Got a midnight-blue Cadillac. Special plates."

"A special plate. What does it say?"

" 'Badman.' You know. Somethin' stupid and eye-catchin'."

I closed my eyes, wondering about that HO plate.

"Well," I said, "he's got a new woman, nice car, all that money. Viv must be taking it pretty hard."

"And that ain't the half of it. Just the other day she looked at herself in this mirror—front, back, and sideways—and swore she was gonna take up joggin' startin' that very day. Well, the only place she jogs is down to Sylvia's for one a them baby back rib sandwiches and on the return trip, stops by Majestic Take-Out for the catch of the day, plus fries."

She stopped talking long enough to unwrap the towel, put another handful of sweet-smelling stuff on my head, and tie the towel up again.

"Johnnie must be quite a man to cause a woman to fall apart like that," I said in the brief silence.

"Well, I can't say firsthand, but from what I heard —now this is between you, me, and the lamppost, you understand?"

"I understand."

I closed my eyes, leaned back in the chair, and let Miss Bert talk.

If you stand on any corner of 135th Street and Lenox, you will be able to take in the YMCA, an adjoining basketball court, the young trees guarding a ribbon of renovated apartments, Pan-Pan's restaurant, Harlem Hospital, the

Schomburg Research Center, and parts of the Lenox Terrace apartment complex.

A step away from Lenox Terrace is a small bar called Twenty-Two West, a dimly lit but comfortable place in which a woman doesn't mind sitting alone.

The television in the rear near the kitchen is respectfully low, even during a Knicks game.

There were a few men at the bar when I walked in and two couples were having dinner at a table in the back.

I sat at a table near the door, looking up each time it opened. I was early but couldn't help glancing at my watch. I had been studying, trying to catch up on the assignments I'd missed, when Tad called. He had sounded so angry that I'd dropped everything and rushed here to meet him.

I was halfway through a Scotch and soda when he came in. As he sat down, I could see, even in the dim light, the small muscle working the side of his jaw.

"What's happened?"

He rested his elbows on the table and leaned forward.

"They took me off Deborah Matthews's case."

"What?"

"That's right. An hour ago. They took me off and gave it to Danny. God only knows what the Chief was thinking when he did that. Personally, I believe he's getting a little senile and oughtta put his papers in. I don't mean to knock Danny. He's as good as they come but, you know, lately . . . I don't know what to say.

"When I asked the Chief why the case was reassigned, he said Danny had actually asked for it to be given to him. That I was too close to be objective."

"But you don't even know Deborah . . ."

"They know that I rushed over to the hospital to meet you the morning she was attacked. They know she's your friend. And Danny knows how I feel about you.

He's also handling Gary Mark's case and Erskin Harding's case. He convinced the Chief to combine those two into a file called the Choir Murders."

"You're kidding. Seems our boy has a flair for the dramatic. This is a chorus, however."

"Whatever. Chorus. Choir. He's handling it now. What's the difference?"

I shrugged, not knowing if there really was a difference. I'd have to ask Dad when I got home.

"So," I said, "if he breaks the choir case—or cases— he gets the five-minute spotlight and another promotion."

"Seems that way. He's up to his ass in cases already, so he intends to close Deborah's file, saying it was a push-in gone wrong. Suspect dead. The end."

I was speechless. Did Danny really need another case?

"Maybe," I said finally, "Danny needs to fill up every second of his time to take his mind off the problem at home."

"Maybe. Maybe not. Rumor has it that he's got some girl around here young enough to be his daughter and fly enough to take his mind off everything."

"Really?"

"That's right. So he works the O.T. to keep him in the neighborhood. Now he's bucking for promotion so he'll have the money to support her and his Long Island family."

I had visions of his serene-faced wife and wondered if she knew where and how her husband was spending his time in the old neighborhood. I wondered if she cared.

Maybe not. In the picture that Danny had showed me, I could see nothing in her face, not even resignation. Maybe she knew and didn't care. As long as hearth and home was covered, he could screw half of Harlem. Just don't rock her boat . . .

"How long has she been in a wheelchair?"

"A few years now. She has multiple sclerosis and Danny's doing the best he can. I have to give him credit for that. He's paying for that house, a private nurse, the girls' schooling, music and dance lessons, car notes . . ."

"And the girlfriend," I added.

He shrugged and I looked at him across the table. "Tad, I'm sorry. I know you're disappointed, and I'm sorry."

We ordered a round of doubles and I watched him stir the ice in his glass.

As bad as things were, the situation had been somewhat simplified for me now. It was no longer Tad's case, so I was no longer held to my promise to lay off. I could start asking questions again. What happened to Deborah was more than a simple robbery. All the information she had gathered on Gary Mark had somehow disappeared. The envelope I was supposed to pick up from Deborah had not yet been recovered.

I sighed and leaned back in my chair watching Tad. I thought of my afternoon with Miss Bert, which had gone so well that I had tipped her beyond my regular budget.

"A ten-dollar tip to condition two inches of hair?" she had laughed. "Girl, put your money back in your pocket."

"No, this is for the knots in my neck," I said. And the conversation, I wanted to add.

. . . The first thing tomorrow morning, I'll be at the Motor Vehicles Department when my friend Barbara returns from vacation. I'll ask her to run a check on Harding's license and every vanity plate with "HO" and I will wait there until I get the answer. No more telephone calls. What happened to Deborah was enough.

I looked at Tad again and placed my hand over his. It was closed so tightly I could trace the veins that spread like a fine web to his wrist. He was a good detective, a good person, a caring and decent man. This should not have happened to him.

"Tad, listen. Things will work themselves out. They usually do . . ."

It sounded so lame, but there was no more to be said. I gazed at him in the dim light and remembered earlier, at the beauty shop; the "laying on of hands" had left me feeling remarkably free and loose and the effects had not yet worn off.

I leaned across the table now until my mouth was as close to his ear as I could get without going inside it.

"Honey, listen, what you need is . . . a laying on of hands."

My voice was low and my fingers went on to trace under his chin and move lightly along his collar line. "You probably have some knots in your neck as big as boulders . . ."

He turned to look at me, barely able to contain a smile.

"How'd you know that?"

"Just a guess . . ."

"Unh-hnh." His expression changed and he moved closer. "You somethin' else, girl. You want to smooth me out? I got something needs smoothing in the worst way. The worst way, baby . . ."

"Your place?" I whispered. "You know, I've never seen the lights shining on the Harlem River at night."

"And I can't wait to show you. I mean it. Every time I hear 'I've been lovin' you too long to stop now,' I hear that song and say to myself, I haven't even got started with this woman. Haven't even—"

"Wait. Don't tell me in here."

I rose from the table.

I imagined us lying among soft pillows on the terrace, splits of Moët, a little Wynton Marsalis blowing in the background, and in the glow of the candles, my fingers working a fragrant oil into the small of his back . . .

"Let me make a call. Let Dad know I'll be out awhile. You know how it is. Kid could be ninety and the parent still worries."

I made my way to the phone near the back of the bar. It rang twice and Alvin picked it up before the second ring was complete. His voice sounded small, as if he had been running and couldn't catch his breath.

"Mali. Listen. Mrs. Johnson, Morris's mother? She just called. Clarence is in trouble. He just got arrested."

"What?"

"She wants you to go to the precinct. To find out what's going on. Maybe do something to get him out . . . Mali, you gotta—"

"Alvin, listen to me. Nothing bad is going to happen to Clarence, you understand?"

"Yeah, but—"

"We're going there right now."

I heard the relief as he said good-bye.

I hung up the phone and pressed my forehead to the wall. Sound filtered from the television into the narrow corridor: a commercial had come on singing the praises of dental floss or freshener or something and I listened to the joyful noises of a man who didn't have to worry anymore, thanks to . . .

I wanted to laugh.

Then I wanted to cry and press my head further into the wall as the images of fragrant oil slipped away. I opened my eyes. The river lights would have to wait.

On the way to the table, my neck started to hurt again.

chapter twelve

T ad convinced me to visit Mrs. Johnson before going to the precinct, considering I was persona non grata there and he had just been relieved of his assignment.

There were eight buildings of twenty-one stories with ten apartments on every floor. The faded red brick exteriors looked deceptively calm and orderly but I remembered responding to at least sixteen calls in one month alone when I was on the midnight shift.

Urban planning said pack them in, contain them. Ignore the pressure and pathology that builds in confined space. In controlled experiments, when conditions become intolerable, rats will bite off their own tails, eat their young, kill each other. But the planners didn't consult the scientists. Then again, perhaps they did.

The elevator was out of order but luckily Mrs. Johnson lived on the fourth floor. We made our way up the fire stairs and listened as people on the landings who had no business being there fled at the sound of our approach.

In the dim lighting we saw the cinder-block walls scarred with a dizzy mosaic of red, yellow, and orange graffiti and signed with bold tags. Every square inch of the stairwell was covered. On every landing, we stepped on crack vials that spilled out from the crevices between the steps where the concrete had chipped or worn away.

The smell of different kinds of food cooking drifted into the stairwell, competing with the pungent odor of dried urine.

On the third floor, there was a loud outburst and a young man slammed open the door to the stairwell.

"Goddamn place ain't worth shit! We oughtta go on a rent strike till they git these damn elevators workin' right. People up on them top floors ain't been downstairs in a week."

He was about to pass us, then stopped and jabbed a finger in our faces. "Now whatta you think'll happen if there's a emergency and the ammalambs come. Then EMS don't be climbin' no stairs. They pull up, they be yellin' C.O.D.! Come! On! Down! They ain't hikin' up these stairs, not even for they mama!"

He was so angry I thought he was going to kick a hole in the concrete wall.

"Listen, brother," Tad said calmly. "The reason why they get away with stuff like this is because we let them. I don't live here, but if I did, I'd be jammin' the wire. The fire department, the housing authority, the police department, health department, and all the politicians I could think of. I'd be on the horn lettin' everybody know I'm droppin' a dime to the newspapers and television stations if something isn't done within twenty-four hours. I'd get the neighbors on the case too. And keep at it, get everybody to holler till something's done. You know it's the squeakiest wheel gets the most grease, but nobody can hear you yellin' in the stairwell."

The man looked at him and shook his head. "You right, brother. You on the money."

He continued on downstairs, quiet now, and I wondered how much of Tad's advice he intended to follow.

On the fourth floor, the lighting was bright enough to at least distinguish one's features and read the numbers painted on the anonymous steel doors lining the narrow, whitewashed corridor.

The noise of a television snapped off and a peephole slid open in response to our knocking.

"Yes?"

"Mrs. Johnson? It's Mali. And I have a friend with me. Can I—"

The door opened and Mrs. Johnson, wearing a faded housecoat, thong sandals, and pink rollers in her hair, stepped aside to let us in.

The apartment was small and neat. From the living room, I saw a galley-style kitchen with a rack of pots and pans suspended from a circular ring in the ceiling. In the carpeted hallway, there were two doors which probably led to the bedrooms. Morris peeped out from one door, waved hello, and disappeared again.

"This is Detective Honeywell, Mrs. Johnson."

She looked at him and murmured, "Oh my. My goodness . . . wait a minute. Have a seat, I'll be right back."

She disappeared into the second room off the hall and emerged minutes later wearing lipstick, a vividly patterned caftan, and a matching scarf that covered the hair rollers.

The living room was sparsely furnished but what furniture there was was well kept. A television console dominated the room and a calendar picture of Malcolm X hung on the wall over the set.

The caftan flowed as she moved. She stared at Tad

as if I was not even in the room and I wondered if he knew what effect he had on some women.

"Well. Have a seat." She smiled and waved us to the sofa as she went into the kitchen. A minute later she returned with three cans of beer.

"So you got my call?"

"Yes, but we wanted to speak with you first, to figure out what needs to be done. What happened? What did Clarence do?"

Mrs. Johnson settled back in her chair and crossed her legs, lifting the caftan much higher than she needed to.

"What did he do? Somethin' he shoulda done long time ago. He beat the shit outta his mama's no-good boyfriend. Scuse my language, Detective Honey, but I—"

"Honeywell."

"Oh. Yes." She paused and smiled. "Excuse the language but I'm damn mad."

Tad and I glanced at each other as she angrily snapped the tab on the can. The tab broke and the beer foamed out and over her hand.

"Shit! Scuse me."

She returned with a new can and took a long swallow before she spoke.

"That man been punchin' her around for years now and wasn't nuthin' that boy could do or say. Then the man got on that crack, and got her strung out, then started sellin' from her apartment to support they habits. Joint got so busy people was lined up like they was at Grand Central waitin' for the five-fifty outta town.

"We complained and complained, hollered and screamed till Housing finally threatened to evict her. Her man lightened up a little bit then. I mean he still dealin' but from another location now. He stash the cash with her, though.

"So tonight he come there all fired up, claimin' she

stole some from him and started on her with a wire hanger. I mean that crack make you crazy. Well, then Clarence came home, saw what had went down, and started on him. Broke that man's arm in two places and his jaw in three. Man ain't nuthin' but garbage. She shoulda kicked 'im to the curb long time ago . . .

"I was watchin' everything out the window and seen the ambulance take 'im away. Those elevators are workin'. They ain't broken like the ones in this building. A hour later here come the cops and they carry Clarence out in cuffs. Now I ask you, is that right? All that time we complained, they ain't never rushed up here to bust the dealer, but rush in when somebody bust *up* the dealer. I don't understand that shit at all, I really don't."

"Well, depending on what charge they're holding Clarence on," Tad said, "maybe we can get him released in the custody of his mother. Where is she?"

Mrs. Johnson shook her head. "Another ambulance come for her same time the cops took Clarence. She's done in pretty bad . . . plus her other problem . . ."

Tad thought for a minute. "Okay, here's what you do, if you're willing to do it. Clarence will go down to Central Booking in a couple of hours. You be down there when he arrives. Say you're his aunt and that you'll be responsible for his court appearance. If his mother presses charges against the boyfriend, chances are Clarence's argument of self-defense will hold up. Are you willing to do it?"

A look of indecision crossed her face and I held my breath as she weighed Tad's advice. It was a second before she finally spoke. "What the hell. Why not? The boy don't have nobody else."

We were halfway to the door when she said, "You know, that other detective—Mr. Williams—he was here again."

I could see a shadow moving across Tad's face as he turned toward her. "When was that?"

"Couple a days ago."

"What did he say?" Tad asked. His jawline tightened and I wondered how much more he would be able to take.

"Well, he kinda asked me and Morris the same questions over and over. Like he didn't believe what we had said in the first place. Got me real upset when he started in on Morris, and I ended up mentionin' how Clarence had used that language to Dr. Harding the—"

"What? You told him what?"

I hadn't meant to shout and Mrs. Johnson looked at me, bewildered.

"Well, I didn't know I wasn't supposed to say nuthin'. He's a cop, ain't he? And he wanted to know if the man in that car, the one that Morris punched, didn't look like Clarence. And Morris said no. Over and over that it wasn't Clarence. I didn't know we wasn't supposed to say anything."

"Well, it's not that, Mrs. Johnson. It's just—well—" I was at a loss and flashed a glance at Tad, trying to read his signals. He let a moment pass, then he smiled at her.

"It's all right, Mrs. Johnson. Don't worry about it. Just try to get down to Central Booking. Here's the address. Whatever happens, please give Mali a call right away. And it might be a good idea if you didn't mention this visit to anyone else."

She took the paper, visibly relaxing in the warmth of his smile.

We made our way back down the darkened stairs, smelling the same smells and listening to the same scurrying sounds we had heard earlier.

The basketball court was deserted as we strolled through it and I thought of telling Tad how Clarence had stayed out here alone, sometimes past midnight, practicing, not wanting to face whatever it was he had to face when he finally went home for the night.

The trees were beginning to bud out and the long branches created a mesh overhead that would have, on another evening, seemed like a protective embrace. Tonight, however, the shadows from the streetlights fell through the moving branches like stark points of electric current, painting our faces a ghostly gray.

We walked in silence for three blocks before I said, "Why did you suggest she go downtown? You know Danny's working right now to book Clarence for Erskin's murder."

"Danny's not that sloppy. He has information but he needs something to make the charge stick. I know how he works. He doesn't like for a case to blow up in his face. He's too ambitious. Wants to move straight to the top and breaking this case will help do it."

"We'll see," I whispered.

chapter thirteen

The auditorium had filled up fairly quickly and I was lucky to slip into a seat in the last row.

Everyone settled down as Lloyd Benton pulled out a handkerchief to wipe his brow. He tapped the podium for quiet and the last scattered murmuring subsided once he began:

"I want to thank all of you for being here today. As you know the Chorus has been through a very difficult period, having lost two very distinguished members of our staff under tragic circumstances. It was only fitting to close for three weeks not only to honor their memory but also to work closely with the police to assure the safety and security of our choristers. Thanks to some very fine detective work, a suspect was apprehended ten days ago and is facing charges in the death of Dr. Harding."

There was a low murmur and he paused to gauge the response before he added: "And the young man, a former member of our chorus whom we tried very hard to rehabilitate, may also be implicated in the death of

Gary Mark. Needless to say, this person has been expelled
and we can only hope that justice will be done.

"We would like to put this terrible period behind us
now and concentrate on the future. I called this meeting
to inform you of our plans to reopen and resume rehearsals in preparation for our upcoming Christmas tour. As
you know, we regularly meet on Saturdays, but since
we've lost three weeks, I'm asking for an additional three
hours on Friday afternoon for the rest of the month. This
is a small sacrifice. Again, let us put this period behind us
and look to the future."

There was a mild smattering of applause and I
knew the parents were not satisfied with this explanation.
Everyone had read the papers. Everyone knew that Clarence had been arrested and was being held on high bail.
But based on the street news—which was the real news—
very few believed he committed the crime.

"Violent Animal" was how one downtown scandal
sheet had headlined him, with very little information to
back up the description. "Troubled Home Life of Chorister," reported another paper. Both had had Clarence's picture plastered across the front pages but there was no
story. His mother had checked out of the hospital and
could not be found, and Mrs. Johnson, to her credit, had
refused to be interviewed. So this had left the reporters
with their usual "unnamed sources" and vivid imagina-
tions to fill in the blanks.

The night of the arrest, the ten o'clock news had
shown Clarence being led from the precinct by Danny
Williams, looking stern with badge pinned prominently to
his lapel.

It looked good on television but to date there still
was no confession.

"What's going to happen to Clarence? Where is this
leading? Danny must know he's not guilty."

I had put these questions to Tad and was desperate for answers.

Danny, he said, was not discussing anything with him, but he suspected that Clarence was being used in order to draw in the real thing.

"Sacrificing Clarence seems more like it," I said. "The boy has been locked up nearly two weeks already."

"Mali, I don't know what to say. Sometimes, ambition can get the better of the best of us . . ."

I wondered where Danny had gone that night after the camera's bright lights had faded. Home to his ailing wife to complain about how tough life was in the big city or to his fly girl's bedroom to celebrate. Probably went to the girlfriend. A shorter trip made for a longer night.

The crowd in the auditorium stirred impatiently, waiting for Lloyd to conclude, eager to ask questions.

I scanned the audience, trying to find Mrs. Johnson, but she was not there. I looked around at the faces nearest me and from their expressions knew that the director was in for some hard questions.

"How do you intend to secure the safety of the choristers?" a tall man with the heft of a linebacker asked. "There are nearly three hundred children here at any one time. Do you intend to have three hundred cops stationed at each rehearsal and ready to walk each student home? What's to prevent another attempt at kidnapping?"

His question was met with loud whistles. Some parents stomped their feet as if they were at the Garden in the crucial minutes of a Knicks game.

Lloyd drew his breath and held up his hands for several seconds before quiet was restored. "Let's try to deal with the reality of the situation," he said. "We all know that total security is not possible anywhere. Not even at the U.N. Or the White House in Washington. And we all know that it is up to us, the parents and friends who care enough for our choristers, to assume the responsibility for their safety. There are some things that we must do for ourselves. No one else should be made to assume those roles."

"But that boy they holdin' wasn't charged with no kidnap. He was charged with manslaughter," another parent said, rising quickly to his feet. "Where do the kidnap fit in? The cops got 'im in jail but the guy that did the snatch is still on the loose. Remember them two little kids that disappeared from that playground down on Lenox? They ain't been found to this day.

"You sayin' we gotta put this and put that behind us. That's what them politicians always be sayin'. Well me, I ain't no politician so I ain't puttin' nuthin' behind me. I'm just a parent, worried about my son and lookin' for some answers . . ."

More shouting and applause until someone else, a middle-aged woman with graying hair, rose. "I'm sorry. I came today to see what was gonna be done about the kidnapping. You're right we got a responsibility, otherwise we wouldn't be here. But we don't need to be wastin' any more time talkin' about who's in jail. That other man is still walkin' these streets. We need to know that our children are gonna be safe. We're taxpayers. Our kids got a right to be safe while they on these streets."

I watched Lloyd's eyebrows come together in the telltale line. The meeting was not going as planned so this session would be drawing to a close. Fast.

"The police have promised unmarked cars, more plainclothesmen patrolling the area, and random auto checks," he said, trying to control the edge creeping into his tone.

"Random checks." A woman next to me laughed aloud. "Now, that's a joke. We've been having these so-called random checks on our streets for years. I haven't seen any improvement, have you?"

She turned away from me and I shook my head,

beginning to feel sorry for the director. Still, he had a point. It was up to us to think about our children's safety. I stood up to voice my opinion, and more to the point, to let Lloyd and everyone else know that Clarence was innocent until proven guilty—arrest or no arrest.

But the director held up his hands again. "I expect to see those choristers on Friday after school who are ready, willing, and able to work." His eyes flashed beneath the black line. "And I suggest to those who are concerned with public safety—safety in our streets as taxpayers—to please contact the captain of your precinct or your local politician. Our most important tour—the Christmas tour—will be here before we know it. I intend for it to be our most successful event ever."

He thanked the parents for coming out to such a successful meeting and turned and left the stage.

Two weeks later, four weeks after Clarence had been arrested, the *City Sun* revealed that a bond had been posted and he had been released.

I spread the paper out on the dining table and gazed out of the window. Who had posted the bail? Who?

It was time to see Bertha to catch up on the latest street news but I needed some other information first.

The lobby of the World Trade Center was jammed with a noontime crowd, and a line of tourists and business types waited behind the red velvet rope for the private elevator to take them to the restaurant on the 106th floor.

I had been surprised when Melissa Stewart agreed to meet me and was further surprised as she approached. We were the same age, give or take a year or two, but her hair, done up in a conservative French twist, was already streaked with gray. Only her high heels and the mauve skirt hovering just at her knees indicated how young she really was.

She was not exactly pretty and she had never gone in for the latest makeup fads—just lipstick and perfume was all she needed, she said.

Apparently that had been enough, the proof being her recent engagement to a civil court judge. She raised her hand now to brush a strand of hair back in place and the flash on her finger was the brightest thing I had seen outside of Tiffany's.

Her embrace was genuine and she held me at arm's length: "Well, look at you, Mali. My goodness, it's good to see you even if you are still thin as ever."

She laughed easily and I tried to act casual as the speed of the elevator caused my ears to sing. The doors finally opened and we stepped into the mirrored and curtained foyer of Windows on the World where relays of maître d's moved with impeccable swiftness to guide us to our table.

The murmur around us was low and expensive and the floor-to-ceiling windows radiated light from a sky that resembled an artist's mixture of pink and purple. Across the Hudson, New Jersey looked like beautiful country.

I turned away when the Goodyear blimp floated by close enough to cast a shadow across my plate.

"Nice place. You come here often?"

"Not really," Melissa said. "Only with the out-of-town clients who want to see what this is all about. Most days, I'm buried in paper in the office."

The waiter leaned over four pieces of crystal stemware to hand me a gold-embossed menu.

"Well, I wish I could say 'Let's just enjoy lunch' but I need to know something about someone who was recently killed uptown."

"Oh yes. Gary Mark. I know who you're talking about. He was something of a legend down here. Young, single, seen everywhere with the model of the moment. Gary was a trader who knew everybody and who hosted some of the wildest parties this side of . . . well, they were just wild. Even by Wall Street standards. Rumor had it that he never served food, but there was a menu listing every kind of drug you could dream of and some that didn't even have a name yet, just colors. The parties lasted for days at a time."

She looked at me and laughed. "No, I wasn't there, never attended and didn't intend to attend. But his parties were never meant to be secret. Gary never hid anything. He simply did what he wanted because he made millions for his firm. Millions. He was, so to speak, the genuine, original golden boy. Weekend cruises for one hundred of his closest friends and chartered ski trips to Aspen with fifty or so people meant nothing to him."

"What happened?"

"He had managed an investment account which made a lot of money for his company. Then he either got greedy or careless. He bet that certain stock prices would decline, but when the market moved against him, he didn't cover his risks. Instead, he increased the size of his bet again and again. By the time he was found out, the losses amounted to nearly $145 million. A lot of money. And word had it that he owed someone uptown or somebody uptown owned him and he was trying to buy his way out. Who really knows . . . He's gone now and we'll never know . . ."

The filet mignon dissolved on my tongue like butter and the mimosas were served in the largest champagne glasses I'd ever seen. By the second drink, I had resolved to dedicate my life to achieving one goal: becoming rich.

"But that was a terrible thing to happen to the Chorus, Mali. We're one of their corporate donors. In fact, it was Gary who approached us. What are their plans now? Do they intend to resume their program?"

"Yes. Of course they do. It'll take time to recover from the fallout but I was at a meeting the other day. The Christmas tour is coming up and they're preparing for it. My nephew's in the Chorus, that's why I wanted to speak to you about the director of development. I had heard that he had an uptown connection, but I don't have a name . . ."

"Well, neither do I. The only thing I can tell you is that as wild as Gary was, he was also a nice guy, wouldn't hurt a fly. Had a loft in SoHo filled with a spectacular collection of African American artwork. He was an early and avid collector. God knows what became of all that.

"Folks felt sorry when they heard what had happened . . . but knowing human nature, I don't know if they were sorry about the way he died or sorry that he went before he could make a comeback and earn them another hundred million."

She picked delicately at her food, then caught my gaze and shrugged. "I'm sorry to put it so baldly, but down here, pressure is so great, the dollar will make you holler."

Later, I thought about that on the elevator coming down and considered hollering myself. I had spent my monthly allowance to hear that Gary was just a nice guy whose only imperfection was that he had let a couple of hundred million dollars go to his head and much of it up his nose.

If that was all there was to it, why did someone waste two bullets . . .

In the lobby, I said good-bye to Melissa and walked a few blocks to Motor Vehicles to see Barbara, another friend I had grown up with. Although she had left the crowd and married young and now had two boys in high school, we remained telephone friends, playing catch-up in semiannual marathon calls.

We were glad to see each other now and I got a chance to admire her St. Thomas tan.

I looked at the vacation photos while she searched the computer for "HO," and thirty minutes later I left with a small printout of several combinations and the names and addresses of the plates' owners.

Tad's name was there but Johnnie Harding's name did not come up at all. There was one uptown address for a HONEY vanity plate and I circled that in red.

chapter fourteen

For the rest of the week, I talked long and hard to persuade Alvin to return to rehearsals. What with Clarence and Morris out and Erskin no longer there, it was a tough sell.

Also, I wondered how many other kids would show up. Lloyd's attitude at the meeting hadn't exactly endeared him to the parents. Afterward, someone had whispered that he seemed more concerned about the corporate funding than about the kids. But then, since times were hard and with the current city administration acting tight enough to put Scrooge to shame, everyone was scrambling for dollars. The Christmas tour would be Lloyd's big gamble. Either it puts the group back on top or they're out of the picture all together.

Alvin made up his mind after I said I'd walk with him and Dad would be there to bring him home later. I also promised to speak to Mrs. Johnson about Morris, but when we arrived, I was surprised to see him already there.

"Mr. Lloyd called my mama," he said.

"Wonderful. Glad to see you back," I said, wondering how many others he'd called and what promises he'd made. I counted seventy kids in the auditorium, clustered in noisy knots, and Alvin went to join them.

I decided to stroll uptown to the Pink Fingernail Beauty Salon hoping that, for a Friday afternoon, it would be crowded enough for me to pick up some gossip. Deborah's visiting hours were limited to Sundays now that she had been transferred to the rehab institute and I planned to see her then.

The warm spring air flowed across the wide expanse of Adam Clayton Powell Boulevard, and cars, cabs, trucks, and buses competed for road space as they chased the next light.

The numbers runners were also out in force. Every few blocks they darted in and out of the three Bs of commerce: the bars, barbershops, and beauty parlors. The runners were mostly the old-timers, well dressed, quiet, and still very efficient.

I spotted TooHot, a runner from back in the sixties and still going strong. Dad said that at one time folks called this man WeeWillie, but all that changed one day when he popped into the Rock Tavern on 8th Avenue to announce to Sugar, the barmaid, that her ship had come in. Loaded. So get set to party.

But WeeWillie must have missed a few payments to the precinct and so the law had been waiting in the back booth to slap the bracelets on the minute he opened his mouth to yawn.

Sugar had blinked toward the rear and yelled, "Shit! It's too hot!" WeeWillie blinked also, and was gone before the cops had a chance to look his way. The next day, reincarnated as TooHot, he paid off Sugar, took a pass on the party, and a week later resumed business as usual.

The Rock Tavern was on 8th Avenue around the

corner from Minton's Playhouse. Both are long gone but TooHot, sixty-nine years old, is still taking the single action, partly because a lot of folks still prefer to play the traditional (nontaxable) way.

I detoured at 145th and walked up the hill past the Bradhurst pool. Its wide white tiles accentuated its emptiness, but in less than a month, the wrought-iron gates would be open and the water would be shimmering under the broad-leafed trees. After many false starts, Benin and I had finally learned to swim here. Alvin had learned much faster because he hadn't been distracted by the lifeguards the way we had been.

The hill seemed steeper than I remembered and I strolled, slower, past the crowd emerging from the subway at St. Nicholas Avenue, most of them joining the take-out line of the chicken and chips place next door to the old Brown Bomber bar.

I passed Convent Avenue Baptist Church and paused to admire a wedding party pulling up in blocklong, silver limos.

On Amsterdam Avenue, the doorway of the Pink Fingernail could be seen a mile away. At the entrance, I lingered long enough to decide what alterations I needed and how long it would take. A shoulder-length hair weave would earn me several hours of gossip but the idea of piling someone else's hair on my head did not appeal to me.

I scanned the list in the window again and settled for a "natural mud baked facial mask," which, according to the large print, was guaranteed to erase laugh lines, frown lines, and signs of stress and aging. Plus, it was cheap.

Once that miracle was accomplished, and depending on how deep the gossip got, maybe I could stay for a manicure.

The owner of the HONEY license plate was listed

as Maizie Nicholas and her address was the same as the Pink Fingernail, but when I opened the door, I thought I had stumbled by mistake into a Mary Kay Emporium. The salon had a bit more pink than Bertha had described.

A ballroom-size chandelier with tiny pink shades hung from a gloss-red ceiling, and the floor was carpeted with an abstract swirl of pink tile. The walls were pale pink with dressing-room-style mirrors. Chairs, shampoo bowls, and display cases were varying shades of the color, as were the soda dispenser in the rear and the air-conditioning unit above the door.

The shop was twice as large as Bertha's but seemed just as crowded with seven workstations, a dozen hair dryers against the wall, a manicurist's table, and a chaise lounge near the rear done up in a pale rose pattern.

Four pink-clad operators were busy when I stepped in and all looked at my hair and flashed me a professional you-need-a-weave-be-with-you-in-a-minute smile.

I smiled back, letting them know that when I walked out, my hair would not be flowing or glowing. All I was interested in was a facial.

The thinnest one waved and I hoped she was Viv's replacement.

"May I help you?"

"I don't have an appointment but I hope you can accommodate me. I'm interested in a facial."

"Sure. My name is Maizie. Have a seat and I'll be with you in a minute."

She slid down off the high stool and motioned me to the chaise. I looked at her and at her extraordinary waistline and wondered if she had ever had an X ray or if her doctor simply had her stand near a strong lightbulb when he examined her.

She was at least my height and must have weighed all of ninety pounds—truly Johnnie Harding material. I always felt fat when I was with Deborah, but looking at

Maizie, I felt at least twenty pounds overweight. Bloated was a better word.

Maizie was not exceptionally pretty, but rather ordinary-looking with shoulder-length hair, regular features, and makeup artfully applied to a medium brown face. Her smile was exceptional and she seemed outgoing.

"Did anyone recommend you to my place?"

"No. I saw an ad in the *City Sun*."

She smiled again, brighter. "That's great. You're entitled to a discount with the ad."

"Well, to be honest, I didn't bring it with me."

"Not to worry. If you mention the ad, you're still entitled."

"Well, thank you."

I felt terrible lying about something I never saw. I don't know why I did it. I must have gotten carried away by all that pink. I made a mental note to read through all my old *City Sun* copies to make sure she hadn't caught me out and was playing me along.

I took a seat and picked up a magazine but was too nervous to read. Every time the door opened, I glanced up. Three more women had come in by appointment only to find their operators working on earlier customers. No one complained and the conversation flowed. The music was low enough for the talk to carry.

". . . and I told 'im, somebody went to the mat with him to knock them three caps off 'cause they was on tight," the woman in Maizie's chair said. "And gold too? With that big-ass diamond in it blindin' you every time he open his mouth? Shit! Couldna been nobody else but his other woman. Anybody else, he'd a sliced 'im and I'd a heard about it by now."

"So you think it musta been his other stuff?" Maizie asked sympathetically.

"Sure do," the woman said, "and the only reason she survivin' is because he don't wanna take them two kids he got by her . . . He did the right thing 'cause if she die, I sure ain't takin' 'em. Got two a my own . . . you know what I'm sayin'."

Maizie nodded. "I hear you, Lexi. It's tough all the way around."

I looked at Lexi as she rose from her seat, stretched, and walked over to get a soda from the machine. Then she settled back in, allowing her soft weight to spill over the sides of the chair. Her arms could not fold across her chest and the double chin and vanilla-pudding face were all the more exaggerated under the elaborate shoulder-length hair weave.

"Diamonds is okay but you know all that damn gold don't do nuthin' but make your breath stink," Lexi went on. "I'm glad they out even if somebody had to knock 'em out. Ain't nuthin' like dog breath when you tryin' to git a little piece."

"Ain't it the truth," Maizie said.

She put the last few waves into the mass of hair, then held a large hand mirror up to allow Lexi to see her handiwork from all angles.

"Next week, when you come in, I'll have that auburn piece for you. Right now, I'm fresh out of 'em." She unfastened the pink towel from Lexi's neck. "And you tell Nightlife that I said for him to behave—teeth or no teeth."

"Aw, his teeth is still in. It's them caps he still beefin' about and this happened over a month ago. You'd thought he'd a forgot about it by now. That's why I think it's his other woman and he can't do nuthin' but talk on it."

"Well, don't let it go gettin' your pressure up. He ain't moved nuthin' out so he's still your man. Besides, you gotta take care a yourself and your kids first, you know what I mean."

"I hear you. See y'all next week."

She pressed several bills in Maizie's hand, waved, and stepped out. I wanted to step out behind her, see where she would lead me, but Maizie beckoned and I moved to the chair.

"Now, you wanted the stress-erasing facial?" Maizie asked, preferring not to call it a mud pack.

"Yes." I looked at my watch. "About how long will it take?"

"Oh, a little over an hour if you really want it to penetrate the dermis. I see you have very fine pores, so this will take a while to get all the built-up dirt and impurities out."

She placed cotton pads over my eyes and turned on a blinding bright light. She examined me closely, and the more she talked, the angrier I felt. Dirt. Impurities. Pores. Crow's-feet. Already. Lines around my mouth. I was beginning to wonder if I had left my real skin at home and stepped in here covered with crocodile hide.

I grew depressed, wondering if plastic surgery might not be the answer to all the problems I didn't know I had.

When she finally started the process, the mask felt good. Warm, herbal-scented, and thick enough so that when it dried, she warned me to remain still to prevent it from cracking.

It was hard to stay awake but I'm glad I did because the talk started as soon as the door closed on Lexi.

"Girl, please. She comin' back next week for auburn? Gimme a break . . ."

"Well, it's only gonna be a streak." Maizie smiled, not exactly discouraging the talk.

The woman who had just taken a seat in the next chair whirled it around to face everyone in the room. "Now, I don't want you to think I'm raggin' my girl. I mean we tight, and whatever I say here, I already told her to her face."

"I know you did, girlfriend. Y'all go back a long way, but what I can't see is how she put up with what's-his-name . . . Night Owl."

"Nightlife. Same thing. Real name is Richard Dillmard. Don't matter what you call him, that no-good thief ain't never home where he s'pose to be."

"I wouldn't be home neither if I had to come home and fry that kinda fat."

"And where she get that name Lexi from anyway? Sound like somethin' off a soup can label."

"Well, Lexi come from Lexington. Her mama had did time there back in the day. Big-time dope dealer and the judge didn't give a shit that she was pregnant. Lexi born in federal prison in Lexington, Kentucky."

"Damn. That's one name I'd a changed."

"Aw, ain't nuthin' wrong with Lexi. Least she didn't turn out like her mama. She could stand to lose a few pounds but she works her two jobs and takes care a them kids the best she know how. And that man ain't hardly much help."

"Well, what is he doin' if he in the street? Gotta be into some kinda money."

"Well, he into a little a this and a little a that. You know how it is . . . that is, when he can git out. I heard that when Lexi go to sleep at night, she got that man's neck in a hammerlock. Ain't too often he be runnin' 'round on her."

"So when does he see his other stuff?"

"Daytime and early evening. When Lexi workin'."

Maizie had gotten quiet and allowed everyone else to talk. I watched her face when the talk centered on what Nightlife actually did for a living. She used the time to rearrange rows of nail polish on the shelf under the manicurist's table but her eyes reminded me of a quiet cat.

The subject of Lexi's problems with Nightlife petered out and the talk turned to other things: getting tick-

ets to *Geraldo,* and what they would wear to make
themselves stand out when the camera swung their way.

I was ready to leave. I had gotten a name that could
be tracked. Nightlife, Richard Dillmard, who had the
caps punched out more than a month ago and who had
most likely been in that car when Erskin was killed.

Maizie's silence told me that she knew Nightlife
very well, knew who he worked for, and probably knew
the particular work he did.

I checked my watch. Fifteen more minutes and my
face would be free of this steel casing. Right now, my
neck and my eyeballs were the only muscles I was permitted to move.

When the door opened, everyone felt the rush of
cool air, and the casual conversation turned off as suddenly as if someone had tightened a water faucet.

I inched forward slightly in my chair to watch the
operators bend attentively to their work. The only sponta-
neous movement came from Maizie as she walked toward
Johnnie Harding, looking as if he had just stepped out
of *GQ.*

"Hey, baby," Maizie whispered.

He said nothing but kissed her lightly on the cheek
and beckoned her toward the rear of the shop.

The aisle leading to the back was wide enough but
he still had to pass each workstation. He moved slowly
and gazed at each woman in the chairs as he passed.
When he approached me, a hollow feeling, an unfamiliar,
raw edge of fear, welled up in me.

Perhaps it was the feeling of helplessness, of being
trapped behind the mask with only my mouth and my
eyes showing. My eyes. I narrowed them but it was too
late to pretend to be dozing. He had seen me staring. I
remained still and thanked God for the mask and for the
towel Maizie had wrapped around my head.

He approached, paused, then moved to the back as Maizie called. "Baby, here it is . . ."

There was a quiet shuffling of paper—probably envelopes—and he left as quickly and quietly as he had come.

By the time Maizie removed the mask and the towel, I was drenched with sweat.

chapter fifteen

I was still sweating when I got home but I considered the information I'd gotten and was determined not to let Johnnie Harding's visit bother me.

Dad was in the living room when I walked in, so I asked, "Notice anything different?"

He looked up from the stack of sheet music on the table and I could tell from his expression that my trip to the Pink Fingernail had not been worth it. Cosmetic-wise, at least.

He leaned forward. "Light's so dim in here, I don't know what I'm supposed to be looking at. New dress, new hair, new face, legs? What? I'm an old man, honey. You have to be more specific."

He always fell back on the "old age" syndrome as a convenient way out. I sighed, headed upstairs, and knocked on Alvin's door. He was stationed in front of his computer and did not look around so I couldn't ask his opinion.

"How was the rehearsal?"

"It was good."

I stepped into the room. "So everything went well? The selections and all?"

"Yeah. Except that Mr. Lloyd was mad but nobody knew why. Kept walkin' in and out of the room. Somebody said he was countin' heads." He turned from the machine, frowning. "What's his problem?"

"Nothing he can't handle," I said, touching his shoulder. "Lloyd's under some pressure right now but he'll be all right."

I was feeling a vague anxiety myself, but later a warm shower calmed my nerves enough to settle down and add to my notes everything I had learned in the Pink Fingernail. I had not spoken to Tad much since Clarence had been released. What with trying to catch up with my class assignments to avoid a failing grade, visiting the hospital, and trying to track down things I needed to know, my main contact had been with his answering machine. When he returned my calls, he seemed too depressed and angry to talk.

I avoided asking anything relating to Danny's so-called Choir Murders file but I knew it was on his mind and talking would have made matters worse. Better to sort out the information that came my way, compile my own file, and present it to him all at one time. If he hit a wall at the precinct, then I would go to the district attorney with it.

I put the notebook away when Dad knocked on the door.

"What time will you be ready?" he asked.

"Ready?" My mind went blank. "For what?"

He opened the door a crack, then stepped inside. He smelled of a wonderful lime aftershave. He stood there with his hands jammed in his pockets and I could see his pained expression. "The opening-night gig is at ten o'clock this evening." He pronounced each word individually as if speaking to a child.

"Opening! Oh, Dad . . ."

I looked at him and tried to find the words to apologize. The New Club Harlem on Malcolm X Boulevard was opening tonight and he had been practicing and preparing for this for at least a month.

"Of course I'm going," I said, scrambling for words and moving across the room to my closet. Thank goodness that what few party clothes I still had were hanging just inside on the closet door and I could have reached in blindfolded to pull one off the hanger.

"What time are we expected?" I asked, trying to soothe his hurt feelings. I was on my knees in the closet searching for matching shoes and a handbag when he sighed.

"You'll have to meet me there. I'm expected to meet the boys a little early. Miss Laura is coming to sit with Alvin. I reserved a table for you."

I raced for the door before he closed it and gave him a kiss. "Good luck, Dad. Good luck. I'm happy for you."

The New Club Harlem on Lenox Avenue was built on a site that once held a three-story garage and auto storage warehouse. The present structure was new from the ground up and spotlights flashing on the white stucco facade highlighted the red canopy and carpet stretching to the curb. Large potted evergreens flanked the double-height brass-inlaid doors, and the velvet rope across the entrance suggested that the least expensive drink would cost three times as much as in the local hangout bar around the corner.

Despite the forbidding rope and prices, the opening caused a wave of excitement in the neighborhood—a supper club to feature jazz exclusively was finally back on the scene.

It was silly to take a cab five blocks when I could have walked to the place but it had been a while since my feet had been in four-inch heels. I looked nice standing in front of the bathroom mirror with a thigh-high black silk dress, triple-strand rope of pearls, and silk shoes, but by the time I left the house and walked to the corner, my toes were calling for a taxi louder than I was.

A crowd of onlookers was gathered outside the club and barricades had been set up just like in the movies. The doorman rushed to help me out of the cab and a murmur went up as I tipped lightly down the carpeted walk.

"Oh, I know her, she's—let's see, she's—"

"Yeah, that's her, the model . . . I seen her with that movie star last year . . . You know her, she's—"

I made it to the door amid the whistles and flash-bulbs and without having to sign a single autograph.

The interior was decorated the way Hollywood imagined a Harlem nightclub ought to look: bright red walls with black silhouettes of Savoy-style dancers caught in various acrobatic poses. Wall sconces cast wavering lights on the silhouettes to create an illusion of shadowy movement.

The tables, small linen-covered squares, were set in tiers around the dance floor. The aisle slanted down so that everyone had a view of the musicians in the center. Stars blinked in the painted ceiling and the lighting was just bright enough for a patron to wave and be recognized.

I wondered how much money went into this. And whose money. How much had the liquor license cost? Was there a front? I noticed a table, larger than the others, just to the right of the door, where four men sat—obscured by a tall screen of plants.

I waved to Dad, took my seat, and ordered a vodka martini from a hovering waiter. I slipped my shoes off under the table and Tad came to mind as I wriggled my toes. I missed him, really missed him. He should have been sitting right here with me but Dad was still upset about Deborah. Tad's presence would have reminded him all over again and I wanted nothing to interfere with his night.

A half hour later the lights dimmed and a spotlight focused on the emcee.

"Welcome to the new jazz club. And let's welcome Jeffrey Anderson, our own Harlem-born, -bred, and -blessed. The only man I know who can make a bass sing soprano."

The spotlight faded to a soft magenta and Dad said simply: "This composition is for Benin."

A soft play of fingers floated over the piano, cutting the silence. Sound rose from keys barely touched but lingered long enough to be caught by the edgy call of a trumpet. After the sax opened up, the bass notes could be heard undergirding and holding together everything that had to be said.

In the darkness, I listened along with everyone else. For weeks I had heard the tapping of keys and plucking of bass, disjointed and hollow, coming from his study. At times there was no sound at all and I had wondered if he was all right or if he had fallen asleep. Other days, profanity loud and strong persuaded me to mind my business and leave him and his Muse strictly alone.

Now here was the finished piece—a memorial— washing over everything in small exquisite waves of sound.

I brushed my tears away as the lights came up and applauded long after everyone else had stopped.

The band played five more numbers and then took a break. Dad eased into the chair beside me. "Trio's coming on after midnight. I can check the acoustics, then maybe take my little girl for a spin on the floor."

He meant to dance. My toes wriggled around and found my shoes, and what I had feared most had happened. My feet had swollen one whole size larger than the shoes. I reached under the table and gathered them up.

"Which way to the ladies' room?"

He pointed to an exit near the front and I thanked God that the lights were dim enough for me to hobble away with some dignity. In the bathroom, I locked myself in a booth, took off my panty hose, and gingerly placed a wad of tissue between the toes that hurt the most. All I needed was enough relief to get me through this session and out of the club. I intended to barefoot it home.

I reapplied my lipstick and walked to the door, only to open it and close it just as quickly.

"Damn!"

I leaned against the door, hoping no one wanted to come in, hoping I hadn't been seen. Johnnie and Danny? Together? Damn!

I let a minute pass before I peered into the corridor again. The two had moved a distance away.

Their voices were muted against the sound from the stage but in the dim light I could make out Danny angrily waving his hand in Johnnie's face and Johnnie laughing. The music died, the applause ended, and the voices floated easily above the voice of the emcee.

". . . I'm tellin' you, Danny, I don't know what the fuck you talkin' about!"

"Don't pull that on me. You know what went down. Your name is on that sheet. You put 'im back out in the street!"

"You think I'd be that stupid? Fuck you!"

The music started again and the rest of the conversation was lost.

chapter sixteen

Walking in Harlem at 5 A.M. reminded me of my old midnight shift except now, instead of moving with the weight of a .38, I had Dad beside me rolling his bass.

Much to his embarrassment, I strolled in my stocking feet, trying to make up my mind whether to throw my shoes into the next trash can.

"You gonna have arthritis up to your knees by morning," he said. "You, a city girl, walking barefoot on concrete. Never saw such a thing in my life."

"Dad, if you only knew how much my feet hurt . . ."

"I know you should use something called common sense and buy shoes that fit. You wore a size nine when you were age nine. You're thirty-one now and—"

"Dad. Please . . ."

He glanced at me and whatever else he meant to say was swallowed back in a grumble.

He was right. It made no sense to stroll barefoot,

what with dog gifts and other debris to contend with, but I couldn't think about that right now. I was still surprised to see Danny and Johnnie Harding together. But things being the way they are, it was entirely possible for cops and criminals to sometimes frequent the same place at the same time.

Dad and I continued the short distance. He remained quiet and the silence between us made the walk seem longer.

Two gypsy cabs, one after the other, slowed down, but we waved them on and watched them disappear into the fading darkness. Already, a small pink rim was enlarging in the downtown sky and transforming anonymous silhouettes into real buildings with windows and drawn shades and people sleeping behind the shades.

A bus rattled by, shifted gears noisily, and a minute later we were alone again, crossing Powell Boulevard with the only sound coming from the small rolling wheel of the bass.

This stillness was remarkable for a neighborhood that never slept. Folks usually lounged on stoops, decorated lampposts, and hung out twenty-four seven in front of the all-night bodega, with music and beer and expectant attitudes, waiting for something to happen even if nothing ever happened. Sometimes the crowds were so thick that other folks thought something had already gone down and so came out to join them.

We passed one person, a forlorn figure nodding off a high on the stone steps of a burned-out building. The entrance was cinder-blocked and the windows above yawned open like black eyes. I did not like this kind of quiet.

I thought of Danny. He was operating in Rambo mode, using more muscle than mind, but why had he allowed Harding to laugh at him?

When they had moved farther down the hall, I had

managed to slip from the ladies' room and back to the table, but the rest of the evening had been lost. The music, the applause, and the emcee's voice all seemed to flow from the other end of a long tunnel and I had been glad when the last set ended.

I put the key in the door, waking Miss Laura. Alvin was fine, she said, and she fell back to sleep on the sofa.

The carpet in the foyer felt like a cloud under my feet and I lingered there as Dad went into the kitchen.

"Coffee?"

"No thanks, I'm too tired." What I really needed was solitude.

Upstairs, I sat near the window with my feet in a basin of water and watched the dawn slip over gray-brown branches of the linden trees, turning them red-gold in the new light. The birds came next, with their morning sounds.

And somewhere beyond the trees and the birds, it was midnight again and I was alone in the street as a black Cadillac pulled up beside me. The tinted window rolled down to reveal a clay mask floating in the dark interior, floating like a balloon.

I tried to run but clawlike hands reached out, growing larger as I struggled to move across a street pock-marked with craters. Then I stumbled and fell soundlessly into a gaping manhole, falling deeper and faster and unable to grasp the slippery walls. The clay mask zigzagged down behind me, and the deeper I fell, the nearer the voice behind the mask seemed. ". . . Let it alone . . . let it alone . . ."

The voice sounded familiar and I tried to call out but fractures appeared in the clay and the mask began to fly apart in sharp, cutting pieces. I turned away screaming, afraid to look at the face behind it.

When I opened my eyes, Dad was shaking me by the shoulders.

"See what walking barefoot will get you? Night-mare had you hollerin' so loud you scared poor Alvin out of a year's growth."

I looked down at the basin which had been knocked over, saw the water seeping into the carpet. The metallic taste of alcohol in my mouth was enough to curl my tongue but I managed to apologize.

"I'm sorry. I'm sorry. I didn't realize . . . Is . . . is Alvin okay?"

"Yeah. Go take a shower and get yourself together. Coffee's ready. I'm gonna walk Miss Laura down the block."

I hurried to the bathroom, avoided the mirror, jumped into the shower, and remained under the icy spray long enough to come to my senses. I knotted a terry robe around me and hurried to Alvin's room.

The door was ajar and I tapped lightly before poking my head in. He was sitting in the window seat with his knees drawn up under his chin.

"Alvin, how're you feeling?"

He lowered his legs to make room for me to sit beside him. On the walls on either side of the window he had taped life-size posters of Michael Jordan and Magic Johnson, and directly over his bed, the face of Patrick Ewing with the ball held chest-high glowered into the room. Magic and Michael were smiling, Patrick looked grim, all were sweaty with determination.

I wondered if they ever had to cope with the crushing anger of abandonment or the guilt that survivors sometimes endured. I turned away and gazed out of the window.

"I'm sorry about waking you," I said, not knowing where to begin.

He raised his shoulders slightly and said nothing. The small chorus of bird chatter just outside the window did little to fill the silence.

"It was a dream," I whispered, "something I can't even remember now that I'm awake."

"I remember all my dreams," he said, turning from the window to look at me. His eyes in the slanting sun took on the light brown cast of his mother's eyes. "I remember my dreams 'cause they don't wanna go away." He bent his leg to examine a small scratch on his knee, then began to pick at it absently. "They come two and three times a night. I wake up tired most of the time."

"What do you dream about?"

He hesitated, trying to decide if he wanted to talk about it. Finally, he said, "Mom. Dad. I see them at the airport."

I put my arms around his shoulders and pressed him to me. He was nine years old when that overseas call had come in. He was supposed to stay with me and Dad for two weeks, long enough for his parents to take a quick trip to celebrate the end of William's internship. A trip that had been planned for a long time. And they were supposed to come back. Instead, the phone call had come in the middle of a rainy night.

At times I feel we, Dad and Alvin and I, are still waiting for them to come back. Even though the bodies had been recovered and brought home. Even though Dad and I had scattered that final wet handful of earth on the caskets and listened to the slow squeal of the winch lowering them into the ground, we seem to be waiting. Even though I can still feel the wind, the chill that had settled in me that day and never left, we wait and listen.

We seem to be in a state of suspension, anticipating a tap on the door, imagining that rush of air as Benin and William stroll in, laughing and breathless from the flight, complaining of the cab ride, dropping suitcases and shopping bags heavy with perfume and Paris labels to prove there had been a mistake.

Two years later and we are still waiting.

I catch myself speaking in the present tense. "Your mother wants you to . . . Your father wants . . ." as if they will one day return to say what a wonderful job we did with their son in their absence.

Early on, I had gone back to Dr. Thomas for crisis sessions. There must be a sense of closure, he said. And it would have been better if Alvin had attended the funeral, gone to the burial, as young as he was. It would have helped him most.

But it's too late to change that. Too late. So we must work all the harder toward this closure. But how does one give up the past without giving up memory?

The sun was up now and the shadows had gone. Alvin moved away from the window, gathered some sheet music, and stuffed it in his backpack. He moved with the awkward grace of a child disinterested in a task and going through the motions to please everyone but himself.

"We're doing six songs today," he said.

Breakfast was quiet but I was glad to see that Alvin's appetite had returned. He devoured six pancakes and bacon and eggs while I hugged a lukewarm cup of coffee.

"I'll walk Alvin to rehearsals, if you want," Dad said, looking at me and probably noticing the circles under my eyes.

"No. I need the exercise. I'll go with him."

The truth was I didn't want to fall asleep again and have to fight another nightmare. Fifteen minutes later I left the house and called Tad from a public phone. His voice was as deep as ever.

"I was beginning to give up on you, Mali."

"Don't do that," I said, surprised that he was home to answer the phone. I had expected to leave a message but here was his voice, alive and fresh and concerned.

Listening to him helped push the nightmare, hangover, and aching feet into an unused corner of my mind.

"I have a late tour today. How about lunch?"

"Fine," I said, realizing how suddenly beautiful the day seemed.

"Meet you at Emily's about one o'clock."

Alvin and I took the long way to the rehearsal hall and passed by the ball court. Clarence was there alone, sitting on the bench near the fence, and there was no ball in sight.

He came over when we waved. He looked thinner and he needed a haircut but he smiled as he approached.

"How's it going, Clarence?"

"Could be better, Miss Mali, but I'm not complainin' . . . How you doin', Striver?"

"Okay," Alvin said, smiling. I could see that he was now even less interested in going to rehearsal and wanted to remain right here on the court, but I wasn't having any of that.

"Where's your ball?" he asked.

Clarence shrugged. "Rolled out into the street and car run over it. So I'm just hangin' till some a my boys breeze by. Maybe pick up a game with them . . ."

"How's Morris?" I asked.

"He all right. Seen 'im last night."

Which meant that Mrs. Johnson was still inviting him in for dinner. I did not ask how his mother was.

"Well, I'm glad to see you, glad you're out . . ."

"Me too," he said. He was suddenly very talkative, as if he wanted the world to know what he'd gone through but couldn't find the words to describe it.

"Man, ain't no way to say what it's like in the joint. Got to be down with the program or ready to throw down. Brothers got to go in badder than Tyson if they spect to survive. Some of 'em don't. Wind up swallowin' glass to git to the infirmary. That don't work, they hang theyselves. It ain't like in no movies. In there's the real deal."

I looked at his face, at his dark, young, unlined skin, and knew what he had seen but would never really talk about. The "blanket parties"—gang rapes—drug deals, beatings, blackmail, and thievery that went on under the very noses of some of the guards.

"Who bailed you?" I asked, knowing it was none of my business.

He shrugged again. "I don't know and I don't care. All I know is I'm out and I ain't goin' back. Ever. No, I mean it ain't that I don't care who did it. I do. But nobody never told me. I mean, one minute, I'm in hell, and the next minute, the door open and I'm breathin' real air again.

"Besides, the Legal Aid sister said they ain't even got a case on me as far as this second rap is concerned. I ain't killed nobody. And the other charge is gonna be downgraded to simple assault and they might even drop that once they get a look at—"

He glanced at Alvin and said no more.

Just then, three young men entered the court from the other end and called out to him. They had a ball and bounced it a few times off the rim.

"Be cool!" Clarence smiled, and I watched him lope easily down to the basket and slap five. The ball went up. He tapped it against the rim and the game was on.

I dropped Alvin off at the hall and was glad that more parents had shown up.

"Dad will pick you up," I reminded him, giving him a hug even though he didn't like this show of affection in front of the other kids. Then I headed downtown on Powell Boulevard to Emily's.

On the way, I browsed through the African market

on Lenox and 116th Street where the spring weather had brought out the bargain hunters and a busload of tourists. The pavement shook beneath car-size boom boxes that put out enough juice to power a rock concert. Hot dog and lemonade stands were crowded. The tops of the patterned tents riffled in the breeze, and inside, the tables were piled with fabric, sandals, incense, and hats. I was caught in the festival sounds and found myself stopping at several tables.

"Ah, madam," a vendor called, holding out a wide-brimmed pale yellow straw hat, "this hat is you. It was just waiting to frame your face. No one else would do it justice."

His accent was deep and his English was soft and precise as he held a postage-stamp-size mirror up to me. I smiled and ignored the pile of identical straw hats on the table.

Last year when Deborah had returned from Senegal, she had advised, "You better learn how to bargain if you expect to visit the motherland. That's all they do."

So I practiced. Smiling wider, speaking softer, finally bargaining harder, and ten minutes later the hat was on my head at a price I could live with.

I tilted the hat, glad that the vendors had found this location, but in the shifting political currents, who knows how long they would be here? The city administration had forced them from their original location on 125th Street, and without the festival sounds and tourists and occasional public speakers, Harlem's main thoroughfare now seemed drained of life.

Emily's has large windows which look out on Fifth Avenue and 111th Street and though smaller than Sylvia's, caters to loyal soul food aficionados. It has a fancy bar and a cool, subdued atmosphere. I slipped into the seat oppoite Tad and he leaned over, pushed my hat back, and kissed me.

"I haven't tasted your lipstick in a long while," he whispered, holding my hands against his face. He looked great, as if he had come out of his depression and was ready to talk about important things. Like making love all night long.

"The lipstick's only the appetizer," I whispered.

"I know," he smiled, rubbing my fingertips against his chin. "When can I start on the main dish?"

"Depends. When can you get a day off? I could cut a class. We could take the phone off the hook, and do all those good things we—"

"Miss another class? At this rate, you won't see your diploma before you're fifty."

I sighed and said nothing. He was right, of course. Dad was also beginning to make noise about my sudden slowdown. But with all that had happened—to Erskin, and Deborah, and worrying about Clarence and Alvin—it was hard to concentrate.

"School is one thing. I'm not in class today."

Tad took my hands again. "Sounds nice but I have to make a hospital visit in a few hours."

I gazed at him and knew I'd better change the subject while my temperature was still somewhere near normal.

"Well, okay, some other time—"

"Come on, baby. You know how I feel. Don't—"

I concentrated on his hands. As long as I didn't gaze into his eyes, everything would probably be all right.

A minute passed before I said, "I was at the Club Harlem last night. Dad played the opening. I saw something interesting . . ."

"I know. You saw Harding. You saw Danny. And you were walking around in your stockings. Must've been quite a night."

I stared at him. He said nothing more. "Did Danny tell you?" I whispered.

"No. Matter of fact, I haven't spoken to him in a few days, but as the old folks say, 'All shut-eye ain't sleep and all good-bye ain't gone.'"

I looked away and smiled in spite of myself. That meant he was still on the case, in his own way, and had his eyes and ears working the street even when he wasn't.

He winked and settled back in his chair. "Anything else happening?"

"Well, I was in the Pink Fingernail Friday and—"

"The Pink Fingernail. On Amsterdam?"

"Yes, I—"

"Mali, of all the beauty shops in Harlem, you had to pick that one. What happened to Bertha's place? I thought that was your cool-down spot?"

"It is. It still is. Bertha mentioned the Pink Fingernail and I wanted to check it out. When I got there, I decided I needed a facial . . ."

He stared at me, as if he were examining my pores. I expected at any minute to see him whip out a Sherlock Holmes–style magnifying glass.

"Mali, your skin is beautiful. You needed a facial?"

"Well, thanks for the compliment. Anyway, I heard some talk."

"Such as?"

"A woman named Lexi was getting her hair together . . ."

"I know her. Her mama was a big-time dope dealer when smack first came on the scene. She did time in Lexington and had her baby there. Not too much imagination when it came to naming the kid . . ."

"Lexi's living with a man called Nightlife."

"Small-time thief uses Riker's as his vacation spot. Go on."

"From what she said, I think Nightlife may be connected to Erskin's death. He may've been in the car that day."

Tad leaned back now as his expression changed. His eyes were as narrow as a cat's. "What exactly did she say?"

"Nightlife had some gold caps punched out about a month ago. Lexi was complaining about it. A few minutes after she left, Johnnie Harding came strolling in."

"Harding. What did he do? Did you hear anything?"

"Nothing. He went straight to the back of the shop and Maizie must've had some envelopes or something for him. He left in a matter of minutes."

Tad passed his hands over his face and I decided not to mention that Johnnie had stared at me as if he knew me. Tad gazed out of the window, absently rearranging his knife and fork on the table. I waited. Finally he leaned over and whispered, "Don't go there again. At least not for a while. That's a hot spot."

And just as quickly, his face changed. His eyes were alight and he was on the verge of a smile. "Anything else interesting going on?"

"Yes," I said, glad to change the subject. "Clarence is out. Who stood the bail?"

"You don't give up, do you?"

"Depends on what I'm after . . ."

He shifted in his seat, choosing to ignore the double meaning of my remark and said, "Seems a J. Harding contacted a bondsman—"

"But why would Johnnie—"

"It's not our boy Johnnie. It was Julia Harding that done the deed."

Julia Harding. Erskin's mother. Good for her and bless her soul. I sat back and nodded my head. This was something to think about, take my mind off Nightlife and Erskin and concentrate on something else. Like that time when a very refined woman, much like Julia Harding, had come into the precinct along with the man who had tried to rob her in her elevator. She hadn't screamed, but simply opened her purse and shot him in the arm with a .22.

Naturally the robber fled only to be arrested in the E.R. and naturally the woman had been arrested for carrying an unlicensed handgun. She explained to the detectives that the gun had been a gift from her late husband and she had had no idea that it was unlicensed. When the holdup occurred, she said, there was no time to call a séance to ask his advice. "Just aim and shoot," he had once told her.

And that's what she did.

She was small and thin with striking silver hair and went through the fingerprint process with an amazing calm, wiping her hands as if she were brushing away crumbs at high tea. When she saw me watching, she had smiled. "Honey, I'm not rough or tough, but mama don't take much stuff."

That had been a woman after my own heart. Now here was Mrs. Julia Harding, a woman who followed her own intuition and everyone else could kiss her refined behind.

No need to ask if Danny knew. He probably did. No need to worry about him visiting Mrs. Harding. He probably would. But no need to worry about her holding her own against his relentless, roundabout questioning. Julia Harding, just like that little lady with the .22, would let him know in a few words that she could do as she pleased. She was not rough or tough but she didn't take no stuff.

"You have a look in your eye," Tad said.

"I do?"

"Yes. A look that says you can't wait to fly out of

here to stick your nose in something that doesn't concern you."

The man seemed able to read me but not well enough.

I didn't look up and we ate in silence when the food arrived.

Of course I was going to see Mrs. Harding, but I also needed to know more about Nightlife.

chapter seventeen

The construction near Mrs. Harding's building was finished, but across the avenue, another phase was under way with the slow driving noise of the bulldozers lifting the soil from the community garden the neighbors had started several summers ago.

This time I called instead of barging in unannounced. It was perfectly all right, she said, to come right over.

The place looked the same, the book-lined walls, the fish tank, plants, and the shining baby grand piano that seemed to dwarf everything around it.

"That was a wonderful thing you did for Clarence," I said, settling onto the sofa.

She offered me a glass of sherry but I opted for a cup of tea since I had not fully recovered from last night.

"Clarence doesn't know who you are but he certainly appreciates what you did."

"You spoke to him?"

"Saw him earlier today when I took Alvin to rehearsal."

"Is the boy—is Clarence back in the Chorus?"

"Not yet, but he will be once this . . . situation is resolved. He's very grateful. Wants to know why anyone would do something like that for him."

Mrs. Harding looked at me, then rose and walked over to the piano, where she lifted the lid.

"This is why I did it," she whispered, keeping her voice soft as if someone else were in the room with us. She handed me a small manila envelope. Inside was a four-by-six-inch spiral notepad.

I thumbed through it and recognized Erskin's precise script. There were six pages of numbers aligned in two columns on each page. The numbers were mostly nine or ten digits and some had a line drawn through them. The rest of the pad was blank.

"When did you find this?"

"About two days before I bailed the boy out. It pays to do a thorough housecleaning once in a while. I was dusting and polishing, lifted the lid and there it was, taped to the inside."

I continued to look at the numbers and remembered what Dad had said about an artist recording events that occurred in other people's lives. Erskin had left a record after all, except that the entries were coded—like the message on his calendar.

"There're too many digits to be anyone's address. What do you think these numbers mean?" I asked.

"I have no idea, unless Erskin scrambled them. But those notations, whatever they mean, convinced me that Clarence had nothing to do with Erskin's death and that something far more sophisticated is going on. That's why I posted the bond and that's why I want you to have this book."

"You want me—are you certain?"

She moved toward the window and stared out. The grinding noise of the bulldozers now blended with the other sounds of the avenue and the construction seemed far away.

"I want to know who killed my son, Mali. If I depend on the police for answers, I will be waiting until the middle of the next century. And at my age, I don't have the luxury of time."

She turned away from the window to face me. "There's something I didn't mention earlier because I didn't see what good it would do to tell you, but now I think you should know how my son felt about you."

I looked at her. "Erskin?"

"Yes. He . . . liked you very much. Very, very much. When I asked why he hadn't approached you, he said . . . he said that you were very beautiful and would probably turn him down."

"What?"

"I never intended to tell you because he's gone now, but you know, aside from my pastor and a few members of my church, no one has been to see me since the funeral except you. You were there when Erskin died. You tried to save him. I like to think that the last face he saw was yours. I want you to have that book."

I did not know what to say. Erskin had been shot point-blank. He probably died before he fell to the ground.

A minute passed before I hugged her, then slipped the envelope carefully into my shoulder bag.

"Mrs. Harding, I ought to tell you that the police—probably a Detective Williams—will be here to ask why you bailed a prime suspect."

"Clarence may be a suspect, but not for the murder of my son."

She looked at me now and I remembered the enigmatic smile of the .22-caliber lady at the precinct.

"So let Mr. Williams—or whoever they decide to send—let them come. I'm not as frail as I look. When I get through reading them about their foot-dragging, it'll be a while before they decide to darken my doorstep again."

She walked me as far as the landing. The veined marble walls reminded me of an old sanctuary and I imagined how full and rich Erskin's music must have sounded floating through these halls.

I tried to think back, to recall the times we'd spoken, or recall the look in his eyes. But the only image that came to me was the final blank gaze.

Mrs. Harding touched my arm. "Next time you visit, please bring Alvin. I'd love to see him."

Back home in my own room, I studied the calendar again and compared the handwriting in the pad. Then I went over my notes. When nothing clicked, I began to feel a grudging admiration for Tad and Danny—Tad for being able to take the smallest clue and dissect it until the layers fell away to reveal the answer, clear as day. And Danny for hanging on to a shred of evidence, shaking it like a pit bull would until something finally fell apart.

I felt tired and closed the book.

Maybe I should give this stuff to Tad right now. Let him figure it all out—the Motor Vehicles printout, the calendar, my notes, everything. But then he'd be obliged to turn everything over to Danny and that would bring up too many other questions. Like how I came by the calendar in the first place. And the addresses of the license plates. Not to mention the notepad I got today from Erskin's mother.

And who knows? Despite Danny's ambition, all of this might simply be filed away and forgotten. There's a murder every week. Sheer numbers could grind down the most conscientious investigation. And the dust almost always gathers in an open file. I can't let that happen to Erskin.

I started through my own notes a final time before going downstairs to prepare dinner. Dad would be home soon with Alvin and both would be hungry enough to chew the leg off the dining table.

Two murders, one attempt, and one attempted kidnapping. Morris's hand was bleeding. The bloodstain is probably still in that car, wherever it is . . .

Morris had punched Nightlife but who had actually driven the car? Who pulled the trigger? Were Erskin and Gary killed by the same gun? By the same person? And how come the police are moving so slow on this?

I closed my notebook. Sometimes, moving away from a problem brought the solution. Sometimes when I least expected it.

At dinner, I nodded politely at intervals as Dad talked about the Club Harlem. He was negotiating for a steady gig at their Sunday brunches and I only half listened until he said, "Bunch a gangsters, all of 'em, but I'm not settlin' for nothing less than top dollar."

"Who owns the place?" I asked.

"Who knows? They've probably set up so many dummy corporations, even the IRS would have a hard time trying to figure it out. But the street talk is that it's a laundrymat for narc-dollars."

"You sure you want to work steady in that place?"

"I don't know. Is there any difference between that place and Wall Street? Or some of the precincts? Or some private clubs in Washington where the pols hang out? The very ones who write the laws against drugs? You know how many of those folks are literally drowning in drug money?"

I had no answer but I knew that Wall Street and certain parts of Washington and the precincts were safe from the nightly drive-by shootings that were part of the street-level battle for control of the drugs. They were safe from boys barely in their teens who packed enough heat to start World War III. These kids traded Tec-9s like baseball cards and routinely blew away anyone stupid enough to step to the wrong corner phone.

So if the Club Harlem was in the money game and something went wrong, who could stop an arsonist from easing into the basement and putting the torch to a custom-soaked tablecloth as the band played on?

Dad glanced at me.

"Listen, kiddo. Everything'll be all right. I know how to quit a sinking ship. I know the exits."

It was as if he had read my mind. I did not feel any better.

chapter eighteen

Sunday morning dawned with a gray drizzle but cleared by the time I left the house to visit Deborah. The Lenox Avenue bus turned down Fifth and fifteen minutes later I stepped off into a neighborhood where private homes resembled small museums and the high-rises were guarded by doormen decked out like Russian generals.

The rehab institute was an old converted mansion next door to a private club. The institute's palm-filled lobby and soft music made it seem more like a small posh hotel than a hospital. I wondered if Deborah's insurance covered all of this or if her sister was more well off than she appeared and was paying the cost to be the boss.

On the fifth floor, a nurse, the only person I saw in uniform, left her desk to escort me down a carpeted hallway to Deborah's room. It had been two weeks since anyone except family had been permitted to visit. Although I kept in touch with her sister by phone, I didn't know what to expect.

When I stepped inside, Deborah was sitting in a chair near the window, reading. When she looked up, her eyes were clear and her smile was radiant.

"Mali! Am I glad to see you!"

I stood near the door, shocked to hear the sound of her voice. She was speaking again. Her sister had never mentioned it; just said that she was doing all right.

"Well, don't just stand there," she said, rising from her seat. "Let me give you a hug. Come on now, Mali, don't start crying. I've seen enough of Mama's tears to last me a lifetime."

She had found her voice again, had pulled it back from wherever it had fled that horrible morning.

"Deborah! Am I glad to see you! And glad to hear you, girl! It's been a damn long time."

"To say the least. What I've been through, I wouldn't wish on a dog, but everything—the treatment, the people in this place—has been wonderful. I've even had acupuncture and a few sessions of hypnosis."

"They managed to hypnotize you?"

"Well, let's put it this way. I think they tried. Anyway, the place isn't bad at all."

"How long will you be here?"

"Not much longer. As good as it is, there's nothing like being home, cooking your own food and sleeping in your own bed."

She waved her hand around the room, taking in the small bed with its flowered coverlet. The window had matching drapes and there was a lamp, radio, small television, and a VCR. All it needed was a shelf or two of books and it could have been a well-appointed dorm room on any campus.

She wanted to go home. I nodded but said nothing. Did she know that her sister planned to take her to Washington to live? Maybe not. One step at a time, her sister had said. The main thing was for Deborah to recover, then I suppose they'd deal with the other issues later. One step at a time.

"You're coming home. That's wonderful, that's good news."

I wondered if her sister had already closed up the apartment, packed her belongings, and shipped them to Washington. If she had, might this cause a relapse? Martha had been very closemouthed about her plans whenever I spoke to her, had refused to even stay in Deborah's apartment, preferring a downtown hotel where she said it was safe. When I asked, she never said that Deborah had improved to this point.

I saw a fight looming between these two. But right now Deborah looked great. And she was talking.

"Take a look at this . . ." She pulled the collar of her blouse aside. The scar looked like a long deep scratch, visible in the arc of her neck. "Doctors did a good job, didn't they?"

"They did more than a good job. This is a miracle."

I gazed at the scar and knew then that what the old folks said was true: "Death could be dancin' in your face but you make it on over to that hospital, honey. If you go in squawkin', they guarantee you'll come out walkin'."

But I didn't mention this because when she went in, she wasn't squawking. She barely had a pulse and her blood pressure was the lowest they'd seen in a patient in a long time. They not only brought her back, but there was little physical evidence of the horror she had gone through.

"Another thing," Deborah said as she settled back in her chair. "Someone from the police department came here to talk to me. Asked a lot of questions about what happened before that man assaulted me, wanted to know if he said anything. How am I supposed to remember what he said, if he said anything? Even if that memory returns, I don't intend to speak to the police or anyone about it. Ever. It's over and I want to forget it."

She twisted her fingers and I watched her face change and I cursed Danny Williams again and again. For his ambition and his "don't give a damn as long as a case gets solved" attitude. But why would he still want to question her? What was he after? Finally, I said, "Don't worry. I'll let your sister know what's happening. She can call the precinct and lodge a complaint. The goal is for you to get well, not to be subjected to any harassment."

She calmed a bit and smiled. "Sorry. I didn't mean to start yelling . . ."

"You weren't yelling."

"Well, I'm sorry." She rose from the chair and began to pace the floor. There wasn't much room to walk and I wondered if she did this often. "I'll be all right once I get back to work, get busy again."

"You'll be fine, Deborah. You're all right now. You've been through a lot, but you're coming along all right now."

I guided her back to the chair by the window and held her hands until she calmed down. "You're coming along fine," I repeated.

She looked at me closely and I knew what she was asking.

"Deborah, I've never lied to you. Never. You are getting better. Soon you'll be one hundred percent."

She closed her eyes. Then: "Will you come see me again?"

"I'll come tomorrow."

"No. Sundays are the only days."

I looked around the room. "Do they permit telephones?"

"I suppose they do, but up to now, I haven't needed one." She was relaxed now, able to smile at the joke.

"Well, I'll contact the nurse's station. Maybe they

can call you to the phone. Meanwhile, I'll speak to your sister and have her go to the precinct. There's no reason why Danny Williams should be harassing you."

She looked at me and shook her head, the silver in her tiny earrings glittering in the fading afternoon light.

"No. His name wasn't Williams. It was Honeywell. A Detective Tad Honeywell, who said he knew you. Very charming. And, let me tell you, girl, he was something to look at."

chapter nineteen

When I came in from class, the message light was blinking on my answering machine, and even before I took my shoes off, I pressed the button hoping to hear Tad's voice. Instead, the message that came on was so explicit I wondered where the caller got his ideas from. He couldn't possibly be capable of doing all the things he suggested. Still, I lowered the volume so that the voice lost depth and took on the insubstantial quality of a small, squeaking rodent.

It was a long call and I thought of speeding it up until a phrase caught my ear: ". . . then we'll take care of your father and your nephew . . ."

I replayed it, pressed the save button, and removed the tape. The calls were coming in more frequently now but the phone company had had no luck tracing them. Probably because whoever it was was calling from a public phone. I hadn't cared because I assumed they had come from the precinct in reaction to the lawsuit.

This message was a death threat.

When the phone rang again, I picked it up on the first ring.

"What're you doing this evening? Feel like coming out?"

"Tad?"

"Well, who else would be calling to—never mind, let me start again. How about having dinner? I know a great chef over at a cozy Riverbend apartment overlooking the river . . ."

"Really?" I whispered, already putting my shoes back on and slipping the tape into my bag. "What's on the menu?"

"You'll see when you get here. Take a cab. I'll have the wine chilled, the candles lit, and dinner on the table by the time you ring the bell." There was a pause, and his voice softened. "Mali, I'm sorry about the other day."

"I'm sorry also, Tad. I'll be there as soon as I can." Even as I said this, I was grabbing my jacket.

I needed to tell him about this latest message, this threat against my family, and find out if it related to the lawsuit or my interest in the choir murders. Either way, it was something to take seriously.

The choir murders. I was throwing a few things into my shoulder bag and paused when I realized I had used Danny Williams's own phrase. The Choir Murders. Nice neat file name but what the hell was happening with it?

I looked at the file on my desk and on the way out, impulsively swept the large envelope into my bag already stuffed with hairbrush, toothbrush, red silk teddy, and some strawberry-flavored personal stuff—just in case.

Somewhere along the line, I'd get around to asking about Tad's visit to Deborah and we could go over Erskin's notebook. But all of that would come later in the evening, probably more toward morning. First things first.

Dad took on a grim look when I mentioned where I was going.

"In my day," he said, "young men came to the house, or at least to the door, to pick up their date for the evening. They might even have a few words with the family before stepping out. But, of course, that was in my day—horse-and-buggy era—so don't let me interfere with anything you want to do."

I wanted to count to ten under my breath before I answered but that would've taken too long.

"Dad, please," I called to him as he made his way toward the kitchen. "It isn't as if you hadn't already met him, or didn't know him."

I heard the door of the fridge slam shut and the rattle of jars and dishes and wondered how he could still be hungry so soon after dinner.

"Technically," he called, "you're right. I did meet him. But I really don't know him."

I waited for him to continue but felt my stomach tightening. I was thirty-one years old, not thirteen. Most women my age were already married to or divorcing their second husbands or sprouting a second crop of kids. In nine short years, I'd be looking in the mirror at a forty-year-old face and body and trying to figure out what had happened. Or more to the point, what had *not* happened, and how I had allowed my life to drain away.

Dad returned to the living room and made his way to the sofa with a small tray loaded with spectator food—beer, soda, chips, and a couple of hard-boiled eggs. He turned on the television and settled himself in for the Knicks game. Alvin would soon come down to keep him company.

And once Patrick Ewing hit the court, it wouldn't matter if I stayed home or not. I could go into cardiac arrest right there in front of the set, and if it happened before halftime, I would be out of luck.

"Dad, can we finish this discussion when I return?"

He snapped the sound off and looked up, noticing my heavy shoulder bag. "What do you have in there? Books, I hope. The semester's ending and I don't see you burning the midnight oil."

"Dad, I just spent the entire afternoon after class in the library. The print was starting to swim before my eyes. I can stand to take a break."

He hesitated, then said, "Well, call me if you're gonna be out late."

I reached over and kissed him on the forehead. "I'll be careful. Don't worry."

It had gotten dark fast. The trees were thick with new leaves and the streetlights only filtered through at intervals as I walked toward Seventh Avenue. Most of the houses had their windows shut and curtains drawn against the evening. Cars were parked bumper-to-bumper on both sides of the street, and despite the warm weather, there were no dog walkers or cars passing through. I was the only one on the block.

Twenty feet away from the confluence of Seventh Avenue's bright lights and busy arena, someone came up behind me. Fast and quiet.

"Give it up!"

Before I turned, his hand was already at my shoulder, pulling the bag away.

"No! No! Let go of me!"

He snatched at the strap but my fingers were frozen to the body of the bag.

"Fuckin' bitch! Let it go! Give it up! I'll kill you!"

"No!"

One strap broke as he jerked the bag, the force pulling me off my feet. I fell down, screaming. Two men crossing the avenue looked back, then came running.

"Yo! What's goin' on? You all right, sister?"

"Help me! This man is—"

"Look, brothers, mind your business. This my woman and she got somethin' belong to me. Okay. So step off."

I was on my feet now and trying to ease an inch at a time toward the avenue, toward lights, toward more people.

"No—wait a minute. I don't know this man! He's trying to rob me. He's a thief. Call the police!"

I pressed the bag to me, staring at the man who wanted it. A dark, wiry man of about thirty with thin braided hair who was actually grinning at the other two. Grinning in a brotherly way.

"You know how it is . . . You break up with your old lady and—"

I stared at him, openmouthed, then at the two men, one of whom had begun to hesitate, wondering if he had done the right thing.

"Well, look, brother, I don't know. I don't get between no man and his woman . . ."

I couldn't believe my ears. This thief. This bum, this son of a bitch, was actually convincing them that it was all right to do what he was doing.

"Walk me to the corner," I said to them, "and we'll find a cop and settle this right now. I'm telling you this man is trying to rob me!"

"You ain't goin' nowhere, bitch. You comin' back home with me!"

I saw the two men glance at each other. This thief was convincing.

The taller of the two shrugged his shoulders. "Okay, brother, but you ain't got to disrespect the sister, you know, callin' her out her name and knockin' her down 'n' stuff. You ain't got to—" Then he looked closely. "Heyyyyy, I thought I seen you before. You hang uptown, but I seen you in the joint. Come on, Nightlife. You know this ain't your woman. Sister got too much style. And I mean, you just got out, man. Just got out. Drop it, okay? 'Less you like it better on the inside liftin' them weights."

Nightlife had been holding onto the broken strap but dropped it cold.

"What that prove, motherfucker? You seen me in the joint, so what that prove? You smarter 'cause you out now? Your big-ass mouth wider than the Lincoln Tunnel. Who ast you?" He reached inside his jacket. "I got somethin' for a runnin' mouth!"

"Now wait a minute, Night—don't be gittin' crazy . . ."

The men backed away, instinctively raising their hands as they moved out of Nightlife's orbit. Just then I waved my arms excitedly and yelled, "Police! Over here! Over here!"

The two men glanced around, bobbing and weaving as if they were on a basketball court.

"Is the 911?"

"Uh-oh! Cops! I ain't in this shit, let's split!"

They took off, hustling in different directions as Nightlife quickly stepped back, scanning for the cruiser.

In that half second of confusion, I raised my foot and planted a hard kick to his groin. When he fell to his knees, the knife in his hand clattered to the pavement and I kicked it to the curb beneath a parked car. Then I raised the bag. "Is this what you wanted?" I slammed it hard against the bridge of his nose, and again across the top of his skull. He was still doubled over when I ran to the corner and a passing gypsy screeched and stopped on a dime.

As I scrambled into the cab, I yelled, "Get a Jay Oh Bee, a job, you fuckin' asshole!"

I peered through the rear window as we pulled

away and saw him still on his knees, holding his stomach
and gasping for air.

"Slight disagreement?" the cabbie asked in a flat
voice that implied he'd seen a whole lot worse in his career.

I rubbed my knees. My stockings were shredded
and my jacket was torn at the elbows.

"You might say that," I whispered. "I'm going to
the Riverbend Apartments. 140th Street and Fifth."

I was trying to brush the dirt from my skirt when
the cab turned the corner at Fifth Avenue and 141st Street
and pulled up in front of the Riverbend complex. Modern, gray stone, terraced structures of fourteen stories or
so running for several blocks facing the river and the
Harlem River Drive. Trees and planters lined the avenue
and not even a candy wrapper marred the sidewalks.

The security man in the lobby stared at me as I
signed the logbook. I met his gaze as he dialed Tad's
apartment.

"Yes. Mr. Honeywell. There's . . . uh . . . a Miss
Anderson to see you?"

He hung up the phone but now kept his eyes on the
terrazzo floor as he gestured toward the elevator. "All
right, miss. He's expecting you."

No one else was on the elevator, which was just as
well. When the door opened on the top floor, Tad was
waiting and the expectant smile faded.

"Mali, what the hell happened?"

Maybe it was his voice. Or the touch of his hands on
my shoulder and around my waist as he led me into the
apartment. Or maybe it was the pain that shot through
my swollen knee and the sudden realization that I was in
more danger than I thought. I felt vulnerable, soft, and in
need of protection. And I was angry at having forgotten
everything I had learned in the academy and had allowed
someone to catch me unawares. More than anything else, I

had come face to face with the man who might have killed Erskin. Why was this son of a bitch still walking the street?

The tears came even as I tried to control the hurt and anger.

"Someone, that man called Nightlife, tried to steal my bag. He must have been watching me, followed as I left the house . . . He had a knife but I got away. I—"

"A knife! That's his trademark. Don't say any more. Let me make a call."

I lay on the sofa with a pillow under my legs and stared at the ceiling. He had candles lit just as he had promised and the shadows danced around the room. I closed my eyes and listened.

"Yeah . . . Nightlife. That's what they call him. About thirty years old, five feet eight, medium brown skin with braided hair, one-sixty or so . . . Got out a month or so ago . . . No, he don't walk with no weight. Couple years ago, he used to pack a pistol in his waist— and tried to hop like those Jamaican boys, but he tripped one time and nearly shot his dick off . . .

"Uh-huh. So a blade is all he works with now, but when he swings, you stay cut because he runs that knife through fresh garlic before he steps out . . . Yeah, in front of the Half-Moon. Never has any cash to go in for a real drink . . . Okay. I'll get back to you in two hours."

He slammed the phone down and the room went silent. I could hear him breathing hard, cursing under his breath as he made his way to the kitchen. The refrigerator door slammed and his footfalls were silent on the rug. I kept my eyes closed until he touched my knee with the ice pack, and the pain shot through me and the tears came again.

"Listen, baby. Everything's gonna be taken care of. Your dad doesn't know, does he?"

"No. And I don't want him to know. That's why I

came here instead of going back home. This wasn't a random thing, Tad. When I got home from class today, there was a message on the machine. A death threat."

"What?"

"The tape's in the bag. You can listen to it." I tried to sit up, to reposition myself on the sofa and ignore the pain moving through my leg. "You know, I wanted this evening—this night—to be good for us. Now look at me. I can barely walk. All I did was fall down . . . well, he pulled me down trying to get at the bag, but I didn't expect to become a basket case. I didn't . . . I didn't expect our evening to turn out like this."

He brushed his hand lightly over my face. "You're getting upset. Don't do this, baby." His hands moved over my legs and his fingers pressed my knees.

"It's swollen and right now you're hurting, but just lie still. I'll take care of everything."

The running water in the bath was softened by music drifting in from a Trinidadian steel pan. Someone next door was playing and the quiet clear notes of "Black Orpheus" seemed to float into the room, old and mournful and beautiful.

Tad opened the terrace door and each note became more distinct. The mild breeze from the river caused the candles to flicker and I watched the shadows moving and falling against the ceiling. This was enough for me. No dinner. No champagne. Right now this was enough.

"Can you make it?" he whispered, easing me up from the sofa.

Everything in the bathroom was a straightforward mix of black and white: wallpaper, towels, double shower curtains, and small black rug with a thick knotted fringe spreading over a white carpet. The tub was filled with a scented bubble bath and candles glowed on a glass shelf over the toilet tank. Near the tub, splits of champagne rested in an ice-filled, brass wine cooler.

"I didn't forget anything, did I?"

He stood behind me, opening my blouse one slow button at a time and pressing his mouth to the bare space on my back as his fingers moved.

All at once I started to tremble and could not look around. The scent from the bathwater entered my nostrils and I closed my eyes and breathed deeply as my brassiere came off.

"Eucalyptus," he said. "Best thing for pain . . ."

"No," I whispered, stepping out of my panties and turning to face him. "The second best thing . . ."

In the tub, my head rested on his shoulder. His skin was smooth and I could feel the rhythm of his heart against my back as the water lapped around us.

"Now, let's see . . . We're supposed to be taking care of a swollen knee."

"Uhn-hunh . . ."

"Well, let's see," he whispered again, turning me easily so that I lay atop him. I tightened my arms around his neck, and his mouth tasted sweet from champagne when I kissed him. His fingers moved along my back, tracing a pattern under the water, and I pressed in, moving against him.

"Mali, take it easy, baby. Easy . . ."

"I am. I am taking it easy. You know how long I've wanted to do this, to feel you just the way I'm feeling you now, and tell you how much I love you . . ."

"Mali, as long as I've known you, I never thought I'd wait this long to get to you. I love you, baby. I mean it. I love you, girl."

I rested back on my heels in the water, my legs moving effortlessly. Either the pain had gone to some other place or I was too busy to care. My hands slid beneath the water to the place between his legs and a smile eased across his face in the glow of the candles.

"Aah, yeah . . . come on, baby. Come on. Let's take it to bed . . ."

There were no candles in the bedroom and it was dark except for a tortoiseshell lamp spreading a small circle of yellow light on the floor near the bed. I stood in the dark outside the circle hugging the towel and not understanding this new, hesitant feeling. I was here. In his bedroom. Finally about to lie in his arms. I didn't have to think about Dad putting his key in the door or a bad-news phone call coming out of the blue. I was here. What was the matter?

He came around the bed to stand near me and I tried to look at his face in the dark. I needed to see his eyes as he spoke. I gave up and settled for his nearness. I looked down at his brown legs in the circle of yellow light and wondered what I would have felt for him if we had met under other circumstances: perhaps at a dance, jazz concert, church, or even in a bar where there was no talk of bodies and bullets. No death threats. When I left the softness of this candlelit place, fear would be waiting. Perhaps in the elevator before I even got downstairs.

When he touched me, I jumped.

"Mali, what is it?"

"I don't know . . . I—"

"Listen, if you're hesitating because of what happened to you earlier, I can understand . . . Sometimes things have a way of knocking the good feeling out of us . . ."

He looked at the clock.

"Just a minute, baby . . ."

He sat on the edge of the bed and whoever he dialed must have been waiting for the call because there was no hello or other introduction. He spoke immediately.

"Uh-huh? . . . No, listen, man. Do as I say and nothing else, you understand me? Just that and nothing more. No point in putting him in a wheelchair to cruise around on a check the rest of his life . . . Yeah, couple of hours. When he gets to the hospital, I'll pick it up from there. Talk to you later . . . Yeah, you got it . . ."

"What was that about, Tad?"

He did not look at me but lay back on the bed and pulled me down so that I lay in his arms. My head rested on his chest. His skin was warm and held the faint scent of eucalyptus. I could feel his calm and measured breathing. Very calm. A minute passed before he spoke again.

"How're you feeling?"

"Better, I guess."

He rolled over and leaned on one elbow to look at me. "Earlier tonight, a man tried to touch the wrong woman. And he has to be set straight . . . Had to have someone else do it, though, because if I went uptown and found him, he'd be dead. No question. Nightlife would be dead. Now," he whispered, "let me hear you talk about something else . . ."

His hands moved down and over my stomach. "I want to hear you talking to me in a different language."

When his mouth covered my navel, the things I thought of talking about went completely out of my mind.

chapter twenty

The small clock by the bed glowed Tuesday 4 A.M. I was alone in the room.

"Tad?"

"I'm out here, baby."

The ache in my knee had subsided to a manageable level, low enough for me to ignore.

I picked up the terry bathrobe—large enough to wrap around me twice—and stepped out on the terrace. Fog hung like a ragged curtain over the river, and the wind skimming the whitecaps reminded me that winter had not completely left town.

Tad leaned with his arms folded on the stone balcony, gazing northward toward the dim outline of the 145th Street bridge. A lone tug passed under it towing a line of barges. They slid by in complete silence, moving with the current. Minutes later the last barge disappeared and the water was still again.

I leaned half against the balcony and half against

Tad, waiting. He put his arm around me, but when he finally spoke, it wasn't what I had expected to hear.

"Let's shower, baby, and I'll take you home."

It was more like a sigh, sad and disappointed.

I looked at him. This was the man who had made love to me just a few hours ago, hot and heavy, and who couldn't get enough; who could barely wait for me to get my strawberry-flavored stuff in place. He never wanted to stop, he said. And neither did I. It was not a hurried, hungry, fumbling kind of love thing. He knew what he was doing and made me feel so good I cried.

But I also knew that the morning after could sometimes be dangerous. Sometimes, when two lovers disconnect, midnight euphoria will slide into midday depression, raging and unbearable.

But this couldn't be happening, not to us. Not after what we felt and the things we said. Not unless one of us was lying.

"What is it, Tad? What's happening—"

"I'm okay . . ."

I continued to gaze at him. He was okay. Not good. Not fine. Not coming down from cloud nine. Just okay— as if he'd only just helped himself to a Mickey Dee fast fat snack instead of a three-course, four-star gourmet meal.

I wanted to say something but the words caught in my throat. I turned from him and was about to step into the living room. He caught my arm.

"Wait a minute. Don't make this any harder. I listened to the tape while you slept. I need to talk to your dad."

"Why?"

"To persuade him to lay low and get your nephew out of town for a while."

The resentment evaporated and the fear I had held in check when I stood near the circle of light came back.

"My dad? Alvin? Leave town? What is going on?"

"I'm not sure yet, but I don't want to take any chances. It'll only be for a few days, possibly a week—till I can ask some questions and get some answers."

"How're you going to convince him? My father can be pretty stubborn."

"He's gonna listen to the tape, and then hopefully, he'll listen to me."

I glanced through the terrace door again. Here and there, the impenetrable darkness of the water had softened to reveal narrow streaks of gray-green as dawn burned through the fog. The whitecaps had disappeared and the bridges shone now in high relief. A flock of seagulls spiraled up from the narrow edge of the highway. They flew high then fell away from the rising arc of the sun like old-fashioned fighter planes to skim the flat water. I wondered if they were also searching for something.

"What answers, what are you looking for, Tad?"

He was headed toward the bathroom and stopped and leaned against the door. "Mali, even if I knew for sure, I wouldn't tell you. It's better if you didn't know."

"Even though I've been threatened?" My voice rose. "My family has been threatened and may be forced to hide out for I don't know how long? Next thing you'll tell us is that we may be hustled off into some witness protection program. Don't you think I have a right to know?"

He put his finger to his mouth, signaling me to calm down. "You have a right to know, Mali, but at the moment there's something more important. And don't think about any witness protection program. You can bet your bottom buck it won't come to that. I can promise you." He held out his hand. "Come on, now . . ."

He leaned against the door and closed his arms around me. I could feel him through the robe. I backed away.

"No. I have to be home before Alvin wakes. I usually fix his breakfast and Dad walks him to school."

• • •

Dad wakes early when he doesn't have a gig. When I walked in, he was already seated at the dining table. He rested his morning paper and made a point of squinting at his watch. It was a large, exaggerated gesture, then he folded his arms and waited.

I stood at the entrance to the dining room and my anger flared up immediately. I felt foolish, as if I was sixteen again and unprepared to explain my night out.

"Good morning, Mr. Anderson," Tad said.

"Good morning, young man. Nice to see you again. And you too, Mali."

He stared down at my legs and shook his head. "One of these days, you're going to come home fully dressed. One night it's no shoes, the next night it's no stockings."

I bit my tongue and ignored the remark, preferring to let Tad handle everything.

"I didn't mean to keep Mali out all this time," Tad said, "but something came up—"

"I bet it did."

I closed my eyes, not wanting to believe that my father had actually made that crude remark.

Tad held up his hands. "Mr. Anderson, let me explain. There's something going on, something that may pose a significant danger to your family unless we can resolve it quickly."

Significant danger. Tad had decided to take the official approach, sliding into bureau lingo and using three- and four-syllable words where usually one would do.

Dad's sour expression changed, but not by much. "What do you mean—significant danger?"

"Let's listen to this tape, then we'll talk."

I didn't want to hear the message again with Dad present, so I used the moment to check on Alvin.

He lay on his stomach asleep, with one arm under

his head and the other dangling from the side of the bed. I felt a stab of guilt. I had missed saying his prayers with him. *Now I lay me down to sleep, I pray the Lord my soul to keep. If I should die . . .*

I knelt beside his bed a few minutes longer listening to him breathe. His breath was light and even now, but I wondered if he'd had a nightmare while I had been gone.

He moved but did not wake when I tucked his arm beneath the blanket. I left his bedroom door half-open.

In the kitchen, I poured two cups of coffee and returned to the dining room, where Dad was standing near the window looking out. At this hour of the morning, there was nothing much to see.

"Sure, it could be a crank call, Mr. Anderson, but she's received too many of them."

"But she never mentioned anything." Dad turned to face me, trying to hide the hurt expression. "Mali, you never mentioned anything."

"Because I didn't think the calls were important and you would've worried needlessly. I didn't think they were serious until last night."

I also hadn't mentioned them because Dad hadn't wanted me to pursue the lawsuit. If I won, he was afraid I'd return to the force. But I had no intention of going back. I'd seen too much.

I put the coffee down and looked from one to the other. "They started right after the lawsuit, then slacked off, and I thought that was the end of it. But after Erskin was killed, they started up again, got dirtier—which I still ignored. Until last night, when they got serious."

"Well, let me tell you," my father said, moving away from the window and taking a seat at the table. "I was born and raised a short way from this very neighborhood and I ain't being run out of town by nobody. Nobody, you hear? I've walked these streets at hours when there was nobody out but me; not even a stray dog. I dodged zip guns in the forties when those stupid gang wars threatened to tear Harlem apart. I've been down in the meanest holes, worked the dirtiest joints in good times and bad. I survived all of that. I survived!"

His face was tight with anger and he took a swallow of coffee before he went on. "I don't expect you to know what I'm talking about so let's just say that I've been through too much shit to be done in by some damn punk voice on the phone. Whoever's making those calls can meet me face-to-face so I can kick their ass. They got my number. Let 'im call and make an appointment. I ain't goin' nowhere no time soon."

A zip gun could never compare to a Tec-9, but if a body was hit in the right spot, it was just as dead. I was so proud of Dad for standing up at that moment I could have kissed him. Tad looked from him to me and knew he was fighting a losing battle and I'm not sure I cared.

He abandoned the official mode and moved to sit across from him at the table. "Mr. Anderson, listen. It's more serious than you think."

"Young man, don't presume to know what's on my mind. And since we're on the subject now, I'd like to know what's on your mind."

"Sir?"

"Regarding my daughter. What's on your mind?"

It came out of the blue. Well, maybe not so far out of the blue but I still did not want to believe what I was hearing.

The three of us looked at each other and I could not tell whose eyes were wider and who stared longer. We each looked and the only sound in the silence came from the thin click of the grandfather clock in the hall. It seemed to grow loud yet no one said a word.

Tad looked at me, and finally when he spoke, he was still looking at me even though he was talking to my father. It was as if Dad were standing behind me, leaning over my shoulder.

"I've known Mali a long time, Mr. Anderson. And I've loved her for as long as I've known her. Even before she knew I loved her. Beyond that, I don't know what more to say."

I closed my eyes and let out a deep breath and opened them again when his hand reached over and covered mine. I was glad to have something to hide my shaking fingers.

Dad simply shook his head, and I knew better than to presume—as he said—to know what he was thinking.

Later, much later, after Alvin had woken up and come downstairs in his pajamas to a breakfast of pancakes and bacon and two cups of hot chocolate and the four of us sat around the table eating, we watched the boy as if he were the last living remnant of some endangered species. Finally, Dad compromised. Alvin was to come out of school a month early and spend two weeks with Dad's friend, an artist who, with his wife, shuttled between their homes in New Jersey and the Maryland shore.

If things weren't straightened out by that time, Alvin was to spend the rest of the summer on a schooner in St. Croix sailing with Captain Bo, the neighbor whose steel pan music had filled Tad's apartment.

"If anyone came looking," Tad said, "it would be hard to find the boy."

I sighed inwardly, imagining my nephew swimming off the Maryland shore and eating fresh crab cakes for breakfast. Then sailing around the Virgin Islands on a schooner.

Hell, we're all in danger. Why can't we all go . . .

Dad, as usual, seemed to pick up my vibrations. "Trip sounds nice but I'm stayin' put," he said. "I got obligations, contracts to fulfill. I don't leave no gig undone."

Tad glanced at me and I lifted my shoulders. Music was my father's life. Playing was like breathing and there was nothing more to be said.

Outside, on the stoop, Tad touched my face. "I see now where you got your stiff back. Your old man's hard as a bag of tenpenny nails."

I leaned my head on his shoulder. "That's the way he is. Like a rock. I'm surprised he compromised so quickly."

"Yeah, well, don't question it. Be glad he did."

We were silent for a moment. I knew Dad had given in because another loss would have taken him right over the side. Tad had to struggle to convince him, but I had watched his face and seen the anger give way to concern.

"My father trusts you. He knows you won't let him down. And what you said to him about me. How you felt. You didn't have to—"

We were standing on the top step, side by side, and his hand moved to my waist, drawing me closer.

"Your father asked me and I told him. I usually say what I mean and mean what I say. Or I say nothing at all. I didn't think it would be that easy. I didn't think I'd be able to do it."

"What?"

"To say it. To tell someone again how I actually feel about them. People say I have no sense of humor. I take everything so seriously. Well, maybe I do. I try to—"

He dropped his arms and took one step down so that his eyes came level with mine. His voice was low and I had to lean close. When he spoke, I caught the mild scent of peppermint and wanted to explore the inside of his mouth, feel his teeth, and taste his tongue, quickly, as if last night had not been enough for me. But I thought of the neighbors behind their lace curtains and let the feeling go.

"Listen," he whispered. "The last few hours, the last few hours were the best I've known in a long time. When I say 'I love you,' baby, it's coming from a place inside me I can't even name. I take things seriously because some damn serious things have happened to me."

He turned, touched my face again, and walked away, heading toward Seventh Avenue.

I watched him move in that slow, slightly loping gait until he reached his car near the end of the block. The serious things he'd get around to telling me in his own good time. Right now it was enough to know how he felt.

Back in the house, I tried to salvage the remainder of the morning. Tad was going to visit the hospital. If anything came up, he would call and I was to go to a street phone and call him back. Otherwise, I was to stay close to home. Dad had left to walk with Alvin, and after school, the boy was not to go out by himself, not even to walk Ruffin.

I settled into the quiet to do some serious cramming. Exams were three weeks away and there was one book I practically needed to memorize.

The call came at 11:30, sooner than I expected.

"Listen, meet me at E. As soon as possible."

"E" would be Emily's restaurant on 111th Street.

"Right."

I said nothing more and hung up, beginning to feel like Double-Oh-Seven at His Majesty's beck and call. I showered quickly, dressed, and exchanged my shoulder bag for a smaller purse containing a kubaton—a small retractable blackjack that fit in the palm of the hand. When you swung it, it snapped outward at least a foot. It was illegal but I'd worry about that if I got caught. At the moment, my adrenaline had kicked in so high I knew if I ran into Nightlife on the street, I would make him see orange stars.

Emily's had an early lunch crowd but Tad was already there and had managed to secure seats in the corner facing the street. I moved around the labyrinth of tables and waved. He rose to pull my chair out.

"How're you feeling?"

The polite tone put me on alert. "Fine. What's going on?"

"Everything and nothing. First off, that low-life character they call Nightlife? Well, he must've been either a very strong guy or a very scared one. By the time I got to the hospital, he had signed out AMA—against medical advice. Leg broken in three different places, the doctor said, and he had the nerve to sign out."

I leaned back in my chair and gazed at him, remembering all the telephone instructions last night.

"Well, where did he go?"

Tad glanced out of the window for a minute and his expression changed only slightly.

"Not far. It was a bad move. A stupid move. His body was found an hour ago in an alley behind an abandoned building uptown. From the looks of it, he didn't exactly hobble there. He was taken there and, from his condition, probably thrown from the roof. Some kids chasing their puppy through the alley came across him."

I looked around me. Patrons, some of them probably staff from North General Hospital and from the row of small businesses that had recently opened in the neighborhood, leaned over tables crowded with food. There were crosscurrents of talk and laughter as the music flowed. Some gestured animatedly although I couldn't hear them above the hum of music.

Ordinary people, casually dressed, discussing ordinary things. How would they react to the news of a broken body lying in some filthy alley? Probably the same as if a roach had crawled across their plate.

Thrown from the roof.

My hands were folded on the table and the unnatural weight of the handbag rested heavily in my lap. I wondered now if I would have used the weapon against him. He had been young and violent and involved in Erskin's death and tried to harm me but now he was gone and his passing mattered to no one except Lexi, who was probably, at this moment, screaming in grief and tearing out her auburn-streaked weave.

I wasn't sure what I was feeling but suddenly all the anger I had felt toward him drained away, leaving me empty.

I didn't see the waitress standing patiently by the table until Tad spoke up: "Yes, two coffees . . . and how're the muffins? Fresh?"

The waitress looked at him and did a good job of hiding her annoyance. "They were baked this morning, sir." She put heavy emphasis on the "sir" but Tad ignored it.

"Good. We'll have the muffins."

He waited until she walked away, then pulled out the notebook Mrs. Harding had given to me.

It amazed me how easily he shifted gears. A man was dead and he was concerned about fresh muffins.

He bent his head in concentration and his fingers eased down the line of numbers carefully, then stopped.

"Look at this."

I leaned over to get a better look and to see if I had missed something earlier. It was a nine-digit number—313010489.

"3130 is the address of the building where the body was found. I don't know what the other numbers mean, but I think we're getting close."

I looked at some of the other entries and one in particular caught my eye.

"Excuse me. I have to double-check something."

I left the table, navigated through the tight crowd to the phone near the ladies' room, and dialed Bertha's number. Her voice came on against a background of loud talk and television drama, probably *Sally Jessy Raphael*. Not her favorite, she had said, but it was enough to hold her until the real soaps came on. She had the volume cranked so as not to miss a sigh.

"Bertha's Beauty Shop! It's our duty . . . to make you a beauty! Hello!"

I wondered how she had managed to hear the phone ring.

"Listen, Miss Bert, it's me. Mali. I dreamed about that beauty shop last night. You know, the Pink something or other . . ."

"Fingernail! And you ain't thinkin' about goin' there! You cuttin' out on me? I don't believe it!"

Her voice rose another decibel and I rushed to calm her. "Bert, listen. It's nothing like that. I dreamed about the place and I want you to put the number in for me. Check the address with Viv."

And without moving away from the phone or my ear, she shouted to Viv above the noise. "What's the address of that shop you had? That's right . . . 3370. Okay."

She spoke to me again, her voice still high. "It's 3370 so you gonna have to drop the zero if you wanna combinate it forty-sixty, okay? Or you can drop a 3 and still combinate it. Whichever way you think gonna bring you your million bucks faster."

I listened, unable to decide. It was frustrating to be born and raised in the heart of Numbers City and not understand the first damn thing about combinating a digit. But then, math had never been my strong point and Bert lost me after that last zero.

"Look, however you do it, it's okay. I'll leave it up to you."

"So you want it forty cents straight and sixty cents combo, right?"

"Whatever you say, Miss Bert. I'll see you next week."

"If you hit, you gonna see me tonight. Wait a minute." She left the phone for a second, then came back on, laughing. "Miss Viv say she ridin' your dream with a ten and hope you don't mind. Say she might as well get somethin' outta that dirty deal."

We shared a laugh and hung up. Tomorrow after class was time enough to visit the shop. By then, all the news not fit to print would have found its way into the place. I probably could've gotten more details from the Pink Fingernail but going there was out of the question now.

I made my way back to the table and looked at the notebook again. 3370 was on the second page and 11787 completed the entry. I remembered Bert saying that Viv had celebrated the grand opening in 1987 and "the folks was throwin' down champagne by the truckload and put away enough food to supply ten homeless hotels."

And she had opened on November 7, just in time to attract the big-bucks, fast-spending, Thanksgiving holiday crowd.

"There it is," I said, "our Rosetta stone. The address of Viv's shop is 3370 and she opened on 11-7-87. Nightlife's body was found behind 3130 Eighth Avenue. A phone call downtown'll tell you if the building was bought on 10-4-89."

chapter twenty-one

By the time we left the restaurant, the earlier bright sunshine had disappeared behind a mass of thunderheads boiling up over the East River. The temperature had dropped and I was not prepared to walk back home in my thin jacket. We hailed a cab, moved along 110th Street past the boathouse, and turned onto Powell Boulevard, where the branches of the trees on the traffic island seemed to bend like reeds in the wind.

Tad reached for my hand, and when I glanced at him, his eyes were closed.

"The shit is about to come down," he whispered.

I looked out of the window at the hurrying figures. Two women pushed strollers fast. A lanky boy with a backpack and headphones skated around the cars. A woman with a loaded shopping cart waited impatiently for the traffic light to change. The loungers had pulled their milk crates in, vacating their usual spots in front of the stoops.

I turned to Tad again but his eyes were still closed.

His brow was knotted and the muscle near his jaw was moving like a small stone and it occurred to me that he had not been referring to the storm.

Before I could reach up to touch him, he opened his eyes. The burned brown liquid softness was gone.

"Pack Alvin's things. Have him ready by six tonight," he said.

I looked at him. "Tonight? That's too soon. I thought—"

"Listen, Mali. Please do as I say."

"What do you mean, do as you say? Tad, this is my nephew we're talking about. I need to know something—"

He held up his hands. "You ask me no questions, I'll tell you no lies. Okay?"

I was so angry I could not answer. This had been another of my mother's famous proverbs. The whole thing was getting to be too much. I sat back and remained quiet for the rest of the ride.

I locked my door and listened as the cab pulled away, then went to the bar. It was only two o'clock but I fixed a vodka martini anyway, despite my shaking hands. How was I going to explain this turn of events to Dad when I didn't really know what was happening myself? What was I going to say to Alvin?

The house was quiet and I wandered upstairs to his room. He and Dad had not returned from school and his door was open. Ruffin lay on the floor at the foot of the bed and looked up at me with sad eyes.

"Don't tell me you know something also," I whispered as I dragged a suitcase and duffel bag out of the closet. The boy had so much stuff, and all of it, no doubt in Alvin's mind, was indispensable. I opened the chest of drawers, feeling like an intruder, and emptied all of his underwear, T-shirts, and socks into the duffel.

In the closet were a half dozen or so pairs of jeans on the shelf and as many pairs of sneakers on the floor. I decided that five pairs of each should be enough and that once the bags were packed, there would be no additions, exchanges, or argument.

When I reached for the stack of jeans, a cassette wedged at an angle on the shelf fell to the floor. "Profoundly Blue"—the tape Dad had given to Erskin. I took it and set it aside. This time, after Alvin was safely on his way and I had nothing to think about, I intended to relax and listen.

Oddly enough, at four o'clock when Alvin came home, he was elated when he saw his suitcase and duffel by the door.

"Man! So soon! I can't believe it. I'm gonna be scuba divin' and sailin'. How about that?"

I watched him and thought of Clarence and how it would've been nice if he could have gone also. But the charges were still pending and he couldn't even move across the street without notifying his attorney. He was out of jail technically but still dragging a ball and chain.

I guess I focused on Clarence to keep from thinking about Alvin. In less than two hours, he would be walking out the door.

Dad looked at the suitcase, then looked at me. "What happened?"

"I . . . don't know. Tad couldn't tell me but I think he got some news."

"Unpleasant news."

"He didn't say."

He glanced at his watch and something akin to panic creased his face. But a second later he straightened up and tried to smile.

"Well, son. This is it for a while. I want you to call

me every day, collect. Let me know how the weather is
and how the folks are treatin' you. Call every day. Say the
word, I'll be right there to pick you up, you hear?"

Alvin moved his shoulders and leaned his weight on
one foot, then the other. "Aw, Grandpa, I'm gonna be
okay. I'm gonna be fine. I'll be swimming, sailing . . ."

"Yeah, I know. All those good things. And me, left
here in the city to sweat it out."

We tried to make small talk, but when the bell rang
at 5:45, we fell silent and stared at the door. No one
moved until it rang a third time and Dad stepped forward
to open it.

Tad's car was double-parked and he moved quickly
to place the bags in the trunk. Something rose in my
throat and I struggled to get the right words out and to
hold the wrong ones in.

I thought of Alvin's swim trunks and flippers
packed among his jeans and tees. At least I had taught
him how to swim. At least I had done that. He could
handle himself. He would not die in some faraway place.

"Don't go out too far," I said, hugging him, not
wanting to let go. My throat was about to close and my
voice was barely above a whisper.

They looked at me, and Dad was the first to laugh.
"Don't go out too far? The boy'll be diving from the
rigging of a schooner."

I looked from one to the other. Diving from a
schooner? No! Wait! His mother—!

Just as my panic mounted, Tad put Alvin in the
front seat and came around the car to me.

"Listen, I can see it in your face. Don't get upset. I'll
call you as soon as we get there. Everything'll be all right.
I love you, baby."

He kissed me and I stood in the rainy street watching the blinking taillight grow smaller, then it turned at
the corner of Eighth Avenue and disappeared.

chapter twenty-two

Back in the house, I moved through the silent living room and into the dining room to sit at the table with my head in my hands. Downstairs, Dad was preparing for a special gig. I listened to the small noises and knew that when he left, I would be truly alone. The emptiness of the rooms was already closing around me, and if I listened hard enough, I could hear those peculiar echoes that tend to float on the dead air of unoccupied space.

Let Alvin be safe. Please. Bring him back to us . . .

I jumped when Dad touched my shoulder.

"Everything's gonna be okay, sweetheart."

I shrugged, unconvinced, and he pulled out a chair to sit beside me. "Now listen, you can't become paralyzed every time the boy leaves your sight. What happened to Benin was a one-in-a-million accident. One in a million."

"I know, but—"

"But nuthin'. You gonna think yourself into a nervous breakdown if you keep this up."

Think myself into a breakdown. The wonder is that it hasn't happened already. If I could only describe to him the bits and pieces of memory that won't remain buried, that keep bobbing to the surface when I least expect it. I'm surprised. Nothing had prepared me to deal with that one-in-a-million thing. Everything I ever learned in training went right out of me that day. Everything.

I insisted on identifying her. I didn't want you to do it, Dad. You never would have survived it. You could not have stood in that cold room without flinching when they rolled that steel drawer out. But I did. I had to. I looked at a body with so little skin left that the only recognizable area was the crescent-shaped birthmark on the inside of her left ankle.

I looked but I had not been prepared. The training academy had only prepared me for certain emergencies. And certainly not for that time on my midnight tour when my partner and I had retrieved a broken little body from a trash-filled alley and then talked our way into a roach-infested room to arrest the mother. A woman who could not remember the last time food was on her table. Or the last time she washed her hair.

In the cold room with the steel drawer, I was not prepared but I looked at Benin's hair. She had streaked it with that funny-looking orangy highlight to make the dark part look darker. I recognized her hair. Her face had been . . . left clinging to the sides of that crevasse. I never blinked but absorbed it all—hair, birthmark, and wedding band—took it all inside me to remember. You could not have done that, Dad. I would have lost you too.

"Mali. Are you listening?"

"What?"

"I don't want you to stay in this house alone. You think too much when you're alone. Come to the club. There's something special happening tonight. I'll reserve a table."

"No. I want to wait for Tad's call."

"But they're drivin' to Maryland, not New Jersey. They won't be calling for a couple of hours, at least."

Outside, a horn sounded twice. The club had sent a car for him and he rose to slip his jacket on. "Will I see you later?"

When I didn't answer, he said again, "Don't stick in the house. I'll hold your table."

He kissed me and I watched him head for the door, envying the way he was able to step into his music so easily, the way people stepped into another room.

I turned the lock and leaned against the door. He was right, as usual. Get out of the house.

The club was crowded for a Tuesday night and the rush of excitement seemed to push my anxious feeling aside for a time. I persuaded the waiter to switch me to a table in the corner several rows away from the bandstand, which gave me a less than perfect view of Dad but a far better view of the crowd.

Most of the tables were occupied, and although April had come and gone, many minks, lynx, and foxes had not yet found their way into storage. They were draped over shoulders and chairs in such abundance I began to wonder if I'd missed the warning of a cold front heading our way.

Still, I admired the sisters for looking good.

The set had not started and small talk floated around the tables, talk that stopped completely when the door opened and Johnnie Harding walked in with Maizie Nicholas on his arm. Judging from the fur draped on her shoulders, a serious blizzard was kicking up right around the corner. Her floor-length red-dyed, sheared mink literally flowed over her black satin gown as Johnnie led her down the inclining aisle. They moved slowly, completely absorbed in their entrance. Johnnie waved to someone

here and another there as the manager, smiling and obse-
quious, led the way.

At their table, the manager bowed and whipped out
his handkerchief to flick invisible dust from the linen
cloth before pulling Maizie's chair out. Then he hovered
nearby, ready, it seemed, to drop to one knee on command.

Maizie detached herself from her coat and yawned
slightly, covering her mouth with fingers so diamond-
heavy I wondered how she was able to raise her hand.
The stone on the engagement finger stood out from the
rest, for its sheer size alone.

I glanced around to see everyone else gazing—if not
at the fingers, then surely at the coat. Johnnie leaned back
in his chair scanning the watching crowd, then beckoned
to the manager, who bowed again and left. Seconds later a
bucket of champagne was at their table just as the lights
were dimming. I couldn't see their faces, but when the
two glasses touched, the diamonds on Maizie's hand sent
a small sparkling shower into the darkness.

The ensemble gathered and a brown woman with a
full figure and throaty voice joined them. Her delivery
was cool and relaxed and forty-five minutes and several
songs later the crowd would not let her go. Two hours
later, after much applause, the stage went dark and Dad
sat facing me.

"Glad you decided to come out. The boy's gonna be
okay."

"I know he will but it bothers me that he had to
leave at all."

"Well, your friend said whatever's gonna happen'll
happen soon. And speaking of happenin's . . ." He
turned and nodded in the general direction of Johnnie's
table. A platoon of waiters was wafting down the aisles
with towel-wrapped bottles of champagne and pouring at
every table. "They finally gonna do the thing."

I followed his gaze. Johnnie was lifting his glass to the crowd and they hung onto his every gesture.

"What thing?"

"You know. Tie the knot. Jump that broom."

So that explained the grand gown-and-fur entrance.

"They're getting married? When?"

"Don't know exactly. Rumor has it that the whole happenin's gonna take place right here. Maybe sometime in December. Soon as he gets some details straight."

I leaned forward and folded my arms on the table. "What details?"

He did not answer but slid me a look that said I should know better than to ask. I glanced away and finished my drink in silence. Then I yawned, covering my mouth with my unadorned fingers and pulled my zebra-print faux-silk shawl around my shoulders.

"You tired?"

"A little."

He leaned over and touched my hand. "You had a tough day, sweetie. I won't be mad if you want to head on out. I'll see you around four. The next set's about to start."

He made his way down the aisle, passing Johnnie's table, and Johnnie reached out to shake his hand. I could not see Dad's expression and a minute later I walked to the door.

The phone rang somewhere and I stood straight up in the dark wondering where I was. I stumbled toward the sound, remembering that I'd fallen asleep on the sofa.

"Yes? Hello?"

"Hey."

Tad's voice sounded as if it was being squeezed through a long hollow tube. "I called earlier but didn't leave a message. We're here. All in one piece. He's getting settled in. Talk to you later."

"But—"

Aside from the bad connection, it was like receiving one of those quick-short-and-to-the-point telegrams. Before I could ask to speak to Alvin, he had disconnected, leaving me to listen to the drone of a dead phone. I settled back on the sofa, fully awake now, with my feelings shifting somewhere between relief and anger. We had had to send Alvin away. I wondered about people in the witness protection program. I knew how it worked but never understood how it affected the person who had to move or how that person was able to shed his old life. Just like a snake.

chapter twenty-three

I spent the next several days in my room with my head buried in *The Theory of Modern Social Work* and nearly succeeded in putting my other thoughts where they belonged—in the back of my mind. At least temporarily.

I was making some progress until the phone rang and Miss Bert came on the line.

"Mali. You got to drop by."

"But today is Monday. You're usually closed on Mondays."

"I'm open."

She sounded too subdued. Fifteen minutes later, when I walked into the shop, Bert was there but it was Miss Vivian who invited me to have a seat at her manicure table.

"I know who you are. That's why I'm gonna tell you all this," Viv said as she examined my nails.

"I'm not in law enforcement any longer, Viv. I was,

but now I'm an ex. As in ex-cop. My only interest now is social work."

     We sat face-to-face and knee-to-knee at the table in the rear of the shop. Up front, the drama of other people's lives poured out at high decibel from the 25-inch screen, and, after waving to me when I walked in, Bert had turned back to the television, completely absorbed. Viv and I were the only other people in the shop and Bert was oblivious to us, even during the commercials.

     "Yeah, Bert told me you was a cop," she said. "So what happened? You quit to go into social work. Everybody know that kinda job don't pay diddly."

     "I didn't quit," I said, knowing that Bertha had told her the whole story, word for word, just as I had cried it to her two years earlier.

     "Mmh-hmph. So you was fired for hittin' that other cop. Well, I guess you the right one to tell."

     "But why *me*?"

     She did not answer immediately and I wondered if I had asked the right question. Finally, she said, " 'Cause Bert thinks you might be able to help me."

     "Help you how?"

     "Well," Viv said, "maybe you carry this to a real cop and get somethin' done. Clean up this mess once and for all."

     I looked at her, trying to read her face and figure out why she had Bertha call me. I was surprised when Bert had said Viv wanted to talk, but why to me?

     This mess—as she called it—was Johnnie Harding's drug dealership and I wondered how willing she would have been to talk had she and Johnnie still been together.

     "Did you try contacting anyone else?" I asked.

     "Contact who? Lemme tell you, everybody and they mama know the real deal. That precinct is tied up like a Christmas present, bow and all."

     "By whom?"

"By Johnnie Harding, that's who."

She leaned back in the chair and glared at me for not knowing just how important Johnnie was supposed to be. She removed my hand from the bowl of soapy water and selected an orange stick. I braced myself, expecting her in her anger to push my cuticles back to my knuckles. But she knew her job well enough to not allow her emotions to interfere.

"I was on the force less than two years," I said.

"Two years? A smart cop woulda learned what was goin' down in two days. Everybody know they don't call Harlem the Gold Coast for nuthin'. Least that's what cops used to call it in the old days when they fought to work up here. This beat practically guaranteed they'd retire rich. Scene ain't changed that much. Just went from bootleg booze to numbers to drugs. Still plenty money here. Plenty. And Johnnie's right in the middle of it. I hope he gets his ass smoked."

She swiveled around and picked up a container of yogurt, took a spoonful, then threw it down. "I need me some real food. I'm strung too damn tight for this yogurt diet shit." I said nothing as she wiped her hands and threw the napkin and what remained of the yogurt into the wastebasket.

She rubbed more oil around the edge of my nails and then leaned forward. "Listen. When the wire came that Johnnie was gettin' hooked up and gettin' out the life, just walkin' off with that money—some of which shoulda been mine—I got my pistol and waited in my car all night outside his place. Just waitin' for him. Or her. Whichever one showed their ass up was gonna get six pieces of Mr. Smith in it. Six bullets. Close as I was, I didn't even have to aim straight. I'd a got 'em. But they never came home. Neither one. Probably out partyin' at one a their other pads. And I sat there till the sun come up. Only reason I left was 'cause the sun did come up and the street got busy."

She applied a thin coat of strengthener to my nails and sat back to allow it to dry. No need to hold it under the tiny blower since I wasn't going anywhere.

"And I know what you sayin' to yourself. Here's this fat-ass fool makin' a bigger fool of herself over a no-good nigger. Ready to do time 'cause a him. Well, maybe a couple a days ago, I was. I mean, what go through your head on Monday ain't necessarily there, come next Sunday. Know what I'm sayin'? I walk in here last week and if it wasn't for Bert talkin' to me, I probably woulda put that pistol down my own throat, but Bert said shit, that wasn't how it was supposed to be. Me gone and Johnnie still ridin' high. Hell no."

My nails were dry but the operation wasn't over. She opened another bottle of colorless polish and began to apply it in neat, even strokes.

"Who was Johnnie paying off at the precinct?" I asked.

She continued to apply the polish and didn't look up. Her hands were remarkably steady.

"He wasn't payin' off nobody. They was all equal partners. They paid themselves."

"Who?"

"Ahhh, now wait a minute, Miss Blue Eyes—"

"They're gray. And they're mine," I said, pointedly staring at her blond weave. She didn't miss a beat, just shook the mass of hair and continued as if I hadn't spoken.

"Whatever. Here's where the shit gits sticky. Before I give somethin' up, I gotta know what I'm gonna get."

"What is it you want?"

"My shop back." She tightened the cap on the small bottle so hard I thought it would break in her hand. "I want my business back. It may've been his cash but it was my sweat, the sweat from my fuckin' ass that built the place up. It was goin' so good, Johnnie got his money back less than a year and a half later. Bragged how it was better than the stock market.

"You know it's one thing to open a business, it's another to keep it goin'. Not only did I keep it goin', I made it pay. I got those customers in there. I was the first one uptown to start paintin' gold fingernails and pink nails with rainbow tips. And I can put a head of hair together in no time flat.

"Many nights I slept on that couch in the back to be there for a six A.M. customer who had to be to work by nine and lookin' good. I *worked*, honey. Then for that bastard to tell me to git my fat funky ass out. Those was his very words. I didn't mind so much gittin' out his face, but not out my place. Now he got that skinny no-behind piece a sparerib warmin' my stool, sweet-talkin' the trade I brought in? Well, every dog has its day, and when mine come up, I'm gonna step.

"Now, I'm tellin' you all this so you could see where I'm comin' from. I'm willin' to name it if I can claim it. I need a guarantee I can claim that place when the deal go down."

I interrupted her. "I don't know if it's that simple, Viv. Once a dealer's assets are seized, they're sold to the highest bidder, who—"

"Who's damn sure gonna be me. Don't think I been diddlin' in the dark while he and Miss Stringbean been carryin' on. I got somethin' set aside and I mean to use it. The only guarantee I want is that there be no other bidders on the scene."

"How can they do that?"

"Come on. You ain't as innocent as you look. They do it the same way they do everything else. With money. Money talks and bullshit walks."

"But suppose they determine that the money you

use to pay for this deal is drug money you used to set up the business in the first place?"

"Look, I got my ducks all in a row. They can't prove none a that start-up cash was mine. I got a loan on the side and books Johnnie ain't never seen. I paid my taxes and got a record of every nap and nail that ever needed doin'."

She stood up abruptly, bumping against the small table. "Look at me. You think I piled these pounds on overnight? Unh-unh. It was slow but it was steady. And seem like nuthin' I could do about it. But I saw him lookin' at me, felt him easin' on 'round the way, but the business was so good, I thought we'd remain, you know, partners. Then he started to talkin' about his image 'n' shit. The image of the business. So, for every dollar he collected, I made sure I took my fifty cents. Plus the tips wasn't nuthin' to play with. Those sisters outdid themselves tryin' to see who could leave the largest bill."

I took that last as a not-so-subtle hint and reached for my own purse. "What do I owe you?"

"Nuthin'," she said, moving to pour the bowl of water into the sink and place the instruments into the sterilizer. She turned and smiled, and when she waved her hand toward me, it was like a command. "I know you gonna help me."

I concentrated on my flawless nails as she riffled the pages of her small book, checking her appointments for the coming week.

Never cross a woman. Especially an ambitious one. Viv wanted Johnnie out of circulation. She wanted him signed, sealed, and delivered before he married Maizie. Before that shop got away from her once and for all. But why was she telling me and not the D.A.?

"You can help me 'cause you got that lawsuit goin'," she said as if she'd read my mind. "So you musta got a lawyer who can stand up to the police."

"But his area is civil rights, discrimination, he's not—"

"He's somebody who can stand up to the police," she repeated, settling the issue.

She rolled the small table into a corner against the wall, then reached into her pocket to hand me a card. A line was drawn through the Pink Fingernail logo and a new phone number was penciled in.

"Don't worry about those changes. They only temporary."

Outside, I was glad to breathe fresh air, but the faster I walked, the more my head seemed to hurt. Equal partners on the take. They paid themselves. Shit! What about the other officers, the ones who played it straight, lived from paycheck to paycheck, and stuck their necks out every time they stepped off from roll call? What about those who tried to explain to some of the young brothers hanging out—the ones who would listen—that a low-wage shift at Mickey Dee's was better than a no-wage stretch at Riker's? What about them?

I dialed Tad from a pay phone and left a message: "More news. I'll stop by later," and hesitated before adding, "I missed you. Hope you had a good trip."

I walked down Lenox, then, following my usual zigzag pattern, cut into a block and over to Seventh Avenue, then into another block, and finally onto Eighth Avenue.

Despite the new construction, there were still many old houses with doorways and stoops crowded with too many people who, on a Monday afternoon, seemed to have nowhere to go and nothing to do.

In the middle of one block, a dice game had drawn so many players and onlookers I had to step into the street in order to pass. On some fire escapes, laundry hung limply in the humid air, and rap lyrics, distorted by the high volume, pounded from an open window.

On the corner, a half dozen teenagers, caps to the side and jeans hanging at thug level on the hips, lounged near a pay phone, waiting for that call to put them in their Bronco for a special delivery. No Mickey Dee fee for them. I thought of the parents at the rehearsal meeting, worried about the kidnapper who was still prowling the streets. But something worse than a kidnapper had gotten hold of these kids near the phone.

A squad car sped past, siren blazing, and I wondered if the run was legitimate or if they were rushing to get paid. Equal partners. What could they say to these kids?

I picked up my pace and headed down to 125th Street. The street was without life now that the vendors had gone but Mart 125 was still there. I needed to spend time with the folks and clear my head before going to meet Tad.

chapter twenty-four

What else did she say?"

Tad leaned back on the sofa jotting in his notepad while I sat on a pillow in the middle of his living room floor.

"Nothing else. She stopped short of naming any names."

"But it's interesting that she mentioned your fight with Terry Keenan—"

"She didn't mention him specifically; just that I'd had a fight with a cop."

He was quiet for a minute as his pen moved across the pad. "How much money does she have put away?"

"She didn't say. But she's ready to use it to buy back that place. I don't understand why she won't take that money and open something in another location."

"It wouldn't be the same, baby. It wouldn't have that sweet, deep satisfying feeling of knowing that the girlfriend is out on the street or possibly in jail with Johnnie."

I shook my head. "I hope I never fall for anyone that hard."

I glanced up to catch him looking at me and immediately regretted my remark. He jotted a few more lines and closed the pad.

"I want you to call her, offer to meet with her somewhere away from Bertha's shop."

"Where?"

He thought for a minute, then: "A public place. You'll meet on the steps of St. John the Divine. I'll be with you to offer her a deal."

"She's expecting me to bring my attorney."

"I'll change professions for the first five minutes. At least until I get some understanding of where we're headed. And besides, she spoke to you because you're an officer. Isn't that what she indicated?"

"Ex-cop," I answered, wondering where this was leading. "She spoke to me because Bertha thought it might be a good idea. Viv was about to eat a bullet and Bertha told her I might be able to do something about her problem."

"By taking her story to a 'real cop,' isn't that what she said?"

"Well, yes, but then she mentioned wanting to speak to my attorney. I think that's what she really wants—"

"Well, she's gonna get both. I want you to contact her as soon as possible."

He got up and began to move around me as I sat on the floor. I felt as if I was in the interview room at the precinct and seated at the wrong end of the table.

The silence stretched and finally I said, "I'll get in touch with her tonight."

He yawned and made his way to the small kitchen. He seemed tired and impatient, opening and quickly closing cabinet doors, then opening the fridge to stand in front of it.

"Can I help?"

He shook his head. "No. The problem is, I don't exactly know what I want."

He walked to the window and stood with his back to me. Somehow I knew that under other circumstances, an offer of a massage would have gotten him smiling again. He had driven from Maryland, gotten home around 5 A.M., and had been on the go ever since. His sour mood was probably due to sleep deprivation.

Then again, maybe he was annoyed by my remark —about never wanting to fall for anyone so hard . . .

He turned from the window as I got up from the floor and gathered my shoulder bag, satisfied that Alvin had been settled and out of harm's reach.

"I'll call you later," I said.

"No, wait. Wait a minute. I . . . I want to talk to you."

I looked at him and moved back toward the sofa, moved with the shakiest sensation in my legs.

"What about?"

He sat near me but leaned away and I was aware of the small space between us.

"I need to talk about a lot of things. While I was driving back, I got to thinking. You have time for that when you're in a car at night with only a tape deck and the tailwind of a tractor trailer to keep you up. I listened to some Billie and Dinah and Aretha, mostly their slow stuff. Stuff I'd been hooked on for the last two years. And I thought about Ellen . . . my ex-wife.

"Remember when I said that I'd been put through some serious shit? I didn't mean to drop that on you and leave you hanging like that."

"Well, you didn't leave me hanging, Tad. I figured

if it was something I need to know, you'd tell me at the right time."

"You're right. And I guess this is it. You know, my mother once said that when you meet a person, you meet history and mystery. And we get so caught up in the mystery, we don't bother looking at the history. That person brings to the relationship an entire experience that has nothing to do with you, yet everything to do with you once that history starts to unfold.

"I divorced Ellen—I never told anyone this—I divorced her because of what I found one morning when I came home after a stakeout on Riverside Drive was called off. I'd told her about the stakeout the night before, so she really hadn't been expecting me. Anyway, I got home, put my key in the door, and found her with someone else."

He stopped talking and stared straight ahead, as if the scene was again being played out before him. When he looked at me, I saw not only the pain of betrayal but confusion and anger and his struggle to allow himself to let go again—to free-fall once more into something unknown and possibly dangerous.

"Trust is a great thing, Mali. You can relax and enjoy and say a lot of things when you trust someone enough."

"That's true," I murmured, wondering where this was leading. I remembered he had certainly said a lot of things that night in the bathtub and it wasn't the champagne talking.

He remained quiet for a minute, then: "Listen. Were you and—were you involved with Erskin?"

I stared at him, so surprised I could not speak. Then I reached for his hands and held them against me. "I was never involved with him. I knew he was fond of me, cared for me, but I didn't find that out until after he'd died. I never knew until after."

"Is that why you're so intent on finding out why he died?"

I let go of his hands then, wanting to laugh. "I can't believe you're asking me this, as if you're jealous of a dead man."

"Maybe I am."

I wanted to tell him how ridiculous he sounded, how much he needed to grow up, get a handle on his life, and move on. Hopefully with me. But I didn't say that. If we were going to get anywhere, we needed to talk about a lot more than I realized.

"You found Ellen with someone. Now you trust no one, is that it? Not even the memory of a dead man." I tried to speak softly, to remain calm. "When you found her, what happened, what did you do? What did she say?"

He moved his shoulders in a slight, tired way. "There was nothing to do. Or say. The woman Ellen was with was wearing nothing except a smile and a Marlboro between her teeth. Neither one seemed the least bit fazed that I'd walked in and interrupted them. Neither one seemed frightened. If anything, there was such a casual intimacy, I knew without thinking about it that whatever was happening had probably been going on for a long time.

"I told Ellen to pack and be out before the sun set. Then don't ask me how I did it, but I backed out of there and found myself outside walking along the highway." He waved toward the window. "I walked and walked and wondered why I hadn't pulled my weapon and killed them both. I sat down near one of those old rotting piers and listened to the rats below and I watched the boats on the water and I thought about killing myself. To this day, I don't know why I didn't do it."

He leaned back on a pillow now and closed his eyes. "I read somewhere that life is nothing but a preoccupation with death, that most of us run around trying to do the thing or find the thing that'll hold it at bay for just a second longer. I didn't know that then. I walked and walked and walked until I found myself down somewhere near Wall Street, surprised that I was still alive.

"So I turned around and started back, not sure I was going to make it, but praying every step of the way because those steps were bringing me back to what I thought would be the end of my life."

I gazed at his drawn face, hair at the temples gone gray, and a mouth that never laughed. He had beautiful teeth and I think I touched them with my tongue more than I actually saw them. I wondered if he had ever smiled before he found out about Ellen. A lesbian. Why had she married him in the first place? For convenience? For cover? No one does that anymore. Either they're in or they're out.

Maybe she wanted it both ways and neglected to tell him. Maybe she had meant to and just hadn't gotten around to it. That little bitch. It was hard to listen and not feel what he was feeling.

"I'll tell you, Mali, it was a while before I was able to think about it without feeling that my chest or stomach was being cut open. Once that feeling left, I got scared all over again because I was sure nothing could replace it.

"Maybe that's why you see so many hard-drinking guys on the job. Guys doing drugs. Guys throwing their weight around, needing to be in control. Not to say that what happened to me has happened to them, but a lot of them've got nine-to-five stress on top of dusk-to-dawn shit. And don't mention the brothers who've got to watch their back for the shit within the department, twenty-four seven. I'm talkin' super stuff now.

"So everybody's got problems and some guys head straight for the bar or the bottle as soon as they close their lockers. I was doing it too, until I coughed up that blood.

Ulcers are no joke. It was like having an alligator in your stomach and you're running around looking for something to wire its jaws shut.

"I came to my senses physically but the other stuff, the mental thing, took a hell of a lot longer. When you invest in a thing one hundred percent—anything—job, marriage, friendship, it's hard to swallow betrayal. It's damn hard."

"But you survived it, Tad. You survived it."

"Barely."

"Do you think I'd betray you?"

"No, I—"

"I love you, Tad. Do you believe me?"

"Yes. Yes, I believe you."

We were quiet for a moment before he continued, his voice barely above a whisper.

"I believe you because I remember your expression when I first saw you three years ago. I had just walked in with that fugitive and was preparing the papers to take him downtown. You were looking at me. You didn't smile. Or blink. Or act surprised. Everyone else was milling around, staring at the guy, at how dirty he was, and the fact that his knees were busted. He was screaming about his rights and there was a lot of talking and yelling going on but you were just standing there. Looking. Like no one else was even in the room. And I guess I knew then that the thing that was bothering me could ease up. Not right away but soon enough.

"Your eyes were like a kind of current traveling through water, and when it reached me, it was a direct hit; made me straighten up whether I wanted to or not. But when we finally got to talking, saying more than hello, I wanted to back away. Even when they were putting you through all that shit, I kept wishing you were another man so I could reach out to you brother-to-brother, not man-to-woman, because I was afraid to go beyond and have to swallow that taste of betrayal again . . ." He shrugged his shoulders and lay back with his eyes closed. "So. There it is . . ."

I wanted to ask more questions but didn't know where to begin. I had glimpsed a picture of Ellen one day, a small unframed photo lying faceup on his desk. The photo disappeared and the next thing I'd heard, he was getting a divorce.

"A lot happens in our lives, Tad. Devastating things. With very few remedies to see us through. Love is one of them. I don't know if I upset you when I said I hoped I'd never fall for anyone so hard. I didn't know what you had gone through. But let me tell you now. I waited a long time for you to come into my life. You're here. You're part of me. We're part of each other. Tomorrow it will be you and me. Next week and the year after."

I moved over and lay my head on his chest. His heartbeat was loud and fast.

"Tad, I love you. I want to love you now. Right now. Here. On the floor . . . where I can feel your hands under me . . ."

At midnight, I left him sleeping. I needed to go and lie in my own bed and think about his ex-wife and how she nearly caused me to lose a good man.

On my way home, as tired as I felt, I looked for a phone. I needed to catch up with Deborah, who was leaving for Washington in a matter of days. We owed ourselves one last night on the town, or at least a good dinner and some small talk. Yesterday, when I had called, she had been so furious she could barely speak.

I dialed her number now and she picked up on the first ring. "Yes?"

"Girlfriend? You calmed down some?"

"Oh. Mali. I suppose so." Her laughter was short and dry. "You know, when I got home I found that my sister had packed all of my things, was about to have my furniture crated, and had notified management that my apartment would be available. My apartment! You know how hard it is to get a decent place in this city. I had to run to them and get the order rescinded and then arrange for one of my coworkers to sublet while I'm gone."

"Sublet? Deborah! Did you say sublet?"

"Why not? I'll only be gone a year. After all the stuff I've been through, I do need some R and R. I mean, the Big Apple bit me but I'm gonna grow my teeth long and bite it back. I'm coming back, girlfriend."

"I'm glad to hear that, Deborah. I really am . . . Good friends are hard to come by."

"Amen."

"What's Martha saying?"

"I could care less about what she's saying or how she's feeling. I suppose she means well, but she's too damn controlling, tried to run my life from day one. I don't need to be around her any longer than I have to, but it'll be nice to see my dad. Spend time with him and Mom for a while."

"What about your job?"

"They've given me a leave." There was a slight pause before she continued. "Listen, I know you planned to come by tomorrow but could we make it for the day after? I still have some things to do—"

"Of course, Deborah. You know me, always flexible." I laughed now, relieved that she wasn't leaving the city permanently.

I hung up and dialed another number and Viv came on the line, sounding as if she'd just woken up. Or perhaps she had been crying. It was hard to tell.

"Viv? Is tomorrow okay for what we talked about?"

"Yeah. Let's see. I got somebody comin' in at eleven. A weave. Gonna take couple hours dependin' on what all she want. So best time is ten. Ten sharp, okay?"

I gave her the location of St. John the Divine, hung up, and called Tad. I woke him, and his voice, sleep-soft, seemed to move right through me.

"Come on back, baby. I'll fix a special breakfast in the morning. With whipped cream on top . . . Come on . . ."

"Unh-unh. We're meeting Viv at ten. If I come back, neither you nor I will be in any shape tomorrow."

I managed to stand my ground even though it was shifting beneath me.

"Damn, you're hard, baby."

"Not as hard as you."

"I love you, baby."

He sounded so mellow I was starting to rethink this whole situation, but making love on that hardwood floor had put more knots in my back than it had taken out so I bit the side of my mouth and whispered, "I'll see you tomorrow."

"Well, okay. If you gonna be like that. Leavin' me in all this distress."

"Nine-thirty tomorrow morning, Tad." I was trying to sound firm, trying to break the feeling that was beginning to point me in the wrong direction. After all, I was closer to his house than I was to my own. It would have been so easy to turn around.

"Okay. Okay. I'll pick you up. Wear some glasses and something to cover your head. And you know enough to leave the high heels in the closet."

"High heels. Very funny. Headgear and glasses sounds like *I Spy*. Do I need a trench coat?"

"Maybe. Rain's in the forecast."

•   •   •

The next morning, I wore a light nylon raincoat, hoping for a smile, but when Tad pulled up, he was in police mode again and didn't comment. He was behind the wheel of a nondescript, dark Buick with one headlight dented.

I settled into the front seat. The seat belts didn't work, nor did the locks.

"Where's your car?" I asked, wondering why this one was still on the road. The upholstery was torn and I felt a spring moving under my left hip.

"In the shop. This is on loan."

I looked at the peeling paint on the hood and decided that maybe this car should be loaned to a salvage yard. But when he turned the ignition, the motor was very quiet and the acceleration was quick when we pulled away.

We headed downtown and he moved his hand from the wheel to touch my ear, but said nothing. Crosstown traffic was light on 125th Street and a minute later we turned at Amsterdam Avenue and parked several yards away from the main entrance of the cathedral.

Directly in front, a three-man Con Ed crew was examining a manhole and preparing to set up shop, probably to disrupt traffic for the rest of the year.

We sat in the car watching the entrance as Tad reviewed the plan. When Viv showed up, I was to point her out and Tad would give her a minute to climb the stairs, then he would approach her alone. I was to stay in the car and keep my eyes open. I was disappointed, I wouldn't be involved.

He checked his watch again, and as he did, I saw her turn the corner.

"There she is, Tad. That's Viv."

She moved quickly, with a flowing black silk top billowing around her, but the yellow spandex tights did nothing to minimize the heavy hips, nor did the yellow open-back high-heel sandals help. She looked around, hesitated, then began to climb the stone steps.

She was on the third or fourth step and Tad had his hand on the car door, ready to open it, when two men got out of a black Cadillac and strode up behind her. One touched her arm and the other grabbed her wrist. She turned around and the expectant smile faded to blank panic.

"Tad! She's got company!"

"Shit! It's a snatch!"

For a second, I was speechless. Then I reached to open the door, to run to help her, but Tad grabbed my arm and his grip was like steel. "Don't move. Don't you move!" he yelled.

"What?"

"You heard me! Don't move!"

He flicked his radio and shouted into it. "It's a damn snatch. Move, dammit!"

The Con Ed crew at the manhole slammed the cover on and climbed into the van just as Viv was shoved into the car. The Cadillac drove a half block before the van took off, accelerating with a souped-up roar, and slammed into its rear. The impact set off alarms of cars parked across the street, and people crossing the avenue yelled. A woman with a stroller screamed. Others, probably thinking that the woman had been hit, rushed up and a crowd quickly gathered. A cruising patrol car halted as the two men in the Cadillac rushed out to confront the Con Ed workers.

"Blind-ass motherfucker, didn't you see us? What the hell's wrong with you?"

The largest of the workers grabbed the driver, pinned him to the hood of the Cadillac, and slapped the cuffs on. Then he began to bang his head to the staccato rhythm of his question.

"Who. Uhn. You. Callin'. Mother. Fucker. Uhn. Mother. Fucker?"

The crowd roared.

"Hey, hey, hey! What you think you doin'?" the other man yelled, reaching into his jacket. He withdrew his hand, empty, when he saw the cuffs and the other uniformed police elbowing their way over.

"What's goin' on?"

The Con Ed men had pulled out their police shields and I watched Viv use the moment to scramble out the opposite door. The leather strap of her purse was looped around her neck and she was barefoot. She used her 180 pounds to burst through the crowd and run right past us.

Without a second thought, I rolled out of the car and took off behind her as she cut into the park adjoining the church. She was several feet ahead of me and moving like a linebacker, skirting around trees, crossing dirt paths, and plowing through hedges and whatever else stood in her way.

"Viv! Wait! Wait!"

Either she did not hear me or panic fueled her flight so much it was impossible for her to stop. She scrambled up an incline, and by the time I reached it, she had slid down to the other side, got up, and continued to run.

My breath came in painful bursts and there was a thick pounding in my ears. My chest hurt so much that tears stung my eyes. I became angry, realizing that after last night, I was one hundred percent out of shape and couldn't keep up with her.

Several yards away, she stepped on something— broken glass or a sharp rock—and suddenly went down to her knees. She rolled up against a tree and was trying to get back on her feet. When I reached her, she tried to scramble away.

"Bitch! You fuckin' white-eyed bitch! You dimed me out, didn't you? Didn't you?"

"Are you crazy? Why would I do that?"

"Those are Johnnie's boys. How . . . how did they—"

I sank to my knees beside her and held my hands over my aching chest. "Because, Viv, your line is probably tapped. I made sure to call you from a pay phone but your line is tapped. Seems like every damn phone in Harlem is."

She was breathing harder than I was, and from the look on her face, she was not convinced. I moved closer, not wanting to talk too loudly and knowing that we couldn't stay here. I took off the nylon raincoat, now dripping wet, my head wrap, and my shoes.

"Listen, I wouldn't do that to you, Viv. Here. Put this stuff on."

She reached for the scarf and her hands shook as she tied her hair up. My size 10 sneakers fit her but the raincoat was too small. She tied it as best she could around her waist to partially hide the yellow tights, at least until she could sneak out of here and into a cab. Then she looked around and started crying.

"I gotta git outta here. Away from here . . ."

"I'll help you, but I have to know something."

"Somethin' like what?" Panic caused her to shake and she looked around, listening to every sound that floated our way.

I touched her shoulder and spoke fast. "Viv. You know that Erskin Harding and Gary Mark were murdered. Did Johnnie . . . did Johnnie have something to do with it? Did he kill them? Or have them killed? This is important to me, Viv. Erskin was a friend of mine, a good friend, and I need to know."

She glanced around again, looking everywhere. Sweat poured down her face and neck and her blouse was wet enough to wring out. "They knew I was gonna talk, cut a deal. My ass ain't worth shit now."

"Viv, please—I'll get you out of here in one piece, if I have to carry you. Now tell me . . ."

She wiped her face with the palm of her hand, leaving a thin streak of grime across her nose and mouth. "I know about Gary Mark. I don't know anything about that other guy, Erskin."

"You're sure?"

"I damn sure am sure. Too late to lie now."

I stood up slowly and looked around. We were in a thick enclosure of evergreens and I wondered if she could stay here until dark, or at least until Tad hooked up with her. She saw my face and read my thoughts. "You ain't leavin' me. You said you'd get me out."

And she started to cry again.

I knelt back down. "I'll get you out. There's even a witness protection program that—"

"Fuck witness protection. I got my own program."

"Where will you go, Viv? You have to be careful."

"Down to John's Island. My people there'll look after me."

"St. John's . . . in the Virgin Islands?"

She looked at me and a second later nodded her head. "Yeah. Yeah. Right. That's right."

Then her face and her whole attitude seemed to change.

"Now listen, Mali. Here's what you do for me. I got a paper bag in a drawer at Bert's shop. Third drawer on the right. In the back, behind them jars and tubes and stuff, is a lot of money. Don't know how much. Probably couple thousand. Emergency stash, you understand? Got more in a safe-deposit but this'll do me till I can get out of this shit."

Her breathing had slowed remarkably and she was much calmer now that she had a glimmer of a plan.

"What do you want me to do?"

"Tell Bert to put it in a plastic bag, not the kind you can see through, but a thick black one. Tell her to drop it in the recyclin' can right outside the shop tonight when she close. Tell her to do it the last minute when she lockin' up. I'll have somebody watchin' from somewhere. Then that person'll go right behind her with a bag with some bottles in it and make like they rummagin' through the recyclin'. They'll pick it up for me."

"You sure this'll work? If it doesn't, I don't want to hear you calling me out of my name again."

"Look Mali, I—I'm sorry about that. I thought—I don't know what I thought. I ain't never been in no shit like this in my whole life. That man was garbage from the git-go. Come to think of it, his dick wasn't all that sweet . . ."

"Well, okay, you can get mad but you gotta do it someplace else. We can't stay here. We gonna find a cab and—"

"No. Once we step out, we gotta split up. The shit is too hot. We gonna walk as far as the edge of this park, or whatever it is we in, then I'm goin' out by myself. I know somebody not too far from here. Where we at? Amsterdam Avenue? Yeah. I can make it. That's the only way to do it."

I was amazed at how well she'd taken control of her situation. A minute earlier, she had been blind with panic; now she was like a general, throwing out commands left and right.

She stood up and pulled at the yellow spandex and I closed my eyes, wondering if she planned to stroll down Amsterdam Avenue wearing only that silk top. A second later I was relieved to see that she had worn a black knee-length Lycra bodyshaper underneath.

"This supposed to be a girdle only they don't call it that. If they did, nobody'd buy it."

She balled up the yellow tights and threw them in the underbrush. Then she tightened my raincoat around her middle and we moved along a narrow path, away from the direction we had come. I wondered where Tad was and what he was doing. I'd find out soon enough, but right now first things first.

It was nearly 10:30 when we emerged. Viv went first, stepping quickly out of the exit near 110th Street. I stood near the gate and watched her move fast down Cathedral Parkway until she was swallowed up in the noonday crowd of strollers and college students near Morningside Drive. Then I walked out and circled two blocks in my bare feet. The Cadillac was gone and so was the crowd and the Con Ed crew. I walked to the car where Tad was standing talking to two men.

One had a ponytail and the other wore a small backpack. They were young and looked like college students except that they were carrying palm-size radios. All three turned to look. There were no introductions and Tad walked up to me quickly.

"Are you . . . all right?"

"I think so."

He turned to the two men with a wave of his hand. "Okay. That's it for now. I'll hook up with you later."

They had not walked out of earshot before he whispered in a shaking voice, "Where the hell did you run to? And where the hell are your shoes?"

I saw the muscle moving near his jaw and the look in his eyes and it reminded me of a parent who wanted to hug his kid for having survived a disaster but chastises it instead for having gone near the danger in the first place.

He opened the car so quickly I thought the door would fly off the hinge. We drove three blocks and in the silence I tried to figure out the best time to tell him what

I'd learned: now, when he was still angry, or later, when he had calmed down and could absorb it all.

Suddenly, he pulled to the curb and I sat there, listening as he drummed his fingers against the wheel. Then he exhaled and put his arms around me so tight I lost my breath.

"Mali. Don't—don't do that again. If anything happened to you, it would be the end of me . . ."

As it turned out, there was no need to call Bert with any instructions. There was no need for the black plastic, and no one needed to rummage through the recycling bin, much to the disappointment of the two young college looking boys parked across from the shop in that raggedy on-loan Buick.

When I called Bert from a nearby pay phone, she simply said, "Joe Turner done come and gone."

"What?"

"Just what I said." And she hung up.

Five fast minutes later I walked into her shop. She was working on a plump, middle-aged woman, twisting swaths of hair into thick Senegalese-style braids.

"You all right, Bert?"

"Yeah, I'm fine. Viv sent her two nephews here to pick up that bag."

"A brown paper bag?"

"Yep."

"With something in it?"

"Uhm-hm. A lotta something in it. Matter a fact, they just left. Two young boys wobblin' on them new Rollerblades."

"And they had the cutest accents," the woman in the chair said. "Sorta like West Indian but more like southern. You know, like them Geechees."

"How young were they?"

"No more than eight or nine," Bert said. Her fingers seemed to be flying at the end of the long braids.

I closed my eyes and as hard as I tried, could not imagine two little boys skating down Frederick Douglass Boulevard and over to Amsterdam Avenue with several thousand dollars in a paper bag.

Bert glanced at my face and sucked her teeth.

"Don't you go gettin' gray hair over it, Mali. Viv know what she doin'. Girl been in the game too long not to know how to put one foot in front of the other."

Bert was right. And I had to give Miss Viv credit. She certainly knew how to put her feet in front by several yards. Probably sat in a cab right around the corner waiting for her nephews to join her. All that talk about black plastic bags and recycling bins gave her just the breather she needed to book.

"This is Viv's customer," Bert said, changing the subject. "Decided on braids. Too hot for a weave. This'll hold her till Viv gets back from her emergency."

Beyond Bert was Viv's workstation, just as she'd left it: combs, curling irons, oils, and lotions in perfect alignment on a clean white towel—as if she had only popped out to Laura's Luncheonette on the corner and was expected back momentarily.

Who else knew she was headed out of the country? At any rate, Tad needed to get to her before someone else did.

The next day when Tad called, I could hear the frustration in his voice. "We have people at Kennedy and Newark. Customs was alerted at St. John's, St. Thomas, St. Croix, and Puerto Rico but there's been no sign of her. And she sure as hell didn't swim."

"Maybe," I said, "she didn't go there at all."

"Well, if you think of anything else, page me and I'll come by. She turned out to be one slick sister."

I hung up and went into the bathroom and filled the tub. A few minutes later I lay back in a cloud of scented bubbles, closed my eyes, and tried to recall everything Bert had said.

Which wasn't much, except that Viv knew how to put one foot in front of the other.

. . . Those boys had cute accents, sounded like—

. . . Geechees.

I opened my eyes and stared at the ceiling, trying to remember if Viv had that accent. The few times I'd heard her speak, she was either cursing her diet or the ineffectiveness of it; the loss of her shop and the general bad breaks in her life. Maybe that's why Bert had kept the TV turned up so high. Too much negativity floating around wasn't good for business. People came to get away from troubles and maybe trade some light gossip but not to get bogged down in heavy-duty stuff that no one could do anything about.

Even when Viv had done my nails, I was more affected by her anger than by the information I knew she had. I hadn't noticed any accent.

. . . Even in the park. Word for word. What did she say . . .

. . . John's Island. My people there'll look after me . . .

Dad had once complained about a young sax player newly arrived in New York sporting orange loafers and no socks who could make a horn do everything but cook dinner.

"Hear Manny's axe, knock you out. We even excuse them country kicks, but his Geechee got to go. Got to take it back."

"Back where?"

"John's Island, where he come from. South Carolina

*need to put out a special dictionary just for that bad-talkin'
boy."*

    I climbed out of the tub, paged Tad, and punched in
my number. He would be here in one minute and out of
town the next.

chapter twenty-five

I could not go to Deborah's apartment because the vision of Jackson Lee stepping back behind her door and the sight of her in the bloodstained bathtub was there every time I closed my eyes. I did not mention this but she agreed to meet me at the Pepper Pot Restaurant.

"A farewell dinner? Girl, I'm not leaving forever."

"I know. Any excuse for a good meal."

"Suits me. See you in an hour."

A warm late spring rain had begun to fall, and by the time we met in front of the restaurant, it had developed into a steady drizzle. Inside, the music of Bob Marley floated from the CD and the aroma of cayenne and basil filtered from the kitchen. Except for one other patron—an elderly man dining alone in the corner—the place was empty, probably due to the rain. We took a table by the window and I ordered broiled red snapper again, the dish I had not been able to enjoy the time I was here with Tad.

"I'll have the same," Deborah said, and the waiter left us alone to look out onto the rainy street. There were few passersby and we drank beer silently.

"Moving got you down?"

Except for ordering, she had not said a word since we sat down and I wondered if she was feeling depressed. She reached for her glass again and emptied it before she answered. "Yes. That . . . and the fact that I have something to tell you."

I watched her face, waiting. Was she afraid of going away? Was her father sicker than she realized? Was her sister acting up, threatening her because she had gone against her? I leaned across the table and kept my voice low, although we were alone in the place.

"What is it? What's going on?"

She hesitated, then stared out of the window at the wet shiny pavement.

"You know, I don't even know where to start. I told you I wouldn't talk about what . . . happened to me even if my memory came back. Well, I remember some things—not the event itself—but I remember the envelope."

She looked at me now and I saw a trace of the vacant stare I had seen in the hospital.

"The memory comes and goes, but in the moments when it comes, I'm afraid to write it down."

"Wait. Wait a minute, Deborah." I held up my hands, wishing I could place them over her mouth to silence her. "You don't need to do this. Don't say anything. Not to me. Not to anyone, you understand? Let sleeping dogs lie. I don't want to know."

Of course I wanted to know, if only for Erskin's sake, and it would be so easy to let her talk. But Erskin is gone. Deborah is here. Alive by some miracle but barely able to keep herself together. If she starts to talk, she will remember more than she wants and she'll disintegrate.

I saw how much and how fast she was drinking and I wondered about her medication. I'd find out what I needed to know but not this way . . .

"Please Deborah, let it lay."

She seemed surprised and somewhat disappointed. "You sure?"

"I'm sure, Deborah."

Besides, we already had a solid connection—at least to Gary's murder—and as soon as Viv turned up, Johnnie Harding would be out of business.

A third round of beer arrived and I watched her empty her bottle, pouring quickly. Then she traced a pattern in the tablecloth with the glass, making small circles and merging the wet outlines.

"This has been one hell of a time. I've been through so much. I want to try to get it out of me, out of my system, so I can start to breathe again."

I kept quiet. To say that I understood would have been insulting. But the glass continued in the small circles and finally I had to say something:

"Once you've settled down with your family, talked to your Mom and Dad, you'll begin to heal, but all of it will take time. It will take time. Right now you don't need any more weight on you."

The waiter arrived and, from sheer gratitude, I wanted to kiss him. Food had a way of taking one's mind off a lot of problems.

"We're leaving early tomorrow morning. Martha's rented a car, and I suppose by the time we hit D.C., we'll have smoothed over our differences enough to present a happy face to our folks. Right now she's still fuming, but I can deal with it. I want to thank you, Mali, for being there for me. I'm going to miss you . . ."

I stared out of the window. A few solitary figures hurried past, pointing their umbrellas into the wind.

I thought of the movies, book parties, and plays

we'd attended during those dry spells when there had been no man in our lives. Even when there was a man, we'd burn up the phone wire advising and commiserating.

I thought of the nights when we had rushed from some evening class or other just in time to catch the last set at the Lickety Split. We always sat at the bar with our books on the floor, nursing watery rum and Cokes, whispering and laughing as the finger-snapping riffs flowed through us. Men smiled and phone numbers were doled out and I could hear her laughter way, way above the riff.

The rain had slacked off by the time we left the restaurant but we hailed a cab anyway. We pulled to a stop in front of my place and I got out.

"Have a good trip, Deborah. I'm going to miss you too. Call me when you get settled."

I closed the door and Deborah rolled down the window, touched my hand, and spoke in a rush as if to prevent me from silencing her:

"Listen. What I wanted to say was that . . . Johnnie didn't have anything to do with . . . what happened to his brother."

The cabbie gunned his engine and Deborah spoke faster.

"It was someone else. I think it's someone you know, Mali . . . I can't tell you any more than that. I don't know any more . . ."

The cab pulled away and I stood at the curb, almost dizzy with the words spinning in my head.

She waved from the window and in the distance her arm looked as fragile as a bird's wing. The car disappeared and I wanted to go into the house and get out of the dress clinging to me in the dampness but I could not move.

It's someone I know . . .

chapter twenty-six

Sleep never comes when you want it but when it does, sometimes you wish it hadn't. No sooner had my head hit the pillow than the voices began all at once: a cacophony of sound—shouts and cries and whispers—and none of it intelligible. Then the voice that I had not heard in so long it sounded new broke through:

. . . Careful. Be careful.

. . . Of whom? I wanted to ask, but the voice had begun to weaken even as I tried to call it back. Through all this, I seemed to float in a shadowy ether, not peacefully but fighting the successive waves bringing me to the edge of wakefulness. I struggled to remain submerged, hoping the voice would grow stronger but it got weaker, then faded entirely.

The small clock on the night table read 4 A.M. when I turned over into wakefulness. The house held the peculiar stillness that let me know I was alone. Even the curtains at the open window seemed held in place by small

steel ball bearings, the delicate ones found in the linings of
pricey jackets.

The sound of a car pulling up got me out of bed and
to the window in time to see Dad moving his bass toward
the steps. When he reached the door, I was there to greet
him.

"You still up?"

"I just woke up. Weird dream . . ."

"Most dreams are," he said, resting the instrument
near the sofa and heading toward the kitchen. "So what
was it about?"

He filled the pot with water and put it on the stove,
then opened the fridge to prepare his after-hours/early
A.M. snack. That way, he could sleep until noon and not
be disturbed by any unscheduled hunger pangs.

I sat at the table, thinking of Deborah and what she
said and then thinking of the voice in the dream, and
suddenly I felt tired.

"I don't remember the dream exactly. It was confus-
ing but I remember the voice. I think it was
Mama's . . ."

He closed the door of the fridge slowly and turned
to rest his hands on the table.

"You know. It's funny. Lately, she been talkin' to
me too."

Perhaps it was fatigue or simply an escape mechanism,
but neither the white shafts of sunlight slanting across my
bed nor the chattering birds on the window ledge pre-
vented me from falling asleep again and I slept late. I
came downstairs at noon and Dad had already finished a
second breakfast and gone out with Ruffin.

I looked around me. Alvin was gone. Tad was still
down on John's Island and Deborah was the latest one to
leave. I wondered who was next.

I think it's someone you know, Mali . . .

Her voice followed me as I moved up the stairs and into the bathroom and it grew stronger as I prepared my bath.

Just slip into the water, close my eyes, and concentrate. It will come to me. It will come . . .

Forty-five minutes later I climbed out cleaner but no wiser. Dad still had not returned and I could hear the echo of my footfalls.

In Alvin's room, I retrieved the "Profoundly Blue" cassette and, not wanting to deal with the glaring basketball posters, took it to my own room and slipped it into the tape deck.

The recording was made from a very old 78 rpm wax album. Dad had used a high-quality tape but the nicks and scratches still came through with the notes. Once the music took hold, though, I was able to ignore the scratching and let the somber sounds of clarinet, celesta, bass, and guitar—Meade "Lux" Lewis, Edmond Hall, and Charlie Christian—come through deep and rich.

Two minutes into the tape, there was a click—as if someone had stepped up to a radio and turned the dial to another station. Voices filled the room and I held my breath, listening in wonder to the deep, angry inflection of Erskin's voice:

"Look, man. How many times do I have to tell you? The answer is no! Get it? No!"

"Erskin, this is the chance of a lifetime. Your brother's in charge of the whole setup. You say the word and I'll go to him and things'll start rolling. Believe me, it can't go wrong."

"Wait a minute. Let's get one thing clear. He's my half brother. Johnnie is my half brother. My father had two wives. And precisely because Johnnie's involved is the reason I want nothing to do with it. He's poison. I'm not that hard up. And

if you know what's good for you, you'll dump this scheme also."

There was the soft sound of laughter, placating but with an edge of tension.

"You know we're not talking hardship, Erskin. We're talking nine hundred grand. Nearly a million dollars. Three trips. Three hundred grand a trip off the top that we split two ways. You and me. The kids won't even know what they're carrying. The stuff is already in Marseille from Lyon and the payoff's in place. They'll blow through customs. I mean, who's going to search through two hundred pieces of luggage belonging to a bunch of young choir kids. No one. I'm asking you, where's the risk?"

A muted, shuffling sound, probably a chair being moved abruptly over carpeted floor.

"Get the hell out of my office, you son of a bitch! Where's the risk? You want to know where's the risk? The risk is when an old grandmother tries to go to the damn corner store, and before she makes it home, some demented crackhead takes her off and leaves her lying in the gutter in a pool of her own blood. The risk is having some young girl give up on life and go with any man who will lead her to her next hit on the pipe. At the hospital just blocks away, nurses are quitting left and right because they can't listen any longer to the screaming of those addicted babies. That's the risk! But you wouldn't know about that. You don't live in this neighborhood so you wouldn't think twice about flooding it with as much shit as you can. They don't do these things downtown where you live, do they?"

And the same voice went on, lower and more deliberate. "And you want to know what the next risk is? If I hear of you approaching anyone else in this organization with your idea, I will personally kick your ass back downtown where it belongs!"

"Now wait a minute, Erskin. You know Johnnie and I go back a long way. A long way. So you watch your words.

And speaking of Johnnie, he lives in the community. Lives large, as they say. How come you're not concerned about the fact that he's flooding his own people with the stuff? You don't have an answer for that, do you? Now let me tell you something else. I have some heavy contacts, Erskin. Some good. Some not so good. It pays to know people on both sides. A lot of people owe me, including some who are very well placed. They owe me!"

"So what? You probably owe somebody also. That's why you're in up to your ass and can't get out. But one thing you can do is get the hell out of my office. Right now!"

The sound of a door opening, a creaky sound, then voices again.

"All right. But just remember one thing. I may be in— as you say—up to my ass, but I've got plenty of company. This is no small thing. Johnnie thought you might be interested, that's all. If you're not, then you better forget I ever mentioned the idea. It's just three hundred grand extra income for a onetime deal, that's all."

"A onetime deal? Gary, you're planning to bring kilos of dope into this neighborhood where it'll be killing people for years and you're calling it a onetime deal?"

"Call it what you want, Erskin. At any rate, I wouldn't take this any further, if I were you."

"But you're not me. You're Gary Mark, ex–Wall Street ex–wonder boy who still thinks he can outslick the suckers. Well, this one's not buying. Now if you don't mind, just close the door on the way out!"

The sound of footsteps. Silence. Then Erskin's voice again, breaking.

"Well, I'll be damned. I'll be damned. They want to use the Chorus. The kids . . ."

There was another click. The fading notes of "Profoundly Blue" came back, and the tape ended several minutes later.

I played the tape again. And again. To confirm what

I didn't want to believe; to hear Erskin's voice again so strong and steady, and to figure out Gary Mark's connections on "both sides" of the line.

Alvin had taken this tape the day Erskin died, and all this time it had lain in the closet. Here were the voices of two men from the grave to point their fingers at Johnnie Harding. Suppose Alvin had played it? Suppose Dad had found it . . .

I took a blank tape, copied it, and took the original downstairs. My hand was unsteady even as I pressed the wall panel near the bar and placed the cassette inside behind an old dusty bottle of cognac that someone had given Dad twenty years ago. Then I got dressed quickly and left the house.

chapter twenty-seven

Do you have an appointment?" the secretary said, reaching for her calendar. "The director sees people only by appointment."

I shifted from one foot to the other and bit my tongue in a losing effort to remain calm. "I don't have an appointment. My nephew's in the Chorus and this is an emergency."

She swiveled her chair around to look up at me. She was new on the job and obviously trying to do the right thing but seemed to have too much attitude for the easygoing atmosphere of an arts organization.

"Is it anything I can help you with?"

"No, ma'am. Please ask Lloyd if he'll see me for five minutes."

I think it was the first-name reference that finally got her to pick up the phone.

Lloyd Benton's office was the same size as Erskin's but it was better furnished. There was the usual leather executive chair behind the walnut desk and the carpet with the muted design on the floor, but where the walls in Erskin's office had been covered with posters and flyers of the various tours, Lloyd's space held several original artworks by African American masters: Henry Tanner, Elizabeth Catlett, and Jacob Lawrence. And there was a small Bearden collage on the wall near the coffeemaker.

I looked around me. This was a cash-strapped organization. Where had this art come from? Had Gary Mark loaned or given it to him? Or had Lloyd been paying himself a salary far in excess of what he was worth?

Lloyd, tall and slim, moved with the grace of a man much younger than his forty-five years. His features were dominated by the shaggy eyebrows, which everyone said were a perfect indicator of his mood.

He came from behind the desk to shake my hand.

"Mali. It's good to see you. I haven't had a chance to let you know personally how much the organization appreciates your support."

"Well, thank you, Lloyd, I—"

"You know, Erskin spoke of you a great deal. Talked about how pretty you were. And he was right, of course." He pulled up a chair and waved me toward it, then he perched on the edge of his desk. "Erskin's sorely missed around here. He was a good man. Dedicated. A shameful, needless death . . ."

"That's what I want to talk to you about, Lloyd. Erskin knew something and it probably got him killed."

When bad news comes calling, some folks sweat, others tremble, and some have eyebrows that speak for them. I watched Lloyd move from the desk to the window, and when he turned to face me, his brows shot up like the back of a porcupine.

"Erskin? He knew something? I thought he was killed trying to prevent a kidnapping. I thought he . . . I mean, you were there. Didn't you say they tried to take Morris and drag him into that car?"

"Yes. But I think the kidnapping was only to get Erskin to cooperate."

"With whom?"

I reached into my bag and pulled the cassette out. "I want you to listen to this."

"What is it?" He checked his watch as if I had taken up too much of his time already.

"Listen to this, Lloyd. It's an eye-opener."

Thirty minutes later he sat with his hands covering his face. When he removed them, his brows had come together in that telltale line and his normally brown skin was flushed a frightening dark red, as if his blood pressure had blown off the chart. His first question surprised me.

"Have you gone to the police?"

Since Tad was still out of town, I had not, so my answer was honest enough.

"No, I haven't. They're not moving on Erskin's murder, and because Gary was so well known, they may not want to move on this. I mean, a prominent Wall Street broker tied to a black drug dealer? Gary's dead. They won't want to tarnish his image. They would probably take the tape and destroy it."

"Where did you get this . . . this tape?"

"I've had it for quite some time. I had it and didn't know what was on it. I heard it for the first time just an hour ago."

"An hour ago?"

"Yes."

I watched him now as he leaned back in his chair, shaking his head, trying to absorb the thing he had just heard.

"I can't believe it! Gary! Mixed up with the biggest thug outside of Attica. And poor Erskin. Caught in the middle. Erskin and Johnnie were like night and day."

"That's true, Lloyd. That's why I came here right

away, to find out what you intend to do about the tour
. . . There's too much at stake."

He looked at me, surprised. "What do you mean,
too much at stake?"

"Well, I was thinking . . . hoping that you'd con-
sider canceling the tour."

"Cancel the tour?" He leaned forward, wide-eyed,
as if I'd just asked him to leap from the top of the World
Trade Center. "The Christmas tour? That's out of the
question. Out of the question."

He rose now and moved again from behind the
desk and paced the floor in a wide circle, his arms held
tightly to his midsection as if he needed to hold something
vital inside.

"Impossible. I can't do that."

"Why not? Who's going to know why you canceled?"

"It can't be done because . . . for one thing, we've
just completed a very successful campaign to underwrite
this tour."

I gazed at the artwork again as he spoke and wondered what his walls at home looked like.

"We need this tour," he said, "to counteract all the
negative publicity we've had the last few months. We
need this so we can get back on track."

I interrupted him. "What about the children,
Lloyd? Aren't you exposing them to a dangerous situation?"

"How can you say that? I mean, there was no actual
kidnapping. There was no threat." He waved his hand as
if dismissing a bothersome fly. "They don't have a hostage
tied up in a hideout somewhere threatening him to make
us do what they want."

"But you heard Gary right there on the tape. You
heard him say the drugs are there. Waiting."

"Whatever Gary said, I don't believe anything'll

come of it. He's dead. The plans have probably been changed."

"How can you be so sure?"

"I can't be. But I'm certain of one thing." He returned again to the desk to lean on it. "Mali, I want you to understand this. I'm not canceling! I'm not calling the police in on this. I'm not doing anything. We've suffered too much adverse publicity already. Any more and we're dead as an organization. Our sources will dry up and our credibility will be zero."

I waited for him to continue. So far he had convinced me of nothing.

"You don't know how it is. You just don't know," he said. "I worked twenty years to get this organization to this point. Twenty years. I'm not about to let it go down the drain over some far-fetched deal which may or may not take place."

It was not so far-fetched. We both knew that drugs had been shipped in the cadavers of Vietnam casualties and more recently in the condom-packed stomachs of couriers. Why not the backpacks of choristers? Especially since someone was being paid to smooth the way.

"Why won't the deal work?"

"I'm not saying it won't work. I'm saying they won't try it. Their main man, their connection, is dead. Gary took two bullets to the head right outside this very building. No one knows who did it. And personally, now that I know what he was all about, I don't give a damn who killed him."

"But don't you care about Erskin?"

"Of course I do."

He moved away from the desk again and began to prowl around the office. Like someone or something suddenly caged and unable to find a bar weak enough to smash through. Then he seemed to remember that I was watching him and he turned to face me.

"Of course I care about Erskin. Of course I do, but Mali, you've got to understand that this organization is larger than that. And it got large because of *me*. *My* sweat. *My* efforts. And I'm not going to let anyone destroy it."

He moved to the window now and stood with his back to me. "You have no idea what went into this. What it took out of me. I have no family. Never had time for one. And I don't miss it because . . . because this is my family."

He turned to face me now and the dark flush had faded somewhat.

"You know that in ordinary relationships, people get married, children are born; there are grandparents, aunts and uncles, cousins, and in-laws all going through the life problems we all must face. Me, I married an idea and it became real because I went through hell to raise the money this idea needed. I smiled, begged, kissed up to people who, under other circumstances, I wouldn't dream of saying hello to. Smiled and kissed corporate asses and sucked up until my jaws ached.

"And even here in Harlem, I went through hell, all the while having to listen to that 'brothers gotta stick together' bullshit; all that empty hype. Smiling at those institutions who initially wouldn't support us, going out and convincing children that it was all right to want to be a choir kid instead of a gangster. All this just to get the damn thing off the ground.

"You know, my father used to be a backyard singer in the old days where four or five of them would travel through the backyards and alleys from tenement to tenement on Sundays, singing hymns. He brought the sound of gospel to folks who didn't or couldn't go to church. I was six years old then and I was the one who ran with my cap held out to collect the few nickels and dimes, but mostly pennies, that were tossed out of the open windows. I picked through the garbage and fought past the rats for those pennies. My father, my mother, and I very nearly starved but we kept at it.

"My folks are gone now but if I learned anything from them, it was the power of faith and a dream and I'm here to tell you it finally paid off. The only family I have is here. And as far as I'm concerned, it's alive and well so I have no intention of letting two men—two dead men— send me back to square one. No way."

He paused and went over to the wall and touched the Bearden collage, correcting a slight misalignment.

"Nice collection," I murmured.

"Yes it is. These pieces were a gift, a very generous gift."

He did not turn around and I knew Gary had loaned them. Now that he was dead, the loan had become a gift.

He finally sat down and we both glanced at the cassette and reached the same conclusion.

"That's a copy," I said.

"Oh."

He leaned across the desk and handed me the tape. "Mali, I can't ask you to keep quiet about this."

"No. You can't," I said, rising from my chair and not at all impressed with his personal history. The power of faith and a dream was one thing, but what about integrity? What about all those strict rules applied to the kids? Shouldn't they apply to the adults also? It was a neatly wrapped speech but as far as I was concerned, it was neatly wrapped bullshit. He was acting as if he'd cornered the market on hard times, but everyone I knew caught hell coming up in Harlem. It was our national anthem.

At the door, I turned at the sound of his voice.

"Well, listen . . . Give me a couple of days. To think about what to do. We can work around this. Perhaps change dates, move the tour up, think about beefing up the group's security or something. I don't know. I just need the time. This has been . . . this has been one hell of a surprise."

His flush had faded entirely, and except for his eyebrows, he seemed to have regained his composure. He was again the administrator in charge.

"Fair enough," I whispered, hoping that Tad would be back by the time I got home. I closed Lloyd's door and walked past his frosty secretary, who did not even bother to look up.

chapter twenty-eight

The news had been a shock to Lloyd, but it had been more than that for me. Outside the rehearsal hall, I tried to decide what to do. Go home or go for a walk. I needed to clear my head and at Malcolm X Boulevard, I turned and headed downtown, walking slowly, with no particular destination.

I looked in the windows of Liberation, the small crowded bookstore I'd visited many times, sometimes dropping in just to chat with the two sisters. I didn't go in now because I needed to concentrate on other things. Erskin's voice, so vibrant and strong on the tape, competed with my memory of his vacant eyes and I needed to come to terms with those conflicting images.

The breeze brought the late afternoon strollers and the usual mobile vendors to the avenue. Stoops were jammed and young girls in front jumped double Dutch, skipping into the ropes, spinning around with braids flying and arms pinned to their sides. Someone called the beat: "Miss Mary Mack, Mack, Mack, all dressed in black,

black, black, with silver buttons, buttons, buttons, all
down her back, back, back . . ." Then the ropers
changed, switching from double Dutch to double orange
and the pace quickened. "Asked my mother for fifteen
cents, to see the elephant jump the fence. Jumped so high,
touched the sky. Never came back till fourth a July."

Sneakers and sandals cleared the ropes, slapping the
hot concrete fast and serious. A tight knot of onlookers
clapped to the beat and I wanted to join the girls, just for
a second, to lose myself in the slapping rhythm and recap-
ture some of their innocence.

At 116th Street, I walked past the mosque and
waved to the bow-tied brothers, several of whom I'd held
serious conversations with years ago in their restaurant.

"*As-Salaam Alaikum,* Sister Mali. You're looking
well."

"*Wa-Alaikum-Salaam,* Brother John. Thank you."

I bought a bean pie and a newspaper and continued
my walk.

At 110th Street, I sat on the grass facing the lake but
my mood did not change and I still had no appetite, despite the pie. I wondered if I had done the right thing
speaking to Lloyd so quickly. Why couldn't I have waited
for Tad? But who knows when he's coming back? Had I
expected Lloyd to do what? See things my way?

And there was Gary, setting up a deal and violating
a trust and not giving a damn about anything. Just like
he'd done on Wall Street, only this was worse. The children had meant nothing to him. Nothing. He had worked
his scene like a cold hawk, yet when I saw him, he'd been
shaken to the bone.

On the tape, he said he'd take the word to Johnnie
and get things rolling. Used Johnnie's name a lot. But I
wonder if Johnnie actually knew what was going down.
Maybe someone else strong-armed Mark with the idea of
using the kids. Using them in exchange for something.

And when Mark couldn't make it work, they took him out. So when I saw him, he hadn't been shaken by Erskin's murder so much as he'd been paralyzed by the fear of his own.

I gave the pie to a homeless man and left the park, heading back the way I had come.

It had been a mistake to try to talk to Lloyd. His program was his life and he intended to do what it took to protect it. Asking me to wait was just a stall.

Heading home, threading my way among the strollers, skaters, and bike riders, I tried to ignore the uneasy feeling that floated out of the humid evening to wrap around me like a cloak.

Night had not quite fallen when I turned into the block and the delicate moment between daylight and streetlight had bathed houses and trees alike in a grainy monochrome. This was the best time of day for me and I'd soon be out walking with Ruffin in quiet solitude.

I climbed the steps and touched the knob and the door swung open even as I fumbled in my bag for the key. I stood there, wondering if I had forgotten to lock it. In all these years, that had never happened, not for me, my sister, my father, or my mother.

In the foyer, I felt my heart race when I reached for the light switch and nothing happened.

"Dad?"

No answer, but that thin, empty-house echo was not there. Another wall light in the hallway leading to the living room was also out.

. . . Try another lamp, one in the living room, then go check the box downstairs . . .

I made my way into the living room, searching in the dark.

. . . Where the hell was the lamp that should have
been on the table near the sofa?

My hand fanned the air and I had a fleeting thought
that I might have wandered into the wrong house but in
all the years I'd lived here, sometimes staggering home
less than sober after a night of parties, I'd never done that.
Drunk or not, I at least knew where I lived.

I had left the front door open but the streetlight
stretched no farther into the room. I kept feeling for the
chairs, the bar, the coffee table. Once I reached the sofa,
the largest thing in the room, I'd get my bearings.

Instead, I stumbled across something soft. I bent
down, touched a form, and backtracked to the foyer to
snatch the large flashlight from the ledge above the door.
When I snapped it on, I took several steps back.

This . . . is . . . not . . .

The large beam swept the living room and I didn't
recognize it.

Dad! No . . . This isn't . . . it can't be . . .

He lay sprawled on the carpet near the bottom of
the stairs.

. . . This isn't my dog. This isn't . . .

Ruffin lay near the fireplace where the sofa should
have been.

The light beam caught the overturned furniture, the
smashed mirrors, the dark stains streaking the walls, and
then wavered. I dropped it and ran screaming next door
to Dr. Thomas.

chapter twenty-nine

The Harlem Hospital emergency room was a war zone. People in various stages of trauma were strapped to gurneys, or slumped in chairs, while others leaned against the walls. The corridors were crowded and every chair and bench was occupied.

Someone with a clipboard and lots of pencils approached, and words like coverage and insurance filtered through to me. I must have answered because eventually the clipboard and pencils floated away, to fasten on someone else.

I moved to a corner and sat on the floor to wait. Dr. Thomas had eased Dad quickly through triage and had gone upstairs with him directly to surgery. I could do nothing but wait and watch the movement curling around me.

A young man was brought in by two others, placed on the floor near me, and abandoned, simply left on his own. His eyes were swollen shut and his tongue protruded, spilling a purple-streaked spittle. He made no sound, and except for the slow rise of his stained sweat-shirt, it was hard to tell he was even alive.

A long time ago, all this would have been part of a night's work: complete a form, file the report, and return to the beat to look for, or at least try to prevent, the next crisis. Now Dad was here and we were in crisis, and there were no reports for me to file.

An overworked nurse and intern stooped over the man, checking his vital signs, deciding whether he was serious enough to move to the head of the line.

The doors to the corridor moved back and forth, each swing bringing in another wave of people. Screaming children pressed against frightened mothers—women who had, by their expression, moved beyond fatigue years ago.

Everyone, those who could speak, talked at once, competing with the sound system, demanding attention. Now. Those who could not speak seemed to sit in dumb amazement, not understanding what had brought them here in the first place.

I closed my eyes to shut out, if not the sound, then at least this vision. But I again saw my living room and door and stairs against the red of my closed lids. A bright red once Dr. Thomas had gotten the lights on. A bright red once the police had come.

"Did your father have any enemies?"

A red so radiant it blinded when Dad was placed in the neck restraint and lifted to the stretcher. In the ambulance, I knelt near the stretcher.

"Did you have any enemies?"

I don't know who asked this question and I did not try to answer. We have enemies the day we are born. I leaned near my father's ear, wiped away the crisp flecks of dried blood, and whispered so that no one but him could hear.

"Daddy? Listen. You remember what the old folks

said? If you go in squawkin', you'll come out walkin'. Remember? Remember?"

There was more red when Dr. Thomas's twin sons had taken Ruffin, barely breathing, wrapping him in a blanket like an oversize broken toy to rush away and be fixed.

Red color thick and dense and turning brown where it had sprayed the walls and clotted there and turning black where it soaked through the carpets.

I could not keep my eyes closed, not even to pray.

Straight ahead, a woman sat in a chair gripping a towel to her left arm. Her gray braids were a bright contrast against her walnut skin. She cried as a small boy rubbed her shoulders and tried to hold the towel in place. Blood had soaked through it to her print dress and I gazed at the fabric. The large pink flower turned dark before prayer came.

Dear Lord! Please. He's an old man. Don't let him go out like this. He's my father and all I have. All I have. Let me . . . keep him a little longer. Just a little longer . . .

When Dr. Thomas approached, his tall, spare frame slowly threading through the crowd, his careful expression told me nothing until he touched my shoulder.

"Mali?" He whispered as if he wanted to wake me from a dream. He pushed his glasses back on his nose and I saw the fine features were wet with perspiration. "He's still in surgery. I came down to let you know. And to see how you're doing."

"So, no one knows anything?"

"Not yet. But be strong, girl. I don't have to tell you that it's not over till it's over. Stay strong. I'll be back soon as they tell me something."

Five and a half hours later he tapped my shoulder and I jerked awake. The lady in the print dress and her little boy were gone, and most of the casualties had been processed and replaced by a new wave.

"Jeffrey's in intensive care. Surgery's over." And without waiting for me to ask, he continued, "Concussion, severe. Compound fracture of the right upper arm, fractured right lower jaw, and there're some contusions on his chest and upper back. He's in serious but stable condition."

Serious but stable . . . serious but stable . . .

I was able to step into his room for five minutes and saw a fighter, mangled and swollen, with tubes spreading like a web. A fighter, serious but stable.

I placed my fingers lightly on his chest, afraid to touch him for fear of bruising him more.

"Dad, I'm sorry. This is my fault. I'm sorry . . ."

In that brief second, his lids flickered. He did not open his eyes but he knew I was there.

"I'm going to take care of everything, Dad. Everything. Don't you worry."

chapter thirty

Sitting at 4 A.M. in the living room of a house I hardly recognize, I listen to the noises of the lock being repaired, furniture being uprighted, and the remaining pictures being taken from the walls and stacked in a corner and I try to make sense of the note one of the twins has pressed into my hand.

"This was on the mantel. Propped there so you could see it. And knowing about your lawsuit, we didn't think you'd want the cops to find it."

BACK OFF. OR WE'LL BE BACK.

I let the note slip to the floor and Dr. Thomas picked it up and read it.

"Mali, do you have any idea who did this? Any idea at all?"

I raised my hands and let them fall to my lap. "I have a lot of ideas but nothing solid, nothing I could—"

"Okay, you're spending the night with us. There's no way you're going to stay in here by yourself. No way."

"But it's nearly morning. I'll be all right . . ."

"No. No way. You've got to stay out of here until this . . . whatever it is . . . is resolved. If you don't want to stay with us, then stay with another friend. Anywhere until you decide what to do about this situation."

He looked at the devastation, then sat beside me on the sofa. The pillows had been slashed and the stuffing ripped out.

"At least Alvin isn't here to see this. Thank God you sent him away."

I nodded my head but did not answer. If Alvin had been here, they would have killed him. Now I thought about Ruffin and what the twins had said. He would survive. A single bullet had passed completely through him and he had lost blood but he would survive.

I looked at the walls again and knew that most of the blood had probably come from whoever had broken in. Ruffin had been shot defending Dad.

"Listen," I repeated, "I'll be all right. I will. I'll call my friend and—"

"The phone's been ripped out. You can use ours."

I looked around and wondered what else had been destroyed. The wall near the piano had not been touched so the tape was still there. The rooms upstairs had been undisturbed. So had Dad's studio. His papers, sheet music, and all his instruments were intact.

After breaking in, the attacker had probably spent most of the time fighting off Ruffin. Didn't have time or the energy to get to the rest of the house.

Still, I looked around the living room and wondered how people managed to bring their lives back together once they had been robbed, raped, or otherwise invaded. How had they managed to touch the things that had been pored over and rummaged through and handled so violently? And the rage they had felt toward the unknowable, how did they prevent it from turning inward? How did they cope . . .

I knew what I had to do, but what did other people do . . .

Rage drained everything from me and I knew if I breathed too deeply, or blinked too suddenly, I would disintegrate.

"I will come next door and sleep for an hour. Then I want to go back to the hospital. I've got to see Dad . . ."

"Good idea. That makes me feel better, Mali."

The twins rolled the carpets up and pushed them into the foyer and I wanted to tell them, as helpful as they were, to stop trying to restore order to this place because it couldn't be done. But I remained silent and concentrated instead on a thin gray streak of light edging through the half-drawn blinds to touch the ruined floors and furniture. The scene resembled a theater set between acts, expertly dismantled.

chapter thirty-one

The hot shower did not help and sleep was out of the question so, despite Dr. Thomas's objections, I returned home to sit in the middle of the living room floor. It was daylight now, and staring at the debris helped me to concentrate on the questions that kept turning over and over.

. . . Who left the note? Who killed Erskin or had him killed? Why was Nightlife taken from the hospital and murdered? Who had taken that envelope from Deborah?

And where was Miss Viv? As slick as she is, she might be hiding out right here in the city. And maybe she decided to get me for setting her up. Why hadn't she been found? Maybe Johnnie's boys got to her before Tad. All of this stuff happening and I haven't heard a word from him.

And Lloyd. As far as he was concerned, he and the Chorus were one and he would die before he'd let anything happen to it.

Or it could have been a message from the friends at the precinct because I had named Terry Keenan in the lawsuit. Too many questions and I needed to tackle them all.

I lay back on the floor and stared at the ceiling.

. . . The shortest distance anywhere is still a straight line. Start at the top with Harding. Start with him or get as near as I can. Then backtrack to Lloyd, and then to Viv, and perhaps the club if I have to. That message was meant for me but Dad might have stumbled onto something he had no business knowing. Get on this now before things get hotter, although I don't know how much worse it can get.

If nothing turns up, look at the precinct and let Tad handle it from there.

Upstairs at my desk, I grabbed a pen and notepaper:

Tad, my father's in the hospital and it's my fault. He has been battered so badly it didn't seem as if he'd survive the night. As I write this, I still don't know. There are so many tubes and wires running in and out and so many machines around him, I could barely get near his bed.

After Benin, I had promised myself that I'd take care of everything. That I'd look after not only her son but our father. So I must do something about this. And do it quickly.

If anything happens to Dad and . . . if I should die, I want you to take care of Alvin. We have no other relatives and even if we had, I would still want you to do this. All the papers are near the piano, near Walker and water (you know where I mean).

I can only remember telling you how much I love you when I was actually making love to you, feeling your strength and the wonder of your

hands on me. You are miles away now and dis-
tance sometimes clears the vision. My vision is
clear. I love you more than ever. Take care of
yourself and take care of Alvin.

Mali

I sealed the letter and returned next door.

"If anything happens, give this to Detective Tad
Honeywell at the precinct. No one else."

Dr. Thomas stared at me, the frown on his face
deepening.

"Mali, enough has happened already. You expecting
more bad news?"

"No. I'm not expecting anything, but things
happen."

I stood on the stoop with him and gazed down the
block. Sunlight had burned back the early morning gray,
and the strong rays now made everything appear postcard-
perfect. The trees were a bright thick green, filled with the
busy peeping sounds of birds. It was so pleasant it made
my head hurt.

In my room again, I went over Erskin's list of numbers. Tad had the original but the copy was plain enough.
My fingers slid down the page and stopped at the address
of the abandoned building where Nightlife had been
found.

In the mirror, I tried not to notice the swollen eyelids on the face staring at me and instead concentrated on
tying a scarf around my hair. Then I placed a wide band
of Velcro above my ankle, attached a lipstick-size canister
of Mace to the band, put on my sweat suit, and left the
house.

At the hospital, I was overcome with a nameless
fear and could not wait for the elevator. I ran up the six

flights to Dad's floor and was shaking as I approached his room. I passed the nurse's station, too afraid to stop.

Inside the room, someone else, another patient, was lying in the space where Dad had been.

"What happened to—where is Mr. Anderson?" I asked a nurse who had stepped from behind a curtain she'd pulled back.

"Mr. Anderson? Oh, he's been moved. No longer in ICU. The desk will tell you what floor he's on."

I leaned against the wall and folded my arms across my chest, weak with relief.

"Are you all right? Do you want a glass of water?"

"No. No. I just—I mean I'm okay. Thank you."

Two flights down, I found him propped in bed near the window in a room he shared with two other patients. Three musicians from the club were standing around him, talking in low voices.

The drummer embraced me. He was short and round and had to reach up to touch my shoulders. "Mali. It's good to see you. This is a damn shame, girl. But your old man is the strongest thing on the block. He gonna make it."

"And thank God for that," the pianist joined in. "We can't afford to lose him just yet. We just now gettin' our second wind, what with the schedule your pop got lined up. Ain't that right, Sonny?"

The pianist was a medium-built, brown-skin man with a large mole on his lower lip. He was seventy-five years old and considered my father a youngster. He always called him Sonny.

My father smiled weakly at the compliment and smiled more energetically when I leaned over and kissed him.

"Daddy? How're you feeling?"

"I've felt better." His voice was a slurred whisper through his wired jaw. "I've felt better, but hell, who's complainin'? I'm lucky. Just plain damn lucky. My arm may be broken but my hands, my hands are okay and my fingers are still moving. Gimme six months and I'll be good to go. Thank God I'm not a horn man. How about you? What's goin' on? You takin' care of yourself? I was worried sick about what might've happened to you."

I patted him gently on the face, rubbed his shoulders, and tried to remain calm. "No. Don't talk. I—I'm all right. I've been staying at Dr. Thomas's house. His sons, you know the twins—they're—"

And I couldn't say any more. One of the three men, the horn player I think, touched my shoulder as I sank into the chair and held my head in my hands. I bit the inside of my mouth until the salty taste of blood came up, but I was determined not to let him see me cry.

The horn man patted my shoulder. "Listen, sweetie. Your pop's tougher than a fried fricassee. He gonna make it. He fought his way outta ICU and he gonna fight his way outta this bed and outta this whole place. Don't you worry."

Most of the tubes and monitors were gone and only the glucose drip remained taped to his wrist. The other medication and pureed food, he was now taking by mouth.

A half hour later the nurse came in and chased us out, saying we could come back tomorrow. I was glad. Dad didn't get the chance to ask me the questions I couldn't answer. And I had something to do. The sooner I started, the better I'd feel.

In the elevator, the three spoke at once, unable to contain the anger. "You know, I seen me some shi—seen me some stuff in my day, but this is deep. Damn deep. Who'd wanna do something like this to your father? To an old man who ain't done nuthin' but good for the folks? Who'd do this?"

"Yeah. Bustin' in and robbin' is one thing. But ain't

no need to go on no damn stampede. But that's what them crackheads be doin' nowadays. They git whack if you look at 'em wrong."

"See, that's why when they come up in my face with they hard-luck story, I give 'em two pennies short of the time a day. Tell 'em take that talk for a walk."

"Can't blame you, man, they nuthin' but a bunch a goddamn roaches."

I nodded but said nothing. Crackheads and roaches don't leave notes.

chapter thirty-two

The basketball court was crowded as I passed, and when I waved to Clarence, he left the bench and ran toward me.

"Miss Mali. Miss Mali. Wait up."

I slowed down but didn't stop and he fell in step beside me.

"Miss Mali. I heard about your pop."

"You did?"

"Yeah, it's on the vine. Bad news. Dag-gone, how come bad things always gotta happen to good people?"

We covered another half block together before he spoke again. "How's he doin'?"

"He's—hangin' in, Clarence. He's tough . . . he's . . . oh, Clarence."

"Aw, please, Miss Mali, don't cry. I didn't mean to upset you. Don't . . ."

He held out the cotton square he had untied from his neck. It was strong with the salt of sweat but I took it and wiped my face anyway.

"Listen, Miss Mali. Striver and me is ace. I had his back all along. He ain't here no more. Least not for a while so I want you to know, if anything go down and you git jammed, I got your back, unnerstan'? I ain't lettin' nuthin' or nobody step up to my little man's sister. Okay?"

He squinted in the sun and tried to smile. I gazed at his worn sweatpants and thin jersey and mismatched laces and wanted to cry some more.

"Thanks, Clarence. Thanks. I appreciate it. I mean it. I'm okay now. I'll see you later . . ."

I returned his kerchief and left him standing there.

Fifteen blocks farther uptown, I stood on the corner and looked at the building across the avenue, a nondescript five-story brown brick structure with a narrow trash-filled alley on either side.

The windows at street level were covered with wood planks but the upper floors had the glass intact and drawn shades. The entrance was closed off by a narrow steel door with a small rectangular panel of wired glass. The building was anything but abandoned and people strolled in and out as if they were visiting the public library.

Two beeper-wearing pitchers or sellers, one on each corner, serviced the carriage trade—mostly Connecticut and Jersey plates. The cars pulled up, engines idling in the open-air market as the two men strolled to the rolled-down windows with unhurried confidence, looking neither right nor left.

A lone spotter scanned the scene from the roof as other customers, the foot trade, walked up the steps to the door.

I moved from the corner and followed closely behind a tall emaciated woman gliding quickly and purposefully up the steps and into the building's dark corridor.

Once inside, the heavy smell of cooking crack was immediate and overwhelming and the woman became more animated.

"Red or yellow?" the man lounging near the stairs asked. He was six feet tall and hovered on the other side of three hundred pounds, obviously the right one for door duty.

"Red," she answered impatiently. "Kenny, you know me. Shit, I been comin' here long enough."

"How much?" Kenny asked. He seemed to know the exact amount but wanted to agitate her even more.

"What you mean how much?"

She reached under her sweater and extracted a faded bill. "Ten dollars, motherfucker. Ten dollars!"

Kenny laughed and placed two red-capped vials in her hand.

"You stayin' or goin'?"

Her hands flew to her hips as she stepped back.

"Why you got to ast me every time? Why you fuckin' wid me?"

"Fuckin' with you? Listen, Carol. I ain't that hard up. I knew you when you was fat and fit. Had big legs. Now you ain't nuthin' but a mangy ho'. Seen more dick than a army doctor and probably tasted 'em all. So don't be comin' on with your funky ass to your shoulder . . . Just answer the question."

"Stayin'."

"Okay. Then that be another two. And I ain't lettin' you slide like last time. I want two damn dollars!"

Carol now reached into a side pocket and brought out two more bills. Kenny snatched them and, laughing, waved her on up the narrow stairs.

I stepped up with my money in my hand, intending to follow her.

"Red," I said quickly before he asked.

"Stayin'?" he asked, giving me a long stare.

"Why not?" I said, even though I felt the sweat running down the hollow of my back. "Yeah, I'm stayin'."

"Good . . . Good." He continued to stare, absently stroking the stack of bills between his fingers.

"Ain't seen you around. First time?"

Before I could answer, he went on. "Listen here, pretty. I be up a little later. You wait. Treat you to somethin' real nice. Real, real nice, you hear . . ."

He leaned close and smiled and in the dim light his teeth glittered like an advertisement for a new Klondike gold rush. I said nothing and backed away up the steps, then turned to catch up with Carol.

The entire second floor had been converted into three large rooms stretching from the front of the building to the back. A small window on the back wall was open, with a sheet of black plastic draped across it, but the slight breeze rippling through did nothing to lighten the odor.

I heard sounds—groaning, mumbling, cursing—and thought of skinny, wide-eyed squeegee men stumbling through screaming traffic for a quarter.

I thought of empty bottles and cans being rushed to recycle for a handful of nickels.

I imagined someone dying and left in a corner to decay.

The lighters flicked like fireflies, casting faces in small yellow circles. A bright glow from a deep, one-second draw, and the faces were swallowed again by the dark.

I stepped just inside the door and tried to get my bearings.

"Watch where you steppin', bitch, else you lose your fuckin' leg!"

"Sorry!" I moved quickly, wondering if anyone ever apologized in these circumstances. More likely, it would have been worse if I said nothing. Nobody likes being ignored.

My stomach was turning and my throat closed against the smell. I took another small step, moving gingerly, and stepped on something else. The odor was overwhelming and I knew that someone had just relieved themselves right there on the floor.

I quickly gave up trying to find Carol and backed out to the narrow hallway to lean against the banister, trying to catch my breath. More people came up the steps and I bent over the railing with my head down. In their rush to light up, they passed me without a backward glance.

I looked in the other rooms, a quick look, and I wanted to cry. There, barely illuminated in the gray light, were the young girls, some no more than eight or nine, performing on a line of men. Other men stood by with their pants open, watching and waiting, while still others had little girls on the floor and against the walls.

The girls' cries filled the room louder than the animal sounds of the men.

I closed my eyes and backed away.

. . . This is how Johnnie gets his money. Driving that Cadillac, walking into that club with Maizie dragging that coat. Sitting there like a king drinking that champagne.

This is how he does it. It has nothing to do with the Pink Fingernail or any of his other businesses. It has to do with nine-year-olds, thrown away. Wiped-out babies. Zombies. This is how he does it . . .

My head began to hurt and I knew what was about to happen. If I didn't get control of myself, I would fly into that crowd screaming, smashing at everything in sight. And I would not leave there alive. I backed farther away and sat on the step in the dark hallway but the hammer in my head would not stop. The flight led to the upper floors and I turned and looked up. If anyone stopped me, I would ask for the bathroom. I needed one, just to throw up.

I slipped the crack vial into my pocket and started to climb. On the second step, a small beep sounded and I froze. I sat down and decided that the best thing to be was sick, if someone came out.

I waited. I heard movement—light footsteps above me—but no one came. I sat on the step a minute longer, with my head propped in my hands. The beep had been nearly imperceptible. If my chest had been pumping any harder, I would not have heard it.

. . . There's a closed-circuit. Electronic eyes. No wonder there're no guards in the halls . . .

I fumbled in my pocket for a Tic-Tac, took some out, swallowed several, and wondered how that looked on the monitor. Pill popping. I certainly didn't need to come in here for that.

I got up, one hand pressing my stomach and the other against my mouth, looking sick for the monitors. I leaned against the wall, doubled over, then moved back up to the second step. Then a step beyond, and this time nothing happened. The monitor was silent.

On the dark and narrow third floor, I moved slowly, still bent over and holding my stomach, still searching for a bathroom, if anyone asked. I heard nothing and moved on.

The fourth floor seemed vacant except for a half dozen large, empty, metal vats at the end of the hall. I climbed up to the fifth floor and voices filtered from behind closed doors but they were muffled, hard to understand. It didn't matter. What I had seen would be enough to pull a raid as fast as Tad could get the warrant.

I turned to leave.

"Say, pretty. Ain't you a little off the track? This is off limits. What you doin'?"

Kenny leaned on the banister at the bottom of the steps, smiling up at me.

"Lookin' for a bathroom," I said, trying to match his whispery voice.

"Well, come on down. I take you to one. I take you to one."

"I don't have to go no more."

"Is that right?"

He moved up the steps now, still smiling.

"Yeah, that's right."

I faced him, looked into his glittering mouth, and knew there was no talking my way out of this. I thought of the young girls downstairs and it wouldn't take much more to get me over the edge.

"So now you got a problem 'cause I don't need no bathroom?"

"Hey!" He held up his hands in mock shock. "What's them pills you just took? Got you real pumped up, baby. Real pumped up."

He moved closer and I refused to back away. If I did, he would know he had the upper hand. He came up the steps slowly, one hand on the banister and the other on the wall, blocking me.

"Look, how 'bout a little bit right here . . . five minutes and you can walk out like nuthin' happened. Otherwise, I got to tag you, got to let the boss know you crossed the line."

The boss already knew and this dog was determined to get his before he turned me over to him.

I sat down on the top step, put my hand on my ankle, and watched him come up.

"Kenny, fuck you and your smelly breath!"

"Well now, ain't that somethin'. 'Cause that's just what you gonna do. Just what you gonna do . . . and this'll soften you up a little. So you can show some respect —you bitch!"

He lunged up the step and swung so hard that if his fist had connected, my head would have gone through the wall. It brushed my face as I ducked down and came up again in a wide-swinging arc. The stream of Mace went directly into his eyes and he fell back down the steps, howling.

"Shit! Fuckin' bitch, I kill you! I kill you!"

I scrambled to my feet and ran along the narrow landing, found another vat, but this one was full, too heavy to roll down the stairs. By this time, doors were opening on the landing below and noise was coming from everywhere.

"Shit, man! Who the fuck did this? Who got to you?"

"Bitch up there!"

He was rolling on the floor pointing and screaming as he covered his face.

I was looking for a way out when another door opened behind me and someone grabbed me around my neck, pressed something to my face, and dragged me inside.

chapter thirty-three

My eyes flew open at the loud cracking sound and the side of my face burned from the stinging slap. For a minute, I saw two of everything: fluorescent fixtures swaying dizzily overhead, two long tables covered with drug paraphernalia, two desks in the corner against the far wall, two doors with steel bars, and four windows, one pair opening onto a fire escape and the other closed.

I was in a straight-back chair with my hands fastened behind me, and when Johnnie Harding stepped in front of me, I saw two of him.

"That ether is a bitch, ain't it? Hope I didn't give you too much, I know what it does to the brain."

He perched on the edge of the table and his image slowly came into focus. I stared at him, trying to get my thoughts together. When I opened my mouth, my jaw hurt and my tongue felt thick.

I tried to reconcile the handsome face, the mani-cured fingers, and the gold Rolex against the shabby image of Carol bargaining her soul away at the door and the children crying in the rooms below.

He continued to watch me and swing his foot lightly against the table leg.

"Kenny's a good man. One of my main men. And you nearly put him outta commission."

He nodded his head casually, speaking as if a fellow corporate exec had met with a slight mishap but was shortly expected back at the desk.

"Yep. Good man. Now—"

He moved from the table and adjusted the overhead light. Long shadows fell across his face as he turned toward me.

"Now, pretty. We don't need no introductions since I already know you. Recognize those eyes a block away. We gotta talk. You was comin' up to do what? Take down my whole operation single-handed? Ain't that somethin'? Damn, I wish you was on my team. I'm tired a these bitches who don't do nuthin' but look pretty. Waste a time.

"Anyway, we gonna talk a little about how much you know, how much you don't know, and dependin' on what you sayin', we might think about lettin' you slide— that is, if you can make it outta here with one foot. Or maybe one arm. Or maybe no arms. So think about it. You got a few minutes. I'm waitin' for my advisers, then maybe you can convince us all." He walked over to the small television, turned it off, and smiled. "Tic-Tacs. Ain't that somethin'? Girl pumped on Tic-Tacs. Gotta get me some a those."

As he moved past me, his cologne was light and smelled nothing like the odor in the rooms below, nothing like the sweat of those screaming little girls. He looked tall and elegant, as if he'd been mistakenly transported into this place by some sci-fi sleight of hand. Then I thought of the sting of his palm against my face.

I watched him wave his hand over the plastic bags, canisters, vials, rubber bands, and scales, as he paced in front of the table.

"I pull a heavy dime from this. Same old story, folks thinkin' they too slick to get sick; too hip to say no; and some fools just don't give a damn . . ." He pressed his fingers against one of the bags. "A lot of money. And like any other enterprise, this has its ups and downs. You know what I mean. Folks get greedy . . . and treacherous. And you have to deal with 'em. Always got to watch your back.

"You an ex so I don't have to run this thing to you. You know the deal. How it works. Who gets paid, who gets laid, and so on down the line. I won't waste your time. And you won't waste mine, right? So what I want to know is, why're you here?"

I looked at him and I had no choice but to remain calm. "You want to know why I'm here. My father's lying on his death bed from a beating and you want to know why I'm here? Johnnie, that man never hurt anyone. Why did this happen to him?"

"And you're askin' me? Well, I got the wire, but I'm lettin' you know, that's not my style. Not my style at all."

"Whose style is it?"

"Well, now. You ain't goin' nowhere just yet so give it five. You give us some answers and maybe you'll get some answers."

He went to the desk near the wall, took out a .357 Magnum, checked it, and placed it back in the drawer.

"Now, I heard you were lookin' for Vivian . . ."

"I was?"

"Yeah. Did you find her?"

His voice was like syrup and I felt a slight chill when he smiled.

"Did you find her?"

"I don't know what you're talking about."

"You want to hear the tape?"

"No, not really."

"Okay, so now we back on track." He returned to perch on the edge of the table and swing his foot lightly in a small arc. "So what did you want from her?"

He wasn't waiting for his advisers, probably because he needed some private information, something he could hold on to for another time.

"Johnnie, I wanted to know . . . who killed your brother. Erskin was a friend of mine. A good friend. I'm trying to find out why he had to die the way he did. I was there. You know I was. I saw him shot down like a dog and left there in the rain. I want to know who did it."

His expression seemed to change and I watched him closely. No one except him had ever referred to Erskin as his brother. I could see it in his face. When he spoke, his voice was lower and the casual menace was gone.

"My brother. Yeah. He didn't have to go out that way." Then almost as an afterthought, he whispered, "Heard he was sweet on you . . ."

"Word certainly gets around . . ." I tried to smile but my face still hurt. "How'd you know that?"

"Like you say, word gets around."

"Then, how come you know that but couldn't find out who killed him? He's your own brother, you know."

"Dammit! I know who he was. I don't need no stupid bitch to preach to me." He slammed his hand into the table and everything on it shook.

"I'm sorry, Johnnie. I wasn't preaching. It's just that I . . . I liked your brother very much."

"Liked him enough to bring me down?"

"I never thought you had anything to do with it, Johnnie. Never."

He seemed to calm down almost at once and his foot started to swing again.

"You know, Erskin was quite a man. Had that . . . quality about him that I wanted. I even wanted his mama to be my own . . .

"When I was little, my mama never cared one way or the other what I did. She was so busy. So I used to stand across the street and watch my brother go to school. Even tried to say hello but he was well trained, he never spoke. I was a stranger.

"I watched him grow up and, you know, I wanted his life, his talent. He never had a dime but I saw how he used his intelligence to get something that was worth something. Now, lookin' at you, I can see what he saw, and I don't blame him. I don't blame him . . . But like they say, there's only one roll of the dice. This is the only go-round we get and we got to make the best of it."

I only nodded because it was too late to go into my "it's not too late" speech that I'd perfected with some of the young brothers when I had been on the beat. Johnnie'd been in the game too long. He had gotten hard, so hard that he no longer heard the small voices in the rooms below. I needed to try something else.

"Who do you think killed your brother?"

He paused, probably trying to decide if he should even discuss this with me. "What the hell. This ain't goin' no further than this room . . ."

. . . *Which meant that I wasn't leaving here in one piece if my hands remained cuffed like this.*

"So you want to know who killed him? Gary killed him. Erskin had stood up on principle and word got to me that Gary took him out because he knew too much."

"And so you took care of Gary?"

"Had to. It was the principle of the thing."

"What if it wasn't Gary?"

"What do you mean by that?" The foot swing stopped and he left the table to stand over me. "What do you mean by that?" he repeated.

"I'm trying to say—listen, could you lighten up on my wrists a little? They're beginning to hurt. My hands are starting to swell up. What I'm saying is what if it was someone else . . . somebody whose name is stuck in an envelope somewhere and you don't know anything about it? An envelope that disappeared when Jackson Lee was killed."

The look on his face told me that I was on the right track. When thieves fall out, watch out.

"That's right," I continued, pressing in quickly, "remember what you said about folks gettin' greedy . . . and treacherous? I don't have to tell you, in fact you said it yourself, those are the ones you have to watch. You don't believe me, just ask your advisers, whoever they are. When they get here, ask them about that envelope. There's something in it you ought to know."

He had begun to pace and I could feel the wheels turning. Here was a man who had gotten by on his wits for years. Played on the fact that he understood human nature and knew how to move one pawn against the other, outslick everybody and run off with the goodies. Like he planned to do in December.

The end of the year. Check the end of the year . . . when the kids return from Europe. When the stuff is delivered. That's when he closes the door on this chapter and opens a new one, probably in Spain or Mexico. Tell everyone he and Maizie are going on a honeymoon and just don't come back. Check the end of the year . . .

"Look, Johnnie. I can't run anywhere. Kenny's boys are downstairs and mad as hell so I'm staying right here. Take these cuffs off my hands before my circulation stops."

He thought about it and glanced at his watch again. "Yeah, why not? Why not?"

It was not out of the goodness of his heart. The news of the envelope had probably persuaded him to switch to plan B, whatever that was. The gold Rolex flashed again as he glanced at it.

"Where the fuck are they? See? Didn't I say that free enterprise is a bitch?"

"Then how come you're still in it?"

"For somebody who don't know if they gonna walk or be carried outta here, you askin' a hell of a lotta questions."

"You said that sometimes we only get one chance . . ."

"But I'm different. I'm movin' outta this shit and into somethin' else. Computers. Right now on the black market, memory chips are untraceable and worth more than gold. More money and less hassle. I don't pay off nobody but the thieves. I'm tellin' you this because you ain't—" He was pacing again but stopped and looked at me. "Okay, listen here. Stay in your seat, pretty. Don't move!"

A beep had gone off and at the sound of the footfalls, he moved to the desk and put the gun in his pocket. He smiled again as the door opened but I stared, speechless, at his advisers.

chapter thirty-four

Danny Williams and Terry Keenan stared at me and then at Johnnie. Danny was the first to speak.

"Man, what the fuck is goin' on? Why is she here?"

"Ask her," Johnnie said, waving his hand lightly toward me.

I watched Terry Keenan as he stood just inside the door, visibly shaking. "Shit, what's goin' on, Johnnie? This your idea of a joke?"

The smile disappeared from Johnnie's face and in a quick step, he was in front of Terry.

"I don't joke with my employees, Terry. Remember that, motherfucker!"

"Okay. Okay. I was just—"

"You was just nuthin'. Watch your mouth, you goddamned—"

Danny stepped between them. "Wait a minute. Listen. Both of you. Calm down. Everything's gonna be all right. Johnnie, how'd she get here?"

"Like I said, she invited herself. But now that she's here, we gonna figure how she's leavin' . . . and that shouldn't be too hard."

Johnnie returned to sit on the edge of the table and it didn't take but a minute for both men to look at Terry. Terry stared at me and began to back away, shaking his head.

"Aw no. Not me. Hell no. She got me down on that lawsuit. The first person they gonna point the finger at is me. And she's Honeywell's woman. Naw. Not me. Get somebody else. Get one a the guys downstairs, but me, I ain't in this."

"Like you weren't in on Erskin's killing," I said.

Wild guess, but if I hoped to walk out of here, I had to mix this dirt up as much as I could. I still had not absorbed the fact that Danny was here. In this room. Long Island Danny who had run from the city because of all the crime. Tad's partner, with the huge "Just Say No" poster plastered on the wall behind his desk.

I stared at him, openmouthed, but he turned away, to concentrate on Terry.

"What the hell are you doin'?" Terry shouted. "You can't pin that on me. That was—"

Danny grabbed him. "Shut the fuck up, you son of a bitch!"

Johnnie watched the whole thing in silence but I noticed he was no longer smiling. The expensive fragrance that had floated around him when he moved had all but disappeared and the air had suddenly gotten thick. Like in the rooms below with all those desperate bodies.

"So, Terry. My man. Tell me about Erskin. What you got to say about my brother?"

Terry said nothing now but Johnnie went on anyway.

"And all this time, I thought it was Gary. I hated to pop him. Gary and me went back a long way. To Wall

Street. Kind of prestigious, you know what I mean, transactin' all that business with a big-time, big-appetite, Wall Street man. No, you wouldn't know what I mean."

He was speaking to Terry, but he had Danny in his sights. Danny had moved into the room to stand near my chair.

Johnnie continued to sit on the edge of the table with his arms folded but he seemed coiled, ready to spring at the slightest movement. Terry leaned back against the closed door. In the silence, I listened to Danny's heavy breathing. I felt his closeness and I felt sick.

Johnnie spoke again and his voice was almost a whisper:

"So tell me, Terry—"

"No. You ask Danny—"

I could hear Danny's quick intake of breath. "Look, that was—it was an accident. We wanted to snatch the kid. Hold 'im until the shipment came."

Johnnie looked at him in disgust. "Hold 'im for eight months? Who you kiddin', man? That's what comes from not followin' orders."

Danny looked at me now and I knew that if they had succeeded, the child would have been killed. They would not have held him for long. Children have a way of growing on you.

Danny ignored the question: "Erskin just happened to be there. Wrong place at the wrong time, that's all."

" 'That's all.' My brother gets killed and all you can come up with is 'that's all.' Plus you gave me the wrong wire. Said it was Gary that did it."

"Well, I knew how you felt about your brother. And besides, Gary had to go. He couldn't produce so he had to go."

"And you got me to do it. As insurance in case things didn't go the way you wanted . . . And you also took that envelope from Jackson Lee. Took it off of him or out of that girl's apartment . . . My, my. Ain't we enterprising . . ."

Danny's eyes were wide, surprised. "Shit, listen now. I—"

"What was in it, Danny?"

"That's just it, man. Nuthin'!"

"Don't hand me that fuckin' shit. What was in it?"

"Just a lotta papers. Old news photos of you and Gary hangin' out in some of the clubs downtown. Articles, clippings about Gary. His court case. His probation report. The fact that he had gone to the Chorus as community service. But it was the pictures of you and him that was blown up almost life-size, almost—"

Danny was talking fast now and Johnnie interrupted.

"Well, where are they? How come I didn't get to see 'em?"

"I got rid of 'em. Like I told you, they wasn't important."

Johnnie rubbed his chin. "Got rid of 'em, you say. Not important enough . . ."

He turned to me now, as if remembering I was still in the room. "Ain't that somethin', pretty? And it wasn't important for him to tell me that he'd killed Erskin."

Danny raised his hand, looked at Terry, and said, "I didn't kill Erskin, Johnnie. Somebody else decided to have a little too much fun that day . . . probably was boozin' it up and overplayed his hand."

I watched this whole chess play, wondering who eventually would be checked. To make sure that Johnnie stayed in line, Danny had set him up to kill Mark. Now Johnnie needed the same thing. He'll force Danny to get me in order to balance the equation. He could've killed me when he grabbed me in the hall. But he waited. He needs this insurance.

I glanced at Terry, still leaning against the door, and

I could smell his sweat from where he stood. His eyes were wide and darting and I could see behind the panic the greed that had brought him to this point: first step was to stop whining, rationalize that "what the hell, everybody else is gettin' some, so take a bundle and walk." Easy money is the easiest thing in the world. It was there. Take it for a little while. Then a while longer. Then maybe transfer to another precinct. But the money bundle kept growing, getting larger. And a little while became a while longer as luxuries became everyday necessities.

Transfer out next year. Or the year after. Or never.

Danny had probably seen the greedy eyes, heard his whiny song of trying to make it on next-to-nothing pay. Got to get the car, the house, the boat, the wife, even the dog taken care of. One small bundle. And he was in . . .

I felt my own sweat sliding down my back, pouring from under my arms, and decided that, whatever happens, they had a fight coming, even if it is three to one. I wasn't about to sit here politely and be taken out.

In my mind's eye, I saw Dad, I saw the note left on the mantel, I heard all those phone calls again, and my adrenaline, already at high level, was now spilling off the scale. My anger always seemed to get me in the most trouble but now it balanced the fear that had had me sitting so quietly trying to think my way out of this. Hell, if there's no way out and I have to go, I'm taking at least one of them with me. At least one. I didn't know how but the sweat was running heavier and I knew that when the deal went down, I wasn't going quietly.

Danny nodded to Terry, who was still leaning against the door.

"Okay. Cuff her. We're takin' her outta here."

Johnnie did not move from the table, but held up one hand.

"Sorry. Whatever you got to do is gonna be done

right here. Where we all can see it gettin' done, ain't that right, Terry?"

Terry looked from one to the other, like someone who had stepped in a fast-closing vise.

"Listen, man. I—"

"You gonna do it, Terry?"

Danny had stepped behind me now and, from the openmouthed look on Terry's face, I knew that Danny had drawn his gun.

"You gonna do it?" he repeated.

Danny drew back the hammer and the click was loud and close against my ear. I turned around quickly to face him, to tell him that nobody was going to tie me up.

"Uh-huh," he whispered, glancing at me for a second and time enough for Terry to decide. Danny aimed just over my head and pulled the trigger, dropping Terry as he pulled his weapon.

"No fuckin' good anyway. Had to go sooner or later."

The shot was so close to my ear I felt dizzy and the echo lasted longer than it should have. I tried to hold my breath as the hot smell of the powder drifted under my nose.

The door slammed open and two men with drawn weapons stood just outside.

"What's goin' on? You okay Johnnie?"

"Everything's cool. No problem . . ."

They glanced at Terry sprawled on the floor but said nothing. Instead, they closed the door, leaving us alone again.

When Johnnie spoke again, the menace was more pronounced.

"So your boy's gone. Now, whatever needs doin', you got to do it yourself. I wondered—"

A beeper went off, sharper than the earlier one, and

Johnnie moved quickly from the table to click on a speaker. A voice crackled into the room.

"Nine-eleven! Nine-eleven!"

Doors out in the hall slammed open and the sound of runners filled the corridors. The two men looked at each other and at the table.

"A fuckin' raid?"

Danny put his gun away and pulled out his badge, but Johnnie glanced at him and laughed.

"That ain't gonna work for you this time, my man. There's a dozen people downstairs know you, plus the video."

"The camera was on? Why, you fuckin'—"

"You know the deal. You shoulda checked!" Johnnie beckoned to me. "Come on, pretty. We steppin'. You my passport."

"Like hell she is—we in this together. Either we all leave or no one leaves."

I was crouched in the chair midway between them, trying to make sense of the noise in the hallway, trying to gauge when the chaos would spill into the room and how quickly I would be able to dive under the table once the stuff hit the fan.

I was closer to Danny and I knew what he was going to do but Johnnie beat him to it, drawing and firing almost instantly.

I fell screaming off the chair and tried to scramble under the table but I felt a hand gripping my ankle and turned to look back at Danny. He looked surprised, as if he couldn't understand this thing that had happened and how it had happened to him. His eyes grew larger and he opened his mouth to say something but a gush of bright red spilled over his shirt.

I looked at Johnnie, who had moved from behind the table and was stuffing a videocassette in his pocket. He waved his gun in my direction.

"Okay. Let's step. We ain't got all day!"

I jerked my foot away from Danny's grasp and my sneaker came off.

"Come on, pretty. We ain't got time!"

Johnnie pushed aside the desk on the far wall and we went through a small door, had to crouch down and crawl through it like one of those old-fashioned dumb-waiters, only this one was made of reinforced steel. In less than a second we were out on the roof and the lookout was nowhere to be found.

"Come on. This way . . ."

He had the gun to my side as we stumbled toward the back of the building. He was heading for the fire escape and I felt the roof slanting imperceptibly under my feet. Even before we reached the edge, the knotted thing rose in my stomach. I saw Benin's face again in that gray room and I froze.

. . . I can't do this . . .

Johnnie pushed me.

"What the fuck's wrong with you? Move! Right now or I'll put you away!"

The sweat was pouring from his face and he had raised the gun to a point beneath my chin. "I'll put you away right now, bitch! One more ain't gonna make no difference!"

"Then put me away, you motherfucker. Put me away."

I screamed and swung hard, to knock the weapon aside, to wrestle him to the ground and hold onto him but he rolled over me and I felt his fingers dig into my neck.

"Bitch! I handled bitches like you. Break you in half . . ."

I tore at his eyes and managed to push myself from under him. The Mace was gone, used up, so I scrambled for the gun but he got to it quicker, dragged me to my feet, and caught me again by the throat.

I felt the steel pressed against my neck and knew he had me and wondered if it was better this way, better than having the roof slanting, falling away.

"Police! Don't move!"

"Fuck you!"

It wasn't better. When he turned the gun away and I slipped to my knees and out of Johnnie's grasp, Tad aimed and fired.

chapter thirty-five

Tad stepped out from the doorway and several members of the Strike Force crowded behind him. He knelt beside me as the others rushed to the edge of the roof and looked down into the alley.

Johnnie had gone over the edge from the force of the bullet.

I lay where I had fallen, unable to move. I felt Tad's hands on me, heard his voice, but could not answer. I looked beyond him, concentrating on the fast-moving clouds racing into the white rays of the sun; followed the flight of a lone circling pigeon and wondered why it was alone.

I watched it and my chest grew tight, nausea filled my throat, overwhelming me as the panic mounted. The birds usually flew in pairs. Concentrate. Breathe. Deep.

It didn't help. The pain of panic crushed my chest, and when the other officers approached, I opened my mouth, but I didn't know if it was to cry or scream.

· · · ·

I had refused an ambulance and now sat in Tad's car, waiting. The area around the building had been blocked off and everyone in the neighborhood was pressing against the barricades. There were police vans, sector cars, three ambulances, two units from the fire department, and more gold-braid officers than I could count. Two service technicians went in with stretchers and I knew the body bags would soon be coming out.

I had left my remaining sneaker on the roof—the other one was probably still in Danny's hand—because I didn't want any of this nightmare to follow me home. I wished I could take off the sweat suit, which gave new definition to the word, but I had nothing to change into.

Tad finally got into the car, ignored the strong fragrance, and kissed me.

"Girl. Hard Head. You're okay . . ."

I closed my eyes and held on. "How'd you know I was in there?"

"I didn't. I didn't know anything. Let's backtrack. When I finally found out where Viv had gone, Johnnie's boys had gotten there first. Johnnie had her whole history and knew just where to look. I wasted a lot of time down there because folks weren't giving up anything. It was only by accident that I came across an old man willing to talk. Small places are like that. Had to sit on his porch three hours sipping that white lightning before he said anything worthwhile.

"Said Viv had taken it on the lam one step ahead of Johnnie's posse. Slick sister's probably right back here, layin' low till this thing breezes over. When I called to tell you, your phone was out and I knew something had gone wrong, so I headed back. I knew something was wrong but I never expected this."

I felt his arms around my shoulders and his hands in my hair and I knew I was safe.

"How did you know where I was?"

"I didn't. And Bertha only knew that your dad was in the hospital. I went there but didn't speak directly to him because I didn't want him worrying. The doctor I spoke to said he could be out of there by next week and I didn't want to risk a relapse.

"Morris's mother hadn't heard anything, but when I was coming out of her building, I ran into Clarence. He told me. He knew you were upset and he had followed you. Right to the door. Said you had stepped into the Inferno. I guess that's what the place is called by the people who know it. Kid was practically in tears because he couldn't believe it. I told him that it wasn't what it looked like."

"Poor Clarence. You mean this raid was pulled because of me?"

"It had been on board all along, but when I heard about you, we moved it up by two days and a couple of hours."

He grew quiet now and I knew what he was thinking. He must have seen Danny's body lying there with his shield in his hand. He must have seen Terry. And tonight he would see the mayor—the same man who had encouraged thousands of policemen to riot, to storm City Hall—this mayor would be on the six o'clock news trying to explain this latest betrayal of the public trust. And it would be tomorrow's banner headlines.

"How do you feel? About Danny?" I asked.

"I don't know. Better, I guess. Now that it's over. No, that's not true. I feel like shit. Once upon a time I really admired him. He was doing all the right things, but something happened along the way . . ." He looked out of the window just as the first bag was brought out. Danny weighed a lot but the two morgue workers were efficient and pushed the bag into the van quickly. Then they went back inside.

Tad shook his head. "You know, they were watching him for a while. As a matter of fact, since I was his partner, they were even watching me. I didn't know anything until a few days after he finagled the Choir Murders file, then Internal Affairs approached me. They had tapped his line and found that he was planning to destroy those files. Man, that was a tough thing. A tough thing . . .

"They clued me but I couldn't say a word to you. And many times, I had to sit back and listen to him when he went into his act. That really got to me, all that slick, crime-in-the-city bullshit. But it wasn't that so much as it was having to laugh and grin in the face of betrayal. When you have a partner and expect him to watch your back . . . man—it wasn't easy to deal with that.

"Danny probably double-crossed everybody he ever said hello to. He figured out how stupid and greedy Keenan was and it was a snap to draw him in. Plus he found out that Keenan had been making those calls to you, so he held that over him. He had Nightlife steal Maizie's car for the snatch so if the license was ever traced, it would eventually lead to Johnnie." He shook his head and turned to watch the scene across the avenue. Kenny was brought out in cuffs, his eyes bandaged. Others followed until the van was filled and another van was backed up to the building.

I had nothing to say. I knew it would take some time for Tad to get over all of this because Danny had once been his friend. Long Island Danny. Who had wanted more money, more prestige, more of everything, and wasn't getting it fast enough. I thought about his wife and her illness, and the daughters with the old-fashioned names, and wondered how they would deal with this. Would they be forced to move? Small towns don't let scandals fade.

A siren started up and I looked out of the window at the flashing lights. An ambulance was pulling out, filled

with some of the young girls. Now they were caught up
in the net and would probably be in the system for years
to come: hospitals, foster care, and therapy if they were
lucky. And their tearstained faces might even be paraded
on the ten o'clock news by an anchorman greedy for rat-
ings.

We heard another noise and turned to watch a wiry
young man, waving a Bible, push his way through the
crowd. He was dressed entirely in black and wore an ill-
fitting clerical collar and dirty white sneakers.

"Where are the mothers, the fathers, of these in-
nocents?" he shouted as the ambulance eased its way
through the crowd. "Where are they?"

Some in the crowd looked at him, but then turned
away as a second ambulance backed to the door. They
were waiting to see how many more victims would be
brought out.

I turned from the window but the sirens, the fire
units, the flash of the squad cars still pushed in.

"Tad. I have to leave. Get away . . ."

"I know, figured as much. How does St. Croix
sound?"

I gazed at him and saw the smile.

"When?" I said.

"Whenever you say."

I rested my head on his shoulder and closed my
eyes. "Two weeks," I whispered. "After exams. After Dad
comes out. And maybe we can take Clarence also. We can
catch up with Alvin on Captain Bo's . . ."

about the author

GRACE EDWARDS was born and raised
in Harlem and now lives in Brooklyn. She is
the author of *In the Shadow of the Peacock*
and three previous Mali Anderson myster-
ies: *If I Should Die, A Toast Before Dying,*
and *No Time to Die.*

I leaned hard on the bell next door to Bertha's Beauty Shop as Ruffin paced nervously beside me. It was four a.m. and except for a solitary figure half a block away who slipped into the shadow of an abandoned building, Eighth Avenue was deserted.

Even the 24-hour bodega across the street that dispensed milk, soda, beer and cigarettes through the narrow slot in its iron shutter had turned off the multicolored strobe light.

One block north, a patrol car turned into 135th Street heading for the precinct. I could hear the thrum of the car's motor in the quiet.

. . . Where is Bertha? She phoned in the middle of the night crying. Where is she?

Through the window of the shop, I made out the circular stairway in the rear that led up to her apartment. The night-light was on but I could see no one.

Ruffin crouched low on the cool pavement, wagging his tail, watching as I reached into my pocket for a quarter, snaked my hand through the metal grill and rapped on the window. The echo sounded as if glass was breaking.

I withdrew my hand and thought again about what brought me here. Bertha had been crying, trying to tell me something about Kendrick. There was noise. We'd gotten disconnected and nothing happened when I'd pressed re-dial. Probably a street phone.

I leaned against the metal shutter and glanced up and down the deserted avenue, trying to keep my thoughts from racing. Maybe she's at the precinct, at

Harlem Hospital's emergency room. Or at the morgue.

Suddenly, Ruffin rose to his feet and let out a short growl, low and deep.

"Ruffin! What's the matter?"

He pressed on the leash and I had to pull back hard in order to restrain him. He didn't exactly relax, but there was less resistance and I eased up. If he wanted to, he could have taken off and dragged me for half a block. But he was a well trained Great Dane.

Still, I held the leash and reined him in tightly when "Flyin' Home" rolled up in his wheelchair powered by his two German Shepherds. The dogs were large and reminded me of St. Nick's reindeer except they were not in the business of delivering Christmas gifts. They spotted Ruffin and were ready for battle. The barking could be heard for blocks.

"Yo! Shut the fuck UP!" Flyin' Home yelled. "Can't take you asses nowhere 'thout y'all actin' up."

"Flyin' Home" was twenty eight years old, with powerful brown arms and the deceptively round face of an angel. Up until three years ago, when he had the use of his legs, he'd been known as The Artist—as in escape artist (specifically fire escape). He was known to scale them up, down, and sideways; pop a window gate, and scoop an assortment of what he called "alphabet appliances"—PCs, TVs, and VCRs. And he usually made it back down to the street in the time it took the snoring victim to turn over.

He worked unarmed and one night came

through the window of an insomniac propped in bed cradling a Mossburg pump shotgun with a twenty inch long barrel.

The blast took care of the The Artist's lower spine and left him navigating in a chair ever since. The chair was motorized but as his legs grew smaller, he'd gotten the dogs because, he said, they moved faster. He traveled at top speed and his girl-friend had stenciled the name "Flyin' Home" on the back of the chair.

I waited as he spoke to the dogs again. In the sudden silence he nodded to me but his eyes were scanning the avenue.

"You lookin' for Bert? She at the Half Moon. Somebody got capped."

"What? Who? Who was it??"

"I 'ont know and I 'ont care," he said quickly, still looking around. "Blueshirts on the scene, bad for my health."

He gave the slightest snap of the leather harnesses and the dogs rose at once.

"Flyin', wait! Who was there? Did you see anything?"

"Hell, no. And you ain't on the force no more so why you wanna know?"

"I'm not on the force, but you and I go back a long way."

"I'm cool with that, Mali. And since we go back, you oughtta know my motto: 'when shit go down, I leaves town.' "

With that, he clicked his teeth and the chair took off, rumbling quickly over the pavement. It picked up speed and in a blink Flyin' Home was half a block away.

I watched as he disappeared down Eighth Avenue.

. . . Somebody got capped. Shot. And Bert had screamed on the phone "they got Kendrick, Mali! They got my brother!"

Huge spotlights cast a blue white glow over the Half Moon Bar and the entire corner of 140th Street and Seventh Avenue was cordoned off as if a major film crew had set up operations. The crowd pressing against the barricades was larger than at most parades and I understood why Eighth Avenue was so deserted. Everyone had run to where the action was.

I couldn't maneuver into the crowd with Ruffin so I skirted the periphery. "What happened?"

A man and a woman glanced at me, then at Ruffin and backed away. "I don't know. Somebody got killed, is all we know."

I kept moving, asking, until someone, a slim teenager seated safely out of reach atop a parked car, looked down at me and nodded. "Barmaid. They just took her from the alley."

And an older woman standing on the other side of the car chimed in. "Today was her birthday. Big sign in the window all week. Somebody said she had just had a birthday toast. Then she got blown away. Ain't that somethin'? Don't know from one day to the next what's in store for you."

I stood there for a moment, allowing the news

to sink in. It was not Kendrick who'd been killed, but Thea. It was Thea, the most popular barmaid in Harlem.

The milling crowd was so thick, I couldn't see beyond the outer edges. Some of the uniformed officers that I recognized on the scene would not have offered me much in the way of information and Tad Honeywell also was not there. I would've spotted him. I moved away. Kendrick had not been killed, but Bertha had said, "they got my brother." Where was he? And where was she?

I circled the crowd again, hoping to catch sight of them. An hour later, only one crime scene van remained and the crowd began to thin out. At 5 a.m. I left also, turning into 139th Street toward home.

The phone was ringing and I knew it was Bertha before I picked it up. Her voice sounded old.

"Listen, I'm home. Can you stop by later?"

"I heard what happened, Bertha. I'll see you in a few minutes."

Dad hadn't gotten in from his gig at the Club Harlem so I propped a note on the piano and left the house again.

Dawn was a weak glow in the downtown sky and the chatter of busy birds kept me company all the way to Eighth Avenue.

Bertha's Beauty Shop was two blocks away situated between a small laundromat and a shop that sold balloons and party favors. Bertha's shutter was now rolled up.

When she opened the door, tears welled up even before she spoke.

"Come on in. You don't know what I been through. You don't know . . ."

"What happened? Thea's dead. How did it happen?"

I followed her inside. The front of the shop was in semi darkness and the cool air had not yet been sucked out into the July heat by the steady opening and closing of the door. Bertha had come downstairs from her apartment wearing a pink silk dress edged in rhinestones. She apparently had not had time to change. The dress was torn and dirty, her hair was a mass of auburn tangles, and her face was puffed from crying.

"Listen," I said. "Go get yourself together while I fix some coffee. Laura's luncheonette is probably open by now. I'll run out for some breakfast."

Without a word, she disappeared up the stairs again. I plugged in the Coffee Master and by the time I returned, the coffee was perking, and Bertha was sitting in the chair by the window in her usual jeans and tee shirt. I handed her a plate of grits, eggs, and bacon.

"So, you heard . . . ?

"Not everything. I still don't know what happened."

"That's what everybody in the Half Moon was askin'. 'What happened?' Well, Thea was shot dead in that alley back of the bar. Kendrick's in jail. Henderson Laws, that son of a bitch, heard the shot and come runnin' out the door sayin' my brother did it, that Kendrick had shot her. I was there. I know he didn't do it. But the cops took Henderson Laws' word and now my brother's in jail."

She put her fork down and leaned back in her chair. She closed her eyes and I was amazed at how drawn her face looked even though she was only thirty-six, just four years older than me.

Kendrick is twenty-six years old and so good looking, that given half the chance, he would put Denzel in the shade. He made you want to holler when he parted that fine mouth to smile at you.

Henderson Laws owns the Half Moon, and Thea and Kendrick had worked behind the bar.

"You say you were there. Did you see what happened?"

"Well, I mean . . . I kinda saw it and didn't see it."

I looked at her. "What does that mean?"

She moved from the chair and toward the counter where the brushes, scissors, hair oils, shampoos, creams, and color charts lay. It was still early, not yet 7 a.m., but from habit, she plugged in the outlet connecting the rack of iron straightening combs. Then she picked up a towel and pointed to her empty chair.

"Listen, I know you don't need it, short as your hair is, but how about a conditioner. I can talk better when my hands are workin'."

I shrugged and sat in the chair and she fastened the plastic cape around my shoulders. She applied an egg and mayonnaise mixture which felt cold but soon warmed up as her fingers massaged my scalp.

"So start at the beginning. You never go to that bar. How come you were there last night? And what happened to your dress?"

"Well, you know—"

Bertha stopped talking when the brass bell over the door jingled and two women came in together. Early thirties and well dressed. I had never seen them before and neither had Bertha, judging from her expression. Neither one had an appointment. I glanced at the clock over the mirror.

7:15, especially on a Saturday, wasn't too early for a "Walk-in," as the beauticians called them. Most small operators—unlike major salons—usually accommodated them, hoping they'd return if they were satisfied with the work.

These women seemed anxious and after a minute or so, I wondered if they were here to find out about Kendrick. Or had they been in the bar, part of the night crowd who decided to drop in for the real deal to take back to their friends?

The taller woman had medium brown skin with longish hair pulled back in a pony tail held by a wide barrette. The other woman was dark and pretty with wide eyes under a close, feathered hair cut.

Bertha did not hesitate. "Good morning. What can I do for you?" She placed a plastic cap on my head, not at all gently, and the mirror reflected her annoyance. She was civil but her straight face let them know that today, she wasn't ready to handle anything except dead presidents—as many Jacksons as possible and preferably a few Grants.

The two woman glanced at each other and it became clear that they were not together. They had simply walked in the door at the same time. The pony tail, the taller of the two, spoke first and wasted no words.

"I want to know why your brother killed Thea."

The silence lasted longer than I expected. It was broken by Bertha's tight whisper. "What did you . . . say??"

"You heard me. I want to know—"

Before the woman got the rest of the words out, Bertha was down from the stool, scooping up a blazing straightening comb from the rack.

"Raise up, bitch! My brother didn't kill nobody!"

Bertha was less than five feet three and Miss Pony Tail was as tall as I am—five nine. But what Bertha might have lacked in height, she made up for in volume.

"You gonna eat them words or eat this heat!"

The other woman, the feather cut, seemed horrified and backed toward the door but did not open it.

"Wait! Wait a minute," I said, stepping in front of Bertha to face the woman. "Who are you? What do you mean coming in here with a question like that?"

The woman looked at me as if seeing me for the first time.

"I have a right. Thea . . . was my friend."

Her eyes were wide with anger and I could see the tears threatening to spill over.

"Look, you're upset. Why don't you sit down. Then we can talk. We can—"

"Aw no!" Bertha said, pushing me aside. "Bitch come in with attitude and you makin' her at home? Fuck her. Let her get her ass on out my door. Right now!"

"Bert, please. Wait a minute. Let me—"

"Let you nuthin'!! Whose side you on anyway??"

A red tinge had spread across her brown face and I knew the last thing she needed was a stroke.

"Okay. Okay. She's leaving."

I intended to walk outside with the woman, get a phone number and contact her later. Any information she had might help, but right now Bertha was too angry to see it.

"So what you waitin' for, bitch? Git the fuck on out!!"

"Don't you dare speak to me like that!!"

"I'll dare the devil if he come on wrong. Now don't you like it, don't you take it. Here's my shoulder, come on shake it!"

I stepped out of the way. Scars have a habit of staying with me so I wasn't about to connect with Bertha's hot comb. The decibel level was so high that no one heard the bell jingle.

Framed in the doorway was a third woman and we all turned to stare.

"Pardon me. Which one of you is Kendrick's sister?"

The four of us already crowded in the small space now looked at this new person. Clearly she did not come to have her hair done. Even under the deep crown of her straw hat, we could see the pale blonde strands pushed to the side. Her thin shoulders were held back as if by a brace and she carried a large straw bag loosely in the crook of her arm. Her blue eyes took in the scene and she seemed undecided about stepping any further into the shop.

"Who are you?" I asked.

She hesitated for a fraction of a second, long enough for me to know a lie was coming.

"I'm . . . Teddi Lovette. His agent."

She tried to smile but her voice shook.

"Come in," I said, even though I knew she was lying.

Bert still had not shifted gears sufficiently to open her mouth without screaming and Miss Pony Tail used the moment to head out.

"Well, okay," I said to no one in particular and followed like a hostess seeing a guest to the door.

Once outside, I caught her arm.

"Just a minute. I want to apologize. Bert's upset."

"So am I," the woman said, and continued to walk. My legs are long, but the woman moved so fast I had a problem keeping up. I trotted beside her, feeling the egg and mayo mixture beginning to ooze down my neck from under the cap.

"Listen, I knew Thea also. She was a sweet person and what happened to her was terrible. An awful thing."

We reached the corner and the light changed.

"I know you're too upset to talk right now but could I call you?"

She fumbled in her purse. When she finally extended the card, I snatched it before the light changed again.

"How well did you know Thea?" she asked.

I stood there, praying for the light to change once more and struggling for an answer that would sound at least half truthful when she nodded her head. "Because you must be mistaken. Thea . . . was not a sweet person."

Then she stepped off the curb, crossed Eighth Avenue and opened the door to a silver Lexus. I rushed back to the shop but when I entered, Bert's hot comb was resting in the rack and Blondie and the dark pretty woman had both disappeared.

BANTAM MYSTERY COLLECTION

Ask for these books at your local bookstore or use this page to order.

Please send me the books I have checked above. I am enclosing $____ (add $2.50 to cover postage and handling). Send check or money order, no cash or C.O.D.'s, please.

Name _____

Address _____

City/State/Zip _____

Send order to: Bantam Books, Dept. MC, 2451 S. Wolf Rd., Des Plaines, IL 60018
Allow four to six weeks for delivery.
Prices and availability subject to change without notice.   MC 2/98